beautifully broken

portia moore

Cover Design:
Najla Qamber Designs

Editing:
Chelsea Kuhel, Madison Seilder

Interior Design and Formatting:
Christine Borgford, Perfectly Publishable

prologue

dexter

I'M GOING TO tell you a story. A story about a boy who was born to be a fuck-up. If you haven't picked up on this yet, this isn't going to be one for children. The boy's biological parents were both dregs of society. His mother dropped out of high school when she was sixteen and had him by a man whose screw-ups were only outnumbered by his kids. The boy was one of six and could have been next in line for the less than desirable family throne. His lot in life was already determined. He should have been following in good ol' dad's footsteps.

At five years old, life was already pitted against him. Born to two asinine parents in an environment filled with fools, there wouldn't have been anything else for him to be—but life intervened. It had a different plan for him . . .

Madison, Michigan is where he eventually grew up. Your typical insignificant town, home to less than a thousand people. The downtown area had a pathetic excuse for a movie theater, library, and city hall. That's where *he* grew up. He was lucky to end up there, some would think. He had been born into an even worse situation; now he had it made. With a *real* mom and dad, and even a dog for a time.

His new parents, *ridiculously in love*, volunteered for every charitable effort that took place in the town, even though they barely made ends meet themselves.

The do-gooders of Shelton County.

Their son, the boy, became a straight-A student, member of every little league team you could think of, captain of the junior varsity football team. The kind of boy you'd want your daughter to date. Popular, but nice to the misfits, and you didn't have to worry about him tainting your daughter's innocence because he was such a gentleman. Almost a character out of a 1950's TV show. They were the *perfect* family. What else could their son be other than perfect? He owed them perfection; they saved him from the wreck that could have been his life. He sacrificed the person nature had made him, for the one nurture would create. He assimilated to become a part of the picture perfect family he had been given. Until one day when everything changed, and the picture shattered. It jarred him—shocked him, even—as he discovered secret on top of secret, the type of thing that breaks most people. It broke him. I'd say it saved him, brought him back to life. He was free.

He was able to escape. And after that he was never going to look back.

Until her.

She changed everything.

chapter 1

cal

FREEDOM.
Most people think they're free, but they aren't. They're slaves—to their jobs, to suffocating families, to misplaced priorities, drowning under the weight of what should be life. I see them. I've lived with them. The pathetic thing is that at one point I wanted to be just like them. Well, a *part* of me at least. Then things changed. I was lost and now I'm found. Many people would wonder how a twenty-three-year-old with no formal education, no background in business, and a pretty shitty attitude—I admit it—ended up with a job making six figures to entertain ass-kissers, all with trust funds from Mommy and Daddy to convince me of why our company should consider saving theirs. My job is atypical, but then again I'm not the typical guy.

I am more than meets the eye. My secret weapon, my gift, and my curse. Every curse can be used to your advantage if you can wield it just right. I had a lot working against me when I was born. The cards weren't stacked in my favor, but if my parents never gave me anything else, they passed along a good combination of their genes, which has given me a little bit of an edge up in the world. Regardless of your personality or

February 28, 2008

your IQ, the right looks will get you everywhere—but, without the right mentality, you can only go so far. Lucky for me, a combination of looks and IQ have taken me from under-paid farm hand in a town most people never heard of, to one of the greatest cities in the world, with the best food, the most interesting locations, and—my favorite part—the most beautiful women you have ever seen.

I wouldn't trade my life for the world. Besides, I've already done that once.

I wasn't always like this. I used to be like everyone else, suffocating in a shell of a man. A yes-man, until he broke in two. He couldn't handle the pressure of life—the real side of it, not the sanitized made-for-TV version of life that was created for him. He couldn't handle that reality is ugly, which worked great because the new me handles that part just fine. But the beautiful part of life, I'm telling you, is what I love. The life some people never experience. My favorite part of this job is being among the most gorgeous women Chicago has to offer. Like an ice-cream shop, that has any flavor you could think of, and I've tasted so many I *should* be embarrassed. Distractions that make me put up with the irritating part of my job.

My prospect tonight is already pissing me off, most of them do. Fucking babies. All used to having their asses kissed. I'm like a breath of fresh air for them, I guess. Somehow not giving a fuck works. And Dex pays me a whole lot to not give a fuck. The first time I went out with him to a business venture boring dinner, the client was a dick. I didn't even work for him yet, and the guy who had my job was just about ready to get on his knees and suck it. *I* told the client to go fuck himself, and that's how I got my first job. Not your typical interview, was it? But Dexter Crestfield isn't your typical boss, and his training isn't your run-of-the-mill HR BS.

" . . . a deal with Crestfield even possible, Cal?" This guy's voice irritates the hell out of me. It's like a cross between a pissed-off teacher and a fast-food worker. His expression looks like he hasn't taken a shit in about four days. He looks irritated, and now I'm irritated. Why the hell would I waste my time if a deal weren't possible?

"Another drink, gentlemen?" One of the bottle girls interrupts us, but what a welcome interruption she is. *Did I say how much I love Chicago?*

I forgot her name. I've seen her here a few times before. Michelle, Mallory, something or other. My two clients eye her tits.

"Not right now, hon. Make sure you come back in couple of minutes," he says with a sly grin. Mr. Constipated, his counterpart, gives her the eye, and I try to contain my laughter. I must admit whoever does the hiring needs a raise—a big one.

"And you, sir?" her voice drops an octave as she flashes her bright green eyes at me. I have a thing for women with beautiful eyes, but I can tell she's a pro as she leans into me, slightly licking her lips, a bold red, the same color as her hair.

"That'll be it," I whisper in her ear, sliding a bill in her hand. She smiles appreciatively and stuffs the fifty into the valley between her tits before sauntering away.

"What? Do I need a pair of Double-D breasts to get his attention?" Mr. Constipated says. If he weren't so fucking cheap, he'd be the one she'd be pressed up against tonight.

"The terms of the agreement you're offering . . . I don't think it's worth the risk," I state simply.

"Well, to be frank, we'd rather discuss this with Mr. Crestfield, and in a proper place of business, not this swamp of Jersey Shore elite," Mr. Constipated says tightly. I grin and signal another bottle girl back to the table.

"Can you pour Mr. Freeman here a drink? Because I think he needs to cool the fuck off."

"Look, Cal, we don't mean any disrespect, we're really anxious to make this deal happen," the less annoying one says. I hate guys like Mr. Constipated, men with degrees that cost more than people's mortgages. They know I'm not one of them, they can tell—sense it, blue blood—bull shit. Good thing is, I don't give a shit. So I smile, the same smile I could flash his wife and have her on her knees in ten minutes and still play it cool. After all, it must suck being him.

"I've taken time out of my schedule on my day off to hear a proposal, a legitimate offer to take back to Dexter, and you bring me this shitty deal? Bottom line is, we have better options to review," I say before standing up.

"Wait. Wait, everyone. Calm down. Tensions are high. Cal, we really appreciate the fact that you've come out to hear our proposals. This is actually one of our properties. Cegan, how about we go see if the property holders are in, and how things are going?"

This is how it usually works. They're caught off-guard. They think the deal is off the table and now their heads are spinning. I pull out my phone as I make my way from the table. I shoot Dex a text saying he has them exactly where he wants them.

I make my way from the VIP area down to the main area of the club. VIP is exclusive and all of that shit, but the main floor is where the fun is and, once work is done, it's time to play, and there are so many toys out tonight. I feel a hand slip around my stomach and turn to see the sexy red head from earlier.

"Are you looking for Tori?" she says, leaning into me.

Tori's a bottle girl who works here. She's supermodel-hot, fun, easy, gives me space, but answers when I call. She's one of my regulars, and when I'm in the mood for something different than her for the night, she doesn't cause a scene or throw a fit. Hell, sometimes she'll come with me and my flavor of the night. Bad thing about her, she likes to drink on the job, if it wasn't for me sliding her manager a couple of hundreds to look the other way, she'd have been out on her ass.

"Maybe," I tell her as I watch her hand slide down my arm and land on my Cartier watch, her finger lingering over it. I immediately know this girl is looking for a cash out, not fun, and I don't play with her type.

"She got canned today. She spilled two thousand dollars' worth of champagne," she says with a gleeful smile on her face.

What the fuck, Tori . . .

I liked that she walked on the wild side of life, but there's nothing sexy about getting wasted. It takes you off your game, makes you a different person, and I have enough quirks in that area. Needless to say, it was irritating that she always wanted to get shit-faced. Tipsy is cute. Drunk off your ass is fucking disgusting. I'm not the type to hold a girl's hair up while she pukes.

"Don't look so sad. I can keep you company tonight," she purrs in my ear. Not interested. I forgot this girl's name, but I'm pretty sure she was Tori's friend, and nothing's more of a turn-off than disloyalty.

"I'm going to go get a drink," I say, pushing her hand out of my way and heading to the bar. There are too many other prospects in here. If I want to take someone home tonight, it won't be a money-hungry back-stabber. I push my way through the crowd, and a few women catch my eye. I don't want a drink, but the bar is the place to be, so that's where I am. Tori's friend squeezes beside me. She shoots me a flirtatious grin. She either didn't take the hint or is desperate.

"How fucking long does it take to get a shot?" some drunk guy next to me shouts, loud enough to be heard over the music. People around me grumble. It looks like they're backed up.

"Steven's out sick," the girl whose name I forgot says, leaning into me before her hand roams up my thigh. If she keeps it up, I might just let her give me a blow job before sending her on her way.

"The owner has waitresses covering," she adds. I shrug and turn my body away from her. She's starting to annoy the fuck out of me, and besides that, she's blocking other girls. I need to find someone to make her get lost quickly. I start to head away from the bar, but as I do, the girl behind the bar catches my eye. She more than catches it because I have to double-back to reclaim the space I just lost at the bar.

Who the hell is she?

"I'm so sorry for the wait, everyone. Please be patient with us." Her voice is light and airy, and her smile makes my heart skip a beat. She's sexy as hell. Creamy white skin, long dark wavy hair, and she has a cute, tight little body. She's short, too. I always had a thing for short girls— 'Fun sized.' Not only is she sexy, she's fucking gorgeous. Most girls are either one or the other, but she's both. Add to that her mesmerizing brown eyes, big and bright ones that make her look innocent. She's only in front of me a few seconds, apologizing to everyone again before she goes to the other end of the bar and does the same. My eyes follow her. Her face is clean. She's not wearing pounds of make-up like most of the other girls in the club. She has perfectly plump lips and on her feet, my favorite shoes on a woman, 'come fuck me pumps.'

"She's taken," Whatserface says in my ear.

Too bad.

There's too many single chicks in the world to bark up that tree, but I decide to play around, just to make 'Whatserface' jealous. Since she won't leave me alone, I might as well have a little fun.

"That's never stopped me before," I taunt her, and her face scrunches up like a finished bag of chips.

"She's not like that," she says defensively.

"Really?" I say sarcastically.

"No, really. She's not. She's all into the other bartender that works here. She doesn't talk to any other guys, not even to flirt for tips," she counters with a satisfied grin on her face. Beautiful and loyal . . . *hmmm*.

It's been a while since a girl seemed unattainable and that piques my curiosity.

It doesn't take more than a smile, a little attention, and a few shots, and Whatsername has given me all the details I want.

Lauren, I like that name, is dating a dude named Michael. I've seen him before at the club. Typical pretty-boy douchebag. The frat boy type, screwing anything that walks. I don't know this girl, but seeing any beautiful, loyal woman attached to some ass-wipe who does any chick he can, ticks me off. This time, it irks me more than it usually does.

My first impression is right. He's a creep if I ever saw one. The type of dude that makes a girl fall for him, traps her in a dead-end, crappy, one-sided relationship, screwing anything that moves but telling his girlfriend he loves her every chance he gets.

Don't get me wrong, I'm no fucking Prince Charming, but I never lead girls on. I don't make promises I'll never keep. I don't lie. Each one knows to expect nothing from me but a good time. I have no desire to play with a girl's emotions. No need to tell them I love them when I don't mean it. And a guy who is fucking someone else definitely doesn't mean it. You can't love someone else and screw around just because they make your dick hard. I've seen enough girls get screwed over by the pricks in disguise and unluckily for Michael. I was going to have a little fun.

I have to admit, dude had balls. I watched him for three nights, and each night he'd pull some girl drunk off her ass into the storage room and come out like he just won a prize. Cheating is routine for most dudes, but doing it in the place your girlfriend works, takes a lot of fucking nerve.

Night four I decided it was time to watch the show. It only cost me fifty bucks to get one of the waitresses at the club to point *her* in the right direction of the storage room. A cute little Asian chick was his meal of choice for the night. I have to hand it to him. He has good taste. Every girl I've seen him with was a fucking ten.

I signal the waitress I paid earlier and see her go over to Lauren. I'm not sure what she said, but it makes Lauren smile, and I feel my palms start to sweat. Not a reaction I expected.

I'm nervous . . . and I don't get nervous.

Screw it.

I'm ready to see the fireworks. I can't wait until she catches this jerk-off. I glance at my watch. It shouldn't take more than five minutes until she finds them.

I'm right.

It only takes two before Lauren is flying out of the storage room, but she's crying. I expected profanity, yelling, maybe a cat-fight, but none of that happens. I thought she'd just be pissed off instead of . . . *this*. I thought the aftermath would be funny, entertaining, that the joke would be on this Michael dude but this girl . . . she's devastated. A few other waitresses chase after her, seeing how upset she is. The other girl in the storage room runs out adjusting her dress and disappears into the crowd. Michael looks confused as hell and frantic.

"Lauren!" he shouts, looking around for her. He goes in the other direction.

This is what I wanted.

Entertainment. But this doesn't feel right.

I feel like a bigger asshole than her boyfriend. I think . . . I feel bad. It's a foreign-ass feeling *and* I want to make up for it.

This girl has no clue who I am or what I've done but, shit, I feel fucked up over it. This is the first time I've cared how someone feels when it doesn't affect me. I want to make it up to *her*. I want to make her feel better. The only problem is, I don't make things up to people. I sure as hell don't make situations better. I fuck shit up, and I have no fucking clue how to not do that.

chapter 2

lauren

I CAN'T BREATHE. How do you stop your heart from beating a thousand miles a minute? How do you escape feelings that are wrapped around you like a noose? I have been swallowed up whole. One sentence was all it took for me to know it was him. My gift and my curse, my ending, my beginning, my best dream and my worst nightmare all wrapped in one. Cal Scott, in all of his glory—I knew it. From the moment I heard his voice on the phone, anxiety crawled up my spine. As I made my way up each floor level, I knew it was him. I imagined this moment *so* many times. I dreamed about it, prepared for it to happen, but never *ever* expected for it to happen like this, which is fitting since I never know what to expect from him.

He's watching me, his eyes narrowed on mine, his gaze locked there. It's like time has stopped; the atmosphere has changed. It's quiet, too quiet, just like the moment before lightning strikes from the sky and all hell breaks loose.

I've seen him almost every day for the past two months, but not like this, not with this intensity in his gaze. His presence overwhelms me, causing fear, excitement, and anxiety to course through my entire body. The icy glare on his face sends chills down to my very core. I'm frozen in place as I look at him.

What the hell happened? All of this time Chris is here and then, just like that, he's gone and this happens, right after I slept with him.

I'm confused, I'm nervous and, with the way Cal's looking at me, a little scared—scared of what's to come because the energy exuding from Cal lets me know it's about to be bad.

Cal.

He's the one I married. The one I'm in love with, the man who I spent years of my life with, but I'm trembling because my body can barely contain the emotions crashing against one another inside of me. The man I loved and loathed. I want to say so many different things to him, but my tongue is stuck to the roof of my mouth. I don't know what to do, and oh my God, what happened to Chris?

Last night we made love—well, Chris and I made love—and I told Chris he was the one I wanted.

Does Cal know what happened?

Shit, shit, shit!

Why the hell do I feel guilty? They're both the same fucking person, but the way he's looking at me, with disdain, anger, and maybe even disgust makes me feel like the lowest creature on the planet. He unfolds his arms and approaches me, each step making my heart try to stampede out of my chest. I expect him to touch me as he gets closer, but he steps around me and closes the door that I left open.

"What happened?" I ask, my voice barely over a whisper. His hand firmly grips my wrist, and he turns me around to face him.

"You tell me." His voice is low and stings me, but I try not to show it.

"What do you mean?" I ask, feeling my hands quivering in his grasp. I know Cal would never hurt me, but he's so angry.

"I love you, Chris. You're the one I want, Chris," he says, mimicking my voice.

"Are you kidding?" I let out a nervous chuckle. I wish he wasn't serious; but I know that he is.

"You think I'm fucking kidding?" he asks tightly as he quickly relinquishes his hold and shoves me away, causing me to stumble. He storms across the room with his hands on his head, but in a split-second, he whips back around.

"How could you do that to me?" he shouts, and I have to fight to breathe. His voice is deep and strong like it always is, but from the look in his eyes, I can see his vulnerability. His anguish is hitting me like a truck. I've never seen him like this. He's hurt, and I don't understand. That's a lie because I get it. I don't fully understand it, but I do get it. It's the only thing shutting me up right now. I try to think of something to say as tears swell in my eyes.

"You don't get to cry, Lauren!" he says angrily.

"Cal. I—I . . ."

"What? What do you have to say? Tell me!" he demands, walking closer to me, but before I can even answer, he starts again.

"*I loved you for years*, and all it took was for him to smile your way a couple of times, tell you how much *I* love you, and your legs fly the fuck open for him?" he asks. "You tell him you love him. That *he's* who you want!"

I try to command the tears forming in my eyes to stop. "You don't understand," I squeak out.

"*You* don't understand!" He gestures his finger towards me. "I—I can't even look at you right now," he growls before grabbing a pair a keys off the table.

"Where are you going?"

"You can't just leave!" I shout, grabbing his arm.

"Don't touch me," he snarls, snatching away from me.

"So you hate me now? Is that it? You hate me?" I'm actually crying now.

"I wish I could hate you," he says bitterly, but this time he heads into the bedroom instead of out of the door. Before he crosses the threshold, he turns to face me. "You were supposed to be different," he says, shaking his head. "But you're like everybody else," he adds quietly, and the look in his eyes causes my breath to hitch.

He looks broken, and I think I am the cause. I broke Cal, and I broke Chris. His dad's right. I'm not good for either of them. I try to stop the wail coming from my mouth as my emotions try to escape from my body. I'm trying to keep too much energy pent up inside, but I can't let it out. I slowly sink down to the floor.

How did things get like this? How did I end up here?

When did I become the villain?

He's looking at me with bitterness, disgust, and something bordering on hatred. He's never looked at me like that before. How can he be so angry at me, like I was with another person? I love him so much. I've loved him every day—*every* part of him. The good and the bad.

I hate myself for crying, that I'm sitting here like a sad little girl. How did things get like this? Today everything was supposed to be better. After being with Chris, things were supposed to be good, and I have a feeling they're about to get worse.

I don't know what to do. Do I call the Scotts? Do I call Dexter? Did sleeping with me cause Chris to run away and hide? A part of me is glad that Cal's here, but how can I not feel terrible knowing that Chris is gone and Cal is in a rage? I don't know what he's going to do. I think back to my conversation with his dad. What he said would happen if Cal came back. Oh God, I can't believe I'm even considering what his dad said. I have never seen Cal as mad as he is now. The only thing worse than his anger is his disappointment, but why is he so angry? Because I slept with *him*? After two years of being alone, I slept with *him*, and he's upset with me like I betrayed him?

My phone rings, interrupting my thoughts. I pull it out and see that it's Mrs. Scott. How the hell am I supposed to explain this to the Scotts? It's going to be my fault, of course. *Maybe* it is my fault. Not only do I have to tell them that Chris is now Cal again, but I also have to tell them that he's mad at the world, and I have no idea what he's going to do. I guess I never did, but now it's like he's on a hinge that's barely hanging on, and I can't deal with it right now. The hollowness in my chest turns into a burning sensation as tears sting my eyes. I want to scream.

This is almost like déjà vu. Being left on the floor crying, desperate, broken because of this man, and he's done it again. I crawl onto the large sofa, curl up into myself, and close my eyes. I'm emotionally drained, mentally and physically exhausted like I've run a marathon.

Chris wanted me to love him. Cal apparently doesn't want me to love Chris. It's all too much to think about—how I ended up in a tug of war with one man. The man who is my daughter's father, who has a shitload of emotional baggage. The depths of which I don't think I ever fully understood until now. They're the same person, but neither of them sees the other as who they are. Cal really looked at me as if I cheated on him.

How can he not understand it is him I love—whoever he decides to call himself. I hate feeling like this, and really, I shouldn't. I shouldn't just lie here and cry. I don't want Caylen to be this type of woman. I may have hurt him, but it wasn't intentional, and what he's done to me is much worse. I wouldn't even be in this situation if it weren't for him.

If anyone should be hurt, it should be me. How can he have the audacity to say those things to me? Like I didn't wait for him for two years. Like he didn't leave me alone to raise a child. I basically forgave him for having a freakin' fiancée, and the fact that he lied to me about his condition. I sit up and clutch my chest, the hollowness quickly incinerating as my anger washes over and through me. Why should I lie here and cry and worry? I've forgiven him a thousand times over. He can forgive me once, even though I'm not even sure that I need to be forgiven.

He may be furious with me, but he still loves me or he'd be gone. I head up the stairs, anger my new source of energy. I swing the door open. It's completely dark aside from a small sliver of light peeking into the room from the window, but I can see that he's lying on the bed with his hands behind his head, staring at the ceiling. The sight of him makes me pause, my once seething anger disappearing in seconds. This man. This man could easily be the death of me.

"You're still here?" he says. His tone suggests it's a joke, and my dissipating anger starts to grow again. "I thought you'd have run off and tattled to Chris's mommy and daddy."

"You have a lot of nerve," I say as I plant my feet on the floor.

He glances over at me. "Oh, that's a nice welcome. You fuck Chris and want to argue with *me*?" He laughs bitterly. He's switched. The emotion pouring off him earlier has been replaced with this indifferent, arrogant sarcasm. That will make this a whole lot easier.

I walk over to him and stare him directly in the eye. "This isn't about Chris. This is about you," I say venomously.

"It wasn't yesterday," he says sarcastically, as if this is a big joke.

"You're still the same selfish jerk you always were," I say, and he begins to laugh. "You think this is funny?" I yell at him and push his chest. He sits there, firmly planted as if my hits have absolutely no effect on him, and I completely lose it. "How dare you!" I yell at him, pulling at him with all my might, swinging my arms as hard as I can, trying to make him feel a fraction of my pain. "How could you do that to me?" I shout at him as we begin to tussle.

"Calm the fuck down!" he says, trying to contain me. I've gone from helpless fool to crazy woman in the span of ten seconds.

"What is wrong with you?" he says, covering up a laugh that makes me even more furious.

"You're what's wrong with me" I say, throwing fist after fist at him.

"Lauren, stop!" he says, finally grabbing me and throwing me on the bed. A second later he's on top of me, pinning me down. I hate that he's stronger than me, that he can contain me.

"I hate you!" I say, catching my breath, tears filling my eyes again. This man drives me insane, pulls my spirit out from the inside. For him to doubt that I love him for even a second hurts, especially when he pretends to not give a flying fuck.

"*You* left me Cal. *You*. *You* lied to me. I waited for *you* for almost two years. I had Caylen alone. You abandoned me, I didn't have an inkling of an idea of what was going on with you, and still I never gave up on us. EVER!" I shout at him, and I can see his hardened expression soften, but I don't care. I take a deep breath, trying to ignore the feelings that shoot through my body at his glance. My anger's turned into an overwhelming sadness. I close my eyes, remembering how it felt to lose him.

"You almost broke me," I mutter, not trying to hide my emotions. I'm tired of hiding them. I hid them from everyone else, even Chris. Cal, he's the one who needs to see them.

He lowers his gaze to mine, like he's thinking, absorbing my words. He leans down closer to my face, and my entire body is on edge. His lips near mine. It's been so long. So long since we were like this, in this position, but it hurts. His eyes look into mine, almost like Chris did a few hours ago. His hands loosen their grip. Finally, he sits up, freeing me from the confinement his body created as he pinned me down. I scold the part of me that wants to stay in this position. The tension is the only thing in the room thicker than the silence.

"When I left you, I thought I was doing the right thing," he says, his eyes finding mine. They're no longer the light green I've grown accustomed to over the past few weeks, but deep, dark, and menacing, like the sky before a storm.

"I left you because I knew I'd fucked up. I'd waited too long to tell you the truth, and then I found out the medication I thought would fix me could actually kill me," he says, his eyes leaving mine and finding the floor.

"What medicine?" I ask, and he looks up at me.

"It doesn't matter. It didn't work," he says, his voice quiet but stern. I think about what he means by the medication *not* working.

"You were trying to get rid of Chris?" I ask hesitantly.

"Trust me, he'd do the same thing in a second if he had the chance," he says. A statement I know for a fact is true, which makes this situation even more messed up.

"The day I left you . . ." Cal pauses as if trying to gather his thoughts. "It was the first unselfish thing I'd ever done. I thought I was doing the right thing. I didn't know you were pregnant. I never would have left if I knew that."

I look into the eyes I fell in love with a thousand times over, and as mad as I am, those same feelings are all still there. I sit up and move closer to him on the bed.

"Why didn't you tell me? How could you not trust me?" After everything that happened, that's what hurts the most. He didn't trust me to love him, to not give up on him, on us.

"Because I was trying to let you go," he says, bluntly, his voice stern and unwavering. He lifts his head, his eyes leave mine and sweep over me, drinking me in as if he's been dying of thirst.

"You deserved better than *this*," he says, letting out a long sigh.

"Do you think I would have left you if you told me? You should have given me a choice!"

"There wasn't a choice."

"You're right! I loved you. There wouldn't have been a choice other than being with you!"

"Tell me this is what you wanted, a husband so fucked up he can't even be the same person? That's what you dreamed of for your life?" He chuckles bitterly.

"It doesn't matter. I love you. There isn't a choice for me," I say, standing and meeting him where he is.

"There's a choice now," he says, closing the space between us.

"What are you talking about?"

"Me or Chris?" he says, and the words cause every nerve in my body to blaze. My mouth immediately becomes dry, and I can't speak. That isn't a choice. There is no choice.

"I can't do that."

"You can't?" He looks up briefly before his eyes narrow in on mine. "You chose him yesterday," he says, dangerously quiet.

"That was different. He needed to hear that," I say, feeling tears in my eyes.

"I don't give a shit what he needed to hear. You fell in love with me. Caylen is *my* daughter. This shouldn't be a hard decision!" He's yelling now.

"You're the *same* person, Cal," I say, grabbing his hand, pleading with him. He severs my grasp before he walks away.

"If anyone knows that isn't true, it should be you," he says quietly, and my eyes leave his. He *is* the same man. Making some arbitrary choice won't even matter, it would just hurt . . . one of them . . . both of them. Oh my God, this is insane!

"Don't choose then. I'll choose for you," he says, simply nodding his head, an amused grin spreading across his face, one that scares me more than his yelling. He steps away from me, shoots across the room, and grabs a black jacket and keys.

"What does that even mean? Where are you going?" I say, starting to follow him.

"Ask Chris, whenever he gets back," he says sarcastically, leaving the room.

"No!" I follow behind him, grabbing his arm.

"This. This is what is still wrong with us after everything. You running away, keeping me in the dark, not telling me how you feel!" I yell as he continues walking towards the door as if my words and my tears mean nothing.

"I choose Chris!" I yell at him. He stops in his tracks. He turns around and faces me with the same amused grin instead of the angry, pissed-off scowl I was expecting.

"You choose Chris?" he says, stalking towards me. I stand my ground and lift my head to meet his stare.

"You don't tell me how you feel, you're mean, you're self-centered, arrogant, and an asshole. I choose Chris," I say, commanding my voice to steady, putting on my best poker face. Does he know I'm bluffing? That it's a ploy? He eyes me for a moment, and I think he does, because his grin spreads into a full-fledged smile, and it makes me nervous. I knew what I said would stop him from leaving, but I didn't expect him to look happy about it. For a moment, I wonder if he's gone, and Chris is back in front of me, but that thought leaves as soon as he grabs me by the waist and lifts me up so we're face to face.

"You'd be bored with Chris in six months," he says, his lips inches away from mine, the huskiness in his voice reminding me how much I used to crave this man. And there it is, the one thing that Cal wins at, the electricity between us—an overload of energy in the air. The broken man I walked in on is gone, and the man who knows me, loves me, drove me to crazy and back is here right in front of me, daring me to not want him. He leans in, his lips touching mine, but they don't pull me into his. Just a touch, and my body is going crazy. I'm about to lose it, but he drops me back on floor. I land on my feet but stumble because I'm shaken, startled, and in a haze.

That's it?

The haze doesn't last long.

In a moment, he snatches me forward, and I crash against his chest. It's like an explosion. His hands are everywhere. His lips all over me. My clothes, his clothes, both flying. His kisses are rough but passionate. It's almost too intense. It's been so long since I felt him like this. It's so much, almost too much. My body's on fire, my skin tingles all over, my stomach is doing flips. I try to catch my breath, but he doesn't give me long before I'm against the wall, and he's inside of me. Why is his touch so electric? Why is it so easy for his kiss to cause me to melt?

"Cal," I can't help but moan as he thrusts inside of me. He was just there—well, Chris was just there—but it was so . . . *different*. Yesterday was gentle and sweet. This—it's like I'm being stretched, reminded that I haven't been touched by him in two years, and it hurts but, God, it's the best-feeling pain I've ever felt.

"You belong to me. Just me," he says in my ear as he continues. It's fast and rough, and I can't keep quiet. I'm so loud. God, I'm afraid everyone on the floor is going to hear me. I try to get my hands out of his grip, but he doesn't let me. He's moving faster and faster, too fast. I can barely breathe, I can't get enough air, but my body can't get enough of him. I feel it coming on faster and faster. I look up at him helplessly, a smug grin on his face.

"Chris could never do this to you," he moans in my ear. I close my eyes and bite my lip but it doesn't help.

"Let's be honest . . . there isn't a choice . . . you don't get to choose. I'm the only option," he taunts me, pushing deeper into me

"Oh my God," I shriek as my legs start to shake. It's happening faster than it's ever happened before. My hands are finally free, and I wrap them around his neck as if I'm holding on for dear life. I bury my head in his shoulder, but he grabs my hair and pulls my head back so I'm forced to look at him.

"I make you feel like this. No one else," he says as I come apart around him. I can't even respond. I breathe in as much air as I can, waiting for my body to return to its normal state, but before it does, he's flipped me around with my stomach against the wall, and he's back inside of me again.

"Cal, wait. Wait," I pant, but he doesn't. His hand slips between my thighs, and he's back inside of me again.

"We're not finished yet," he says into my ear as he starts again, and thank God he's holding me up, because I'm exhausted. Yet, my body still manages to come alive, waking up for him all over again. His mouth is on my neck sucking hard, so hard I know it's going to leave marks, and his fingers trace their favorite spot as he pushes into me. His fingers cause the most perfect pleasure I have felt in such a long time.

"Tell me to stop," he says. One of his hands squeezes my thigh as he goes faster and faster. I can't even speak, just an indistinguishable moan. I want him to stop but never stop, pleasure and pain crashing against one another inside of me.

"I dare you," he taunts me. Everything is spinning around me. I'm on a rollercoaster right at the edge of the highest peak

"You and I are much more alike than you think," he says. He's already so deep, but each thrust feels deeper than the last one. "You're like Chris on your weakest day, me on your best." He's rubbing me faster and faster, and I feel it coming again, tears coming just as I'm about to.

"Where's your fire, Lauren?" he says as I throw my head back, and I come down in waves.

"He put it out. But don't worry, I'll start it again." I hear him, but his words seem far away. I'm far away, like I'm floating. I just want to sleep, but I still feel him. I'm helpless and, as he finishes, his arms wrap around me pulling me back as close to him as possible. I feel like I've been both punished and rewarded. I glance back at him, my eyes barely able to stay open. His expression tells me that it was both. I can't even speak. All I want now is to sleep.

chapter 3

lauren

UNRAVELING. IF I had to describe the state I'm in, that would be it. I'm coming apart. He made me come apart again and again until I fell to pieces. Pieces he broke me into and threw into the deep-end of what's now my life, and I'm drowning.

How did I get here? How did I end up in the most complicated relationship I could have ever imagined? I think back to all of those days when I wondered where he was, who he was with, and if he was cheating. Was he was involved in some type of organized crime? I even entertained the idea that maybe he was doing covert missions for the CIA. I was so far off, but as crazy as all those explanations were, any of those things would have been easier to handle.

Now he's right here next to me, and it gives me comfort, but it also makes my heart skip a beat. This should be a turning point, but in what direction I don't know. Where is Chris? I don't even know if Cal is the one next to me at this point. The last time we had sex, he switched just like that. My life was as easy to flip as a light switch.

When I first saw Cal, I couldn't help but wonder if it were really Chris I slept with or if it was some strange type of mind game Cal was playing. Would Chris sleep with me? If he's still with Jenna, I can't see him doing that. I don't think that's who he is. But who is Cal? Who is Chris? They're one in the same but *so* different. Chris is lost, but I don't think that Cal is. Of the two, I think he knows exactly what's going on. HHe always has, and it's time for answers. If he thought that little display yesterday would shut me up, he has another thing coming. He's been gone for two years. I felt his loss each of those days, and now I need answers, not just for me but for Caylen and for his family.

Last night, it was like he was making up for lost time—two years of us not being together, not having my body—and yesterday, it felt like he claimed me. He owned me. He had to prove that I was his, to prove that he knew me better and in ways that Chris doesn't. The thing is, after all the time I've known him and the little time I've known Chris, I know more about Chris than Cal, and that knowledge alone makes me want to throw up. I'm still hurt that he didn't tell me the truth and disgusted we've fallen right back into our routine—the temporary fix of sex—and I can't let this happen again. He said I lost my fire with Chris, the spark in me was gone. Well if my spark means being a screaming lunatic, no I wasn't that way with Chris. It was nice, even if it made me feel as if I were walking on egg shells most of the time. I felt like I had to be careful with Chris. He was vulnerable, almost fragile, but what would happen once Chris was broken? Would a broken Chris be Cal? Did I break Chris?

"You have an hour to get dressed or I'm leaving you," he says, his voice and tone distinctive and completely different from the voice I've been hearing for the past few weeks. One that was almost forgotten but is etching itself in my memory again, vibrating through me.

I try to think of how the old Lauren would respond and compare it to the Lauren I've been the past few weeks. I can't help wondering . . . who am I now? The Lauren of yesterday is gone, obliterated. He fucked the complete life out of her. I try to find the words of who I should be, but I'm at a complete loss. Nothing I can think of seems adequate, so I stay perfectly still and quiet. That's not something I've ever done before. I turn to see him disappear into the bathroom, bare as an egg, body of a god, and with the attitude of a spoiled six year old.

He's still upset. But from what I've learned about Chris in the weeks I've been getting to know him, Chris forgives easily, and I know from past experiences that Cal holds grudges like a hoarder. I get up from the bed and try to think. What we did last night wasn't making love. It was the opposite, and I don't know how to feel about that.

I don't know what to do, but I have to tell his parents. I can't avoid them because they have Caylen, and I can't tell Cal. I've never been so confused in my life. My eyes make a sweep of the room in a frantic search for my clothes. Of course, my clothes aren't in here. They're somewhere on the first floor of the suite. I grab the sheet, wrap it around myself, and head downstairs. My clothes are strewn all across the room. I grab the pieces from where they lay scattered all over the place and put them on. Out of the corner of my eye, I spot my phone, the alert light blinking, beckoning me. I'm afraid to see how many messages are on it. I take a deep breath and see that I have eighteen missed calls and twelve voice messages. I scroll through and see the numbers from Gwen, Lisa, and Helen.

Shit.

I don't know what to tell these people. I don't expect Cal to tell them anything. I scroll through the numbers and dial Helen's. It goes to voicemail. I call Lisa's. I can't call Mrs. Scott. I can't tell her any of this over the phone. I glance back towards the room.

I don't know why I feel like I have to sneak and do this. Should I do this? Ugh! I'm not going to drive myself crazy about this. It's time to cut the bullshit. I head back up stairs and into the bedroom. I hear the shower running.

"I've been thinking of whether I should call your parents or not," I say loudly enough for him to hear me over the water. He doesn't say anything.

"They have Caylen. I'm going to have to tell them something. I was going to call and tell them without speaking with you, but I'm trying to start something new. I want nothing but open and honest communication between us. So can you let me know your thoughts on that?" I say in almost one breath.

He steps out of the shower, and I force my eyes to stay on his face and go nowhere else, but the wall between us is back up again. His eyes are on me, and I can't read him. His stare is blank, but he steps towards me, completely naked with a sly smirk stretched across his face. My breath hitches as he reaches behind me to grab a towel and wipes his face before wrapping it around his waist.

"Are you going to say anything?" I ask him, feeling my stoic façade begin to crumble beneath me. He bites his lips trying to suppress the smile peeking through. He likes me upset. How could I forget?

"Fine," I say, pulling out my phone. "I'll give them a call." Before I can even get my thumb to touch a button, he snatches it from my hand. I expect him to leave the room or to even flush it down the toilet, but he doesn't. He hits a few keys, and the phone starts to ring on speaker.

"Lauren, where the hell are you, and why haven't you been answering our calls?"

It's Mr. Scott, and my eyes widen.

"Who the fuck do you think you're talking to?" Cal's voice sends a chill through my spine. There's a stunned silence on the other end. Mr. Scott is obviously at a loss for words.

"If you ever speak to my wife like that again, I'm going to break your fucking legs," he says, his grip tightening on the phone.

"We'll be there to get our daughter tonight. I'll call you when we're a few minutes away. Have her dressed and ready to leave." He hangs up and tosses the phone to me before stepping closer, his arm wrapping around my back, pulling me towards him and leaning down to my ear.

"I'm not a little boy. I thought I reminded you of that last night," he says huskily, his grip tightening on my waist.

"Chris's parents don't scare me. Dexter has no authority over me. I can give a shit what anyone else thinks about me being back. You can call and alert the newspaper if you feel the need to. *You're* either in this with me or you're not. Chris won't be back anytime soon," he says, letting me go and leaving the bathroom. My phone begins to ring again. I'm guessing it's probably a not-so-stunned Mr. Scott calling back in a fury, but when I glance down, I see that it's Lisa. She's called me at least four times. I shake my head and pick up.

"Hey, Lisa," I say, trying my best to mask the utter terror pumping through my veins.

"Lauren, have you talked to Chris? I've been trying to call him and . . ." Before she can finish, Cal's back in front of me and snatches the phone from my hand.

"Don't ever call me or Lauren again. I'm not kidding! If you do, I will ruin you. Stay the fuck away!"

I stand in front of him in complete shock. "Do you even know who that was?"

"Don't fucking answer for her," he says bitterly, before leaving the room. I follow.

"What's your problem with Lisa?" I ask, exasperated.

"I mean it," he says pointedly.

"Is this about her not wanting to sleep with you?" I told Lisa I wouldn't tell Chris, but this is Cal. A condescending laugh escapes him.

"Is that what that lying little cunt told you?" he says, throwing on his clothes.

"How about you tell me? How about you tell me about everything?" I say, grabbing his wrist. "About why you hate your parents . . ."

"I don't hate my parents," he says abruptly.

"Your dad," I reiterate. "What happened to make you like this?"

"Like what? Like me? What screwed me up so bad to bring me about? Is that what you're asking me?"

"That's not what I meant," I say quietly.

"No, that's *exactly* what you meant," he spits back.

"Don't turn this around on me. This is bigger than you and me now. We have a daughter, Cal," I plead.

"You're not my fucking shrink, Lauren. You're my *wife*. The woman *I* asked to marry *me*. You know everything now, so let's get past this. I'm ready to get back to normal. No more of this bullshit."

"Normal? What we had is not normal. Just be honest with me. *Please*. Don't I deserve that at least?"

"Why do you think I know everything?" he asks quietly.

I hesitate. He should know everything, right? He has to; he's the alter. But how do I say that without it being an insult? Looking at him, I can't say it. I still don't want to admit it. I am mad at him, but I don't want to hurt him—I *never* wanted to hurt Cal—and if I say it out loud right in front of him, I know it will hurt him. Or maybe I'm just afraid of saying it, of saying those actual words.

"You can say it, Lauren. I won't melt. I'm not a mythical creature," he says with an amused grin.

"I can only go off of what I know, and you haven't told me anything."

"I don't know who your loyalty lies with. So I'll pass for now," he says wryly.

"What are you talking about?"

"You know exactly what I mean. We can save a lot of time if you stop playing stupid. Remember that I know you like the back of my hand."

He has a lot fucking nerve. Of course, he does. It is Cal, after all. He doesn't know who my loyalty lies with? I waited for him for two years after he walked out on me. Yet, he questions my loyalty? I don't understand what else I need to do to prove my loyalty to him. Why am I paying for a mistake I wasn't aware I'd made? I'm trying so hard to keep my emotions in check, especially my anger and my frustration. It's taking nearly all of my willpower to remain calm and not fly off the handle again.

But, like always, Cal has a way of pushing my buttons. He can't think I'm going to go along with this—all his secrets, living a lie, pretending to be happy about the very thing that unraveled our marriage. He steps toward me, closing the distance between us. His gray eyes cling to mine, as if he's reading my mind.

"Don't worry, gorgeous. You'll know everything soon. Just make sure you're ready for it." At that, he leaves me standing where I am with more questions than answers. Cal has always had a knack for leaving me stupefied. His statement isn't a simple declaration; it's more like a threat. But he doesn't get to do this to me anymore. I could easily retaliate with the threat of leaving, but I can't bring myself to do it. I have a daughter to think about. And then there's Chris. I feel a world of responsibility on my shoulders, and I don't know how long I can hold it all up.

"I'll meet you downstairs," he says, as he heads out the door.

How do I do this? I can't walk out on him. He's mentally unstable, but I can't go through a life of secrets anymore! It's Cal, but he's different, a little colder, a little more raw, uncensored and unpredictable, and there's no way I can let him out of my sight.

I TRY TO gather my thoughts as I make my way downstairs. They're everywhere, on everything. I feel powerless, more than I ever have before. I walk out of the hotel and see him sitting in the Audi. I take a deep breath before getting in. I feel like I'm slipping back into my old life. He's *still* angry, but he's *still* here with me and that means all hope isn't completely lost. I'm not as powerless as I thought. We're both at odds, but we *still* love each other. I used to think of it as only my weakness, but now I know it's his weakness too, and I fully intend to use it to try to fix this mess—*if* we can be fixed.

"So what's the plan?" I try to keep bitter sarcasm out of my voice, but I'm sure it's not working. "We just go back to being how we were before? Let's remember, things weren't exactly peachy."

He doesn't even glance my way.

"And I'm supposed to pretend that the past two years haven't happened? That I don't know the truth?"

"Can you just enjoy the fucking ride?" he says as if he is annoyed with me. I exhale and take a breath. I don't know how many breaths I can take to keep from exploding on his nonchalant, arrogant ass! Thank God I have been able to practice exercising my patience with Chris these past few weeks. Talking to him is useless at this point, so I won't say anything to him until I have the right words to say. I turn my attention towards the window, looking out over the city that I drove into with a vastly different man. My thoughts are interrupted when I hear him chuckle. Out of the corner of my eye, I see him with an amused grin on his face.

"What happened to you?" he asks, amused.

"I grew up. You should try it sometime."

He grins. "I think there is more to it than that."

"Don't play psychiatrist with me if you don't want me to play one with you," I spit back at him.

He laughs at that, but he doesn't retort. That is a first. His silence is unexpected and a little unnerving.

"Did you miss me?"

These words surprise me. He even sounds sincere. My eyes trail over to him, and for a moment, I want to call a truce, but we both have our walls up for our own reasons. "Of course I did."

"Did you miss me when you were with him?"

I wonder if it's always going to be like this—a contest between the two of them. I want to comment on it, but I decide against it and I tell him the truth. *"Especially* when I was with him."

He looks over at me, a hint of disbelief lingering on his expression. Did my sleeping with Chris cause him to think that we have nothing, that my feelings for him are gone? There are so many questions I want to ask him, but I know he won't answer most of them, so I ask him the simplest while he's in a talking mood.

"Did you miss me?"

There's a long silence, and right when I think he's not going to answer, he says, "Every day." His tone is quiet and makes me smile, but a sense of sadness washes over me. If he's here, where is Chris now?

"It used to be us before anything. Now it seems like that's changed," he says solemnly.

"We have a daughter now. It can't be like that anymore. Secrets almost destroyed us, Cal. We almost lost each other; I did lose you. I don't want that to happen again."

I wish this conversation wasn't happening during a drive. Are my words affecting him? Or are they going in one ear and out the other? He has always put a huge wall up around himself, one that I could never get behind. Has he changed? Is this the same man that left me on the floor in tears and alone all those years ago? He's quiet, which means he's probably thinking. This is good. So I decide to push a little more.

"I want you to get better because I love you and for our daughter." I see his jaw flinch, and I know I took it too far too fast.

"Better, meaning Chris?" he asks through clenched teeth.

"Better, meaning all of you," I say defensively.

"Why didn't you have this conversation with him?"

"I was going to, but he's not here now—you are. But why does it even matter? This shouldn't be you versus him. We're in this together."

"We are? Well, since we're all in this together, tell me why he left?" he spits out, and my patience is officially up.

"You tell me! Better yet, how about you tell me how this all works? Does he decide? Do you decide? Is there a fucking schedule that I can get a copy of? Because *this* is insane. I thought when you came back, I would have answers. That the big puzzle in my life would be solved, but of course, it's not. That would be easy, and with you, nothing is ever easy."

"There she is."

"Who?"

"The real you," he answers smugly. He's such a smart ass.

Great, he wants me to be a screaming lunatic, and Chris wants me to be a nun.

Fanfreakintastic.

chapter 4

WE SURVIVE THE ride without killing each other, and eventually, I fall asleep. How do you fall asleep in the midst of a storm, surrounded by a torrent of unanswered questions? I don't know, but eventually your mind and body shut down giving you a respite, and I dream. I dream about my world, about how it was, about Chris coming into it, how he changed things and then Cal coming back, flipping things on their head. When I wake, I think about where my world is going. How do I parent in the midst of dysfunction? How do I avoid being pulled back to the place I used to be? I feel like I'm fighting a war, weaponless and against an opponent that knows my very weakness is him. I open my eyes to see that it's dark out. The car has stopped, and my door is open. I look up to see him leaning over me, his hands resting on the roof of the car. I sit up and look around.

"Where are we?" I ask, a yawn escaping my mouth. It doesn't look like we're in a part of Michigan or Chicago.

"Is that something you really need to know?" he quips. He's such a smart ass.

"Yes I need to know where we are in relation to our daughter. You know, the one we were supposed to pick up from your parents."

"Gwen knows we're picking her up tomorrow," he replies.

"You talked to your mom?" I ask, surprised.

"Gwen is one of the few people who doesn't think I'm the anti-Christ," he says sarcastically.

"And we're in Ventian, a shitty little suburb in Michigan" he says.

"What are we doing?"

"You say you want to know the whole story . . . all *my* secrets. Well, this is where it starts," he says, reaching his hand out to me. I look up at him skeptically.

"Is this a game or something?"

"Games are for kids. Welcome to our new fucked-up reality," he says.

Riddles and games, all freakin' puzzle pieces. It'd be too easy get straight answers. I let out a deep breath and watch him walk into the house.

I look around. It's late evening, and the street is quiet. It looks like a lower, lower middle-class neighborhood. I reluctantly follow him. I stop half way and wonder if I should just jump back in the car and speed off to the Scotts'. That would be the logical thing to do, then again, I've never been logical when it comes to Cal and me. If this is a game, though, there will be a winner and a loser. I don't plan on losing.

I stop at the little mailbox in front of the house and look in it. I pull out three letters that all say Cal Scott on them. What the hell? He actually had this place—owns it, maybe? But, for how long and why?

"What? Are you Nancy Drew, now?" he chuckles before disappearing into the house. I begrudgingly make my way up the stairs and follow him into the little two-level home. By the time I'm in, he's flicked on the lights, and I'm actually shocked. The outside of the house looks old and more than a little run-down, but inside, it's completely different. It's decorated in cool grays and shades of blue. I'm impressed. It looks like a professionally decorated space. On one end of the living room is a pale gray sofa with dark-blue pillows. A glass, asymmetrically-shaped coffee table with metal legs fills the space between the sofa and two printed, similarly colored, armless chairs. It looks expensive, like our home, which would mean the furnishings in this house are more than the house is even worth. In the left corner of the room is a fireplace surrounded by black stone. The kitchen is modern, complete with stainless steel appliances and is painted the same grays and blues as the living area with just a touch of lime green in the backsplash mosaic and in the hand towels.

"So when did you get this? Why do you even have this?" I ask, confused.

"It was before us and the area interests me," he says simply, taking off his jacket and putting it away in a closet. His phone vibrates on the counter top. He glances at it, and a wide smile spreads across his face.

"It's Jenna," he says, looking over at me. "You want to get it? What do you think Chris would say to her? Since he's your new soulmate and all," he says sarcastically. I can't believe he's really jealous.

When I make no move to answer the phone, he swipes it from the counter and answers with a curt, "What's up, Jenna?"

"No, it's not Chris. It's Cal. I was going to be calling you soon anyway. Just thought you should know Chris fucked Lauren last night," he says matter-of-factly.

"Really, Cal?" I shout at him. I can't believe he just said that! Well actually I can believe it, but oh my God!

"Yeah, I couldn't believe it either. The pussy grew a dick—a scientific anomaly." He winks at me.

"Hang up the phone," I say tightly, walking over to him. He backs away from me.

"I didn't have anything to do with it. It was all him, trust me," he continues, dodging my attempt to snatch the phone away from him. "If it makes you feel any better. I plan on fucking him right out of her memory," he says with a wink.

"You are such an asshole!" I shout at him. Jenna's not one of my favorite people. She's actually my least favorite person, but she deserves to hear about Chris's absence a helluva lot better than that.

"I'm the asshole?" he laughs boisterously.

"I'm not the one who screwed her fiancé," he chuckles.

"Do you hear yourself?" I say angrily. "You're mad at me because I slept with *you*? I let *you* touch me, *your* hands, *and your* lips. You don't trust me because of that?" I laugh hysterically, and his face hardens.

"I don't trust you because you turned on me!"

"Turned on you?" I ask in disbelief.

"You weren't supposed to give up on us, remember?" he says bitterly. "You told me you'd never look at me like I was the villain," he continues, walking towards me.

"I've never looked at you like that!"

"How do you think you're looking at me right now?"

The quietness is eerie. For a second, I see vulnerability in his eyes. This man hides behind his arrogance, his cockiness, and hard façade. I have to remind myself this unbreakable man I've come to think of as Cal, isn't right. He has a mental illness. He is broken, more broken than I've ever been, and it's entirely possible that he, in fact, sees what I did as a legitimate act of betrayal. I let out a sigh and lean on the counter.

"Are we going to be able to get past this? Are you going to hate me forever and never trust me again? Is this it for us?" I ask him sincerely.

He looks away from me. "I'm going to go get some groceries. Maybe you can make use of some of those cooking lessons you've been taking," he says before walking out the door. How much does he remember? Is it everything? How does he know all, and Chris knows nothing except what Cal wants him to?

chapter 5

April 30th, 2008

I DON'T GO on dates. I haven't had to since I've been here. I like to have fun. I like things to be easy, and I usually like my girls the same way—*easy*. I can see through most girls, but this one's different. I'm not sure if I like it or not, but I guess I do because I'm here with her. It's the first time I've been around a girl who doesn't look like she dressed up for me—that she tried at least. She's still gorgeous; I don't think she wouldn't be if she tried. I haven't been around a girl in a long time who didn't have on a skirt that barely covered her ass, with tits on high alert. Even dressed how she is, she's one of the most beautiful women I've ever seen. In the club, she looked different. There, she was playing dress up. This, I think, is the girl behind the mask. Or maybe I'm wrong. I'm pretty good at reading people, but I read her wrong when I first saw her.

Something about her scares me. She seems innocent, breakable, and that terrifies the fuck out of me. I'm used to dealing with girls that have already been fucked up, so it's not on me. I hope I'm not fucking myself in this. I'm just going to make up for throwing her into the disaster I put her smack in the middle of. That's it. She'll feel better, I'll feel better, and we can both move on. If only she didn't look at me with those wide hazel eyes and that innocent smile. Fuck, I hope she's not a virgin. Nah, she can't be. I couldn't see that douchebag she was with waiting on a virgin.

"Where are we going, Cal?" she asks nervously as we make our way to the bridge. I try to cover the smile growing on my face. Getting her on the back of my bike was difficult. When I tell her what we're doing here, she might freak the hell out. I stop and turn to face her and take her hands. Her eyes widen, and I ignore how my heart speeds up. She lets out a little sigh. I force my eyes away from her lips. They're perfect and begging me to kiss them.

"How open-minded are you?" I ask her, closing the distance between us.

She looks at me skeptically. "You're not taking me to a giant wilderness orgy are you?" she jokes. Huh, she's funny.

"The next best thing," I say with a laugh, and she bites her thumb. I hope she stops doing stuff like that. It's so damn sexy, and I'm not going to sleep with her.

Fuck, I am going to sleep with her.

"We're going bungee-jumping," I tell her reluctantly, and her eyes widen.

"What?!" she says, snatching her hands from me. "No. No, I can't." She shakes her head.

"Yes, you can," I say, taking her hand again.

"Are you one of those people—uh, what do you call them?—adrenaline junkies?" She starts to laugh, holding her head in her hand.

"Something like that, but it's not bad. After you do it, you'll feel like a different person," I promise her.

She looks at me skeptically then past me. "This, this doesn't look like an authorized site. Are we supposed to be doing this here?" she says nervously.

"Okay, so it's not exactly authorized, but Jake here is the man. I've jumped with him a dozen times. You won't die. I promise you," I say, trying to contain my laugh at the horrified look on her face. She lets out a deep sigh and turns away from me.

She's not going to do it. Maybe bungee-jumping was a little too much, but dinner and a movie? That's boring as hell.

I walk closer to her, and I hear her breath hitch. It's a turn on like nothing else. "Afraid of trying something new?" I ask her as her eyes find mine, and she looks into them like she's trying to see what's behind them. It's unnerving and a thrilling rush all at once.

"Okay, let's do it," she says, walking past me towards Jake.

"Really?" I ask, surprised.

"I didn't ride an hour on the back of that death machine to sit and watch you have all the fun," she says, nudging me.

There's more to this girl than I thought.

"Only thing is, I get to go first," she says nervously.

"You're kind of a boss aren't you, Lauren?"

She rolls her eyes at me. "I better survive," she mutters.

"You're in good hands," Jake says as we approach him. He turns to me. "C. Scott, and who is this cute little thing?"

"This cute little thing's name is Lauren," she answers before I can. I smirk at Jake who throws his hands up.

"Feisty?" he quips.

"So you know what you're doing right?" she asks as he picks up the restraint.

"I haven't killed this guy yet," he answers.

"Who's going first?" he asks. As Lauren steps closer to the edge of the bridge, her eyes widen.

"She is," I pipe in, and Jake gives me a knowing smile.

"I am," she says quietly, shooting me a nervous glance.

It only takes Jake a few minutes to suit her up. "You're awfully quiet, feisty," he says.

"I'm praying," she says with a light chuckle.

"It's funny how spiritual people get before doing this," he jokes.

"How many times have you done this?" she asks, after turning to face me.

"Twelve," I answer, and her eyes bug out of her head. "It's not as fun as skydiving," I tell her, and she looks at me in disbelief.

"The first of the month, he's usually out here," Jake chimes in.

"Do you try to scare all your dates half to death?"

"Feisty, you're the first," Jake says, giving her a pat on the back. I shoot him a warning glare.

"So I'm the lucky one, huh?" she asks, nodding her head, and I give her a wink.

"Are you ready?" Jake asks, and I watch as the color literally drains from her face.

"No. But let's do this," she says as confidently as she can.

"You've got this," I tell her as she walks to her jumping point.

Jake stands behind her. "Hold out your arms and take a deep breath."

I can feel my heart pounding, remembering my first jump. After that, I felt like I was better than *him*. That I could do anything. She does as he says, and I can hear how much air she's sucking in.

"I'm going to count to five, and then you're going to jump, okay?" Jake tells her, and I can see she's shaking.

"Kiss for good luck?" I ask her to relieve some tension.

"I'm not so sure what type of luck you are for me yet," she says nervously.

"One two, three, four . . . any last words?" Jake asks.

"If this goes wrong, and I die, I'm haunting both of you," and with that, she sucks in one last breath, closes her eyes, and jumps.

"I thought she'd be a staller," Jake says as we watch her soar through the air, her screams echoing.

My phone rings. It's Dexter. You'd think someone with as much money as he has would find more to do than call me all the damn time.

"What's up Dexter?"

"Gwen has called me about a thousand and one times this week."

"That's nothing new."

"I'm unsure as to why you won't speak with her. From what you've disclosed to me I see no r—"

"I'll talk to her when I have something to say to her. Right now there's nothing," I say plainly, waiting to hear his disapproving huff.

"Helen will be back in town this week. Will you be able to see her?" he asks, and I roll my eyes.

"I have the meeting with the Luxe brothers,"

"Well, this is a little more important wouldn't you say?"

"Sure, whatever. I'll give you a call back. I'm on a date right now, I think it's rude to stay on the phone during it."

"You're on a date?" He sounds skeptical. "Since when do you date?"

I laugh. "Since I felt like it."

"Since when do you *feel*?" he asks wryly.

"Funny. I'll talk to you later Dexter. Always a pleasure," I say, hanging up just as Lauren has been pulled up.

"You survived, feisty. I'm a little sad you won't be haunting me tonight," Jake flirts.

"Hey watch it," I say, warning him. He throws his hands up in mock surrender.

"Oh, my God! That was insane!" she says excitedly as Jake starts to help her remove her safety gear.

"I've got it," I tell him. He frowns but wisely backs off.

"Good insane or . . . ?" I ask her hesitantly but, from the excitement in her face, I already know the answer.

"Amazingly insane. I can't believe I did that! I've never done anything like that before. I just jumped off a bridge and survived!"

"And you jumped without stalling. Not a lot of people do that," I admit, as I free her from her harness.

"Did you stall? Your first time, that is?"

"What do you think?" I ask her curiously, and she takes a moment as if she's really thinking. "No. You seem to do things without thinking first," she says, and I chuckle.

"Is that a good or bad thing?" I ask skeptically, and for the first time since she's jumped, she looks away shyly before meeting my eyes.

"It can be both," her reply is quiet.

I want to kiss her, right here, right now. Usually I would, but *I'm* the one stalling now. Which is strange because I'm not a staller. I don't think; I just do. But something about her makes me stop and think, and I'm not sure what to do with her. I'm not used to being in this territory. The reason I'm even here is foreign to me. I don't do this. I don't rescue girls from assholes. I *am* the asshole—well, not as big as some of them are. I don't think back on the damage I've done. I definitely don't think about fixing it. I don't even date; yet, here I am. Smack dab in the middle of a date with a girl who is too beautiful to not want to sleep with, who has eyes that make you not want to look away but make you stare. She gives me a conscience—one I'm not used to having, one that I prefer to block out. That's a bridge I don't want to cross. She's more than tempting, she's dangerous.

And fuck if danger isn't my thing.

lauren

WHEN CAL FINALLY decides to waltz back in, he has a bag of groceries. He glances over at me sitting on the couch, the TV on as a distraction. I want to bombard him with questions as soon as he walks through the door, but of course, that would be the dumbest thing to do and the very thing that will get me no answers. He brought me here for a reason. I know he loves me; he *has* to. I have to give him time, but how much time?

"Are you going to put some of those cooking lessons to use?" he asks, setting the bag on the table before disappearing into the bedroom. How much does Cal know, what does he see? Does he know everything that happens with Chris? I head to the counter and see that there is a carton of apple juice, eggs, bacon, two steaks, three potatoes, and a bag of spinach. If he were Chris, this definitely wouldn't be enough food.

I start to wonder how long we're going to be here. For a day? Several? I trust that Caylen is fine with the Scotts, but she should be with us . . . shouldn't she? When she is with us, how does this work? Is he going to tell her he's Cal and what will happen if Chris comes back? What happens as she gets older? Does she live with two dads? Do I become the woman with two husbands?

"You're thinking too much," his voice interrupts me from my trance. I try to read him. What's his mood?

He's a blank canvas.

"I try to keep my thoughts to myself these days. It seems to work out better for everyone," I say quietly as I move past him to the sink to wash my hands. He leans back so that he can look at my face. His stare sends chills down my spine. He still has the ability to look at me and un-nerve my thoughts, to unhinge my anger.

"I've been told that can cause serious problems," he says, and I try to stop myself from laughing. I feel him behind me, his chest pressing against my back. I close my eyes and think about how we were before, before all of this. When we were just us. He presses closer against me as his hands move on both sides of me, and he washes them.

I've made up my mind. I won't give him my body if he won't give me the truth. He has my heart, but I can at least deny him my physical self, no matter how difficult it is.

I move away from him and search through the drawers for the uten-sils we need. Without missing a beat, he pulls out a skillet and bowl. It's quiet, eerily quiet, despite unspoken words blaring between us. I don't think we have ever gone this long without talking to the other, unless one of us was pissed off. I don't think he is. However, I am pissed, but more than anything, I'm hurt and still off-balance from everything that's happened. Questions upon questions, unsolved mysteries, disconnected theories that want to burst out of me. I don't voice them, though. I keep them confined in the pit of my stomach, but they swirl around as dinner starts.

He does the hard part of the cooking. He makes the steak and the potatoes. I watch as he goes about doing what I now know he learned from Mrs. Scott, that's one mystery solved. I've tended to the spinach, which was easy.

"There're plates in the cabinet over the sink. You want to put them on the table? I'm almost done, but your spinach is about to overcook."

Shit.

I turn off the stove and, sure enough, there are dishes in the cabinets over me. I grab service for two and lay them out on the table. A few mo-ments later, he brings the food. For some reason, he seems more domes-ticated than he ever was years ago. After he puts the food out and I've made my plate, I quickly say a prayer. A habit I've picked up from eating dinner with the Scotts. When I open my eyes, I catch him observing me as if he's absorbing my every move. I expect him to say something, but he doesn't. I look at his plate, which is the half the size of Chris's, and I can't help but giggle. He eyes me suspiciously.

"What?" he asks, irritated. I shake my head and giggle again.

"What, Lauren?" he demands.

"You and Chris . . . eat so . . . differently," I say, quickly stuffing my mouth with a spoonful of potatoes. It feels different saying his name to Cal. It doesn't feel like a sore subject, but I glance at him to see if I'm wrong. Instead of seeing him frown, a smug grin spreads across his face.

"He ate like a pig because he wasn't getting any," he says, and I try to hide my shock. He's watching me, waiting on my reaction. I'm trying to not give him one, but what is he talking about? I want to play coy but screw that.

"What do you mean?" He can't be saying what I think he's inferring. That's not possible, is it?

"He and Jenna never . . ." I trail off.

"Nope," he says, his eyes directly on mine, unearthing feelings within me that only he has been able to do, with just his stare. I don't know how to feel. Happy? I'm ecstatic, actually. All this time, I tried to never think about him and Jenna. It hurt too much. It made me sick. But, to know that he never . . . that means Cal never . . . and what I did with Chris, he sees as . . . God this sucks.

"Did that have anything to do with you?" I say quietly.

"What do you think?" he says stoically, and I get up from the table. Cal could always be a jerk when he wanted, but now he's like a jerk with PMS. I head to the bedroom and slam the door. Was it a stupid question? How the hell do I know what's stupid or off-limits since he's shut himself off from me? The walls are up again, and I feel lost because I have no idea what to do about it.

I feel the bed shift as he sits down on it. There's silence, so much so that it fills the room. A moment later, his hand touches my back, causing a warm sensation to run through me, but I shift away from him. That's just how it starts, and *that* will not start tonight. There are so many other important things that need to be brought to the table and distracting me with his form of physical comfort won't work.

No more distractions.

"I want to talk," I say, rolling over to face him. He looks me in the eyes. I expect a look of scorn or disdain, but I don't find that at all. He looks away from me briefly, and I slowly glide my hand across the bed and touch his. "Please," I say, as sincerely as I can. Silence passes between us.

"I don't remember a lot of my childhood. I know I had brothers and sisters. Or I remember playing with a lot of other kids, at least," he continues. He doesn't look at me but ahead of him. I wanted to talk, but I definitely didn't expect this answer.

"My mom's name was Isabella. My . . . biological dad's name is Clay. She died when I was five. I've been trying to find Clay since before I met you."

I sit up in bed and move near him. He turns to look at me, and his expression is nearly stoic.

"How much do you want to know? Are you really ready to know? People think they want to know things, but it can be ugly. It can change things."

"There's nothing that can change the way I feel about you," I promise him. He nods his head.

"I know that you want things to be normal for Caylen. I don't want her to be screwed up by me. I know why things have to be different now," he says, looking me in the eyes.

"They have to," I admit.

"What do you want to know?" he asks casually, his posture adjusts with his tone as if he's just said the simplest thing in the world.

"Are you really going to tell me?" I ask him.

"I'll tell you whatever I can," he says, his eyes on mine. I sit up, taken off guard by his openness.

"If you want to?" I ask, still cautious of the turn this has taken.

"If I think it pertains to you," he says simply. There's always a catch. I let out a deep breath.

"Why do you hate your dad?"

"William?" he scoffs.

I nod.

"Because he's an asshole," he answers simply.

I can't exactly argue with that. "But there has to be more to it than that."

"Next question," he says gruffly.

Instead of arguing, I go on to the next question, "When Chris comes out, what happens to you?"

His eyebrow raises, and he looks directly ahead, his hardened expression softens. "I'm still there. I'm always there, it just . . . sometimes I can choose not to be," he says quietly.

"So you don't go in this dark prison or something," I ask, the question sounding silly and immature, but it's honest.

A small smirk spreads across his face. "It's not really like that. It's more like a dream. Sometimes I choose to sleep instead, if that makes sense. When he met Jenna, I was asleep if that's what you want to call it. I didn't want to be around. I'd just left you. Gwen was dying. It was his turn to deal with the shitty side of life," he says quietly.

"So you can choose when you come back?" I ask him with bated breath. My stomach coils. If he says he can, I don't know if I can handle that information because knowing that he could have come back at any time and didn't, will hurt more than anything he's said to me.

"No. If it worked liked that, Chris would have been gone. Like I said, it's like dreaming almost. Sometimes you can control what happens, and other times you're just stuck watching. It used to be easier to keep him from taking control, now it's harder." He stands up and walks across the room.

"Where is he now? Why does he not remember things but you do?" I ask him.

"Can that be enough for now? Just for tonight?" he asks me, looking into my eyes, and I nod. I don't know exactly why we're here, or the fact that a simple piece of information pacifies me, but I feel like what he's just told me isn't so simple. The reason why we're here isn't just a coincidence.

"One more question?" I ask him, and he lets out an exasperated huff but nods. "Do you really not trust me anymore?" I ask, afraid to hear the answer, but it's something that I need to hear. Is loving the other side of him disloyal? I always wanted him to be able to count on me, to let me in, to be there for him. If he doesn't trust me, if what happened between

Chris and me makes that impossible, how can we ever move forward?

"I trust you more than I trust myself," he says before lying down next to me. The space between us feels foreign. I don't cross it, but slowly he does, pulling me closer to him, skin to skin. His touches start slow and my body melts, tension everywhere but disappears as his caresses become firmer, deeper.

His hands move everywhere and find places that haven't been touched like this in so long. It's so different from last night when I could feel his passion, anger, and frustration coursing through me. This time he doesn't claim me but shows me in every way that I'm his. That he knows my body like no one else. I want to give in and break my rule. I'm so close to it . . .

"I'm so sorry babe. I never meant to hurt you. I thought I was doing what was right," He whispers in my ear, and he holds me close and long, I breathe him in and imprint his touch on my memory. I close my eyes, sleep catching up with me.

"I'll never hurt you again. Even if I have to give you up."

chapter 6

I T WAS CLOSE, too close. I tried so fucking hard to not want her. I almost had her, right there, devoured her. She wouldn't have even known what was coming. I can't get her lips out of my mind, how she moaned in my ear, how everywhere I touched her caused her to react, I can't imagine what she'd be like to fu . . .

April 31st, 2008

No. I can't. She's not the type that would get over it. I can't see her moving forward with no strings attached.

Sex won't be just sex.

When I saw that prick's name on her cellphone, I wanted to go break his fucking neck. Me, jealous? One date and I'm jealous? No, jealous isn't the word, he isn't even competition. I feel possessive. I don't want him anywhere near her.

He hurt her, but what the hell am I going to do? Why couldn't she be easy like the rest? But if she were, I wouldn't be interested in her. She's different, and that's why I like her, why I want her. I haven't liked a girl in a long time. I've tolerated them, been comfortable around them, but I *like* this girl. The way she smiles, the way she talks, and how she listens. The way she looks at me, like she sees something that I don't see, that's what bugs me. She sees something that isn't real, that will never be, *that's* not who I am.

I should quit while I'm ahead. She's one of the good ones. She'll make someone a good wife one day. Maybe one day she'll meet a normal guy, with normal expectations, who's not fucked-up. She's the type that wants that life, so why waste time? If only she just wanted fun. I could give her fun. I could give her amazing. I could make her forget about anyone that she thought made her feel anything. I'd do things to her . . . that I'm never going to do because it'll make things worse!

She puts on a tough act, and she's feisty, but I can see beyond it. She hasn't been broken yet, and I don't want to be the one to do it.

"Never on time, are we?"

It's Helen.

I thought I'd beat her here. I'm never on time, anyway.

"I'd hate to surprise you," I say with a wink before flopping on the leather couch in her office. She rolls her eyes. She'd better not be in a pissed-off mood today.

Helen Lyce-Crestfield.

Smart, beautiful, and manipulative. The woman who was able to land one of the richest men in the country. I guess it makes perfect sense that she'd be my *doctor.* Her looks held my attention, but her intellect caught me off guard. She liked to manipulate, and I liked to play. We were a patient-doctor match made in heaven. Somewhere along the way, she became one of the few people I don't just tolerate but like being around.

"So anything you want to talk about? Problems with the medication? Anything new I should be informed of?" she asks off-handily.

"Nope same-o, same-o," I say with a shrug.

"Then that'll make this easy," she says, finally sitting behind her desk. "Did you fill out the med card I gave you?"

"Do I ever?" I ask, playing with the stress ball I picked up from her desk.

"Of course," she says, irritated.

"If I start having hallucinations, vomiting or some shit, I will be sure to call you right then and there," I tell her sarcastically.

"So. How was your date?"

I sigh. Dexter and his big fucking mouth. "It wasn't exactly like a date," I tell her dryly.

"Then what was it like?" I swear she and Dex are a match made in heaven.

"I met a girl. She's hot. We went bungee-jumping, had something to eat, and that was that," I say, bored. "Can we cut this a little short today? I have something to do," I say, standing.

"Cal, let's not do this. You need me to sign off for the okay to meet with the Luxe brothers. There can be a lot of money in a deal like that for you," I sigh and fall back onto the sofa.

"Come on, Helen. It's nothing," I tell her, but I can already see those wheels spinning in her head.

"You have never been shy about sharing your liaisons with women before, which makes this all the more interesting," she says.

I roll my eyes. When I first met Helen, I wasn't sure what to think of her, so I did to her what I did to most beautiful woman. I tried to seduce her. In one of my ploys, I gave her every detail of my nights with whomever I took home. When that didn't work, I thought it'd scare her off. In my defense, that was before I decided I liked Helen. She's one of the only women I haven't been able to screw.

"I haven't done that in a long time," I say, laughing, remembering how young and dumb I was.

"You made me sit through that for hours at a time. Not that Dexter didn't thank you for it," she teases, and I make a vomiting expression. Now I can't see Helen as anything but a sister and thinking of her and Dex having sex is disgusting, especially if I had any part in helping them get going.

"All jokes aside, Cal, a new person entering your life is significant and can impact things. Let's chat."

I stare at her blankly and look at my watch. We can do this for the next thirty minutes.

"Okay. I'll start," she says cheerfully and pulls out a file from her desk.

"Lauren Brooks, age 21, an English major, minoring in Art History at Chicago University, works as a waitress at The Vault," she rattles off, and I want to laugh.

"Dex had her checked out?" I scoff.

"This surprises you?" she asks sarcastically.

"Well then, you guys know she's harmless," I say, getting up to leave.

"I think you like her from the way you avoid discussing her. If you do like her, I bet you're trying to think of another date, and if you are, I'd say an art student would love to attend the AIC gala Saturday."

That could a better date than sky diving. But I don't even know if I should go on another date or call or her again. It'd be doing her more of a favor not to. Damn. I glance back at Helen who gestures to the chair across from her.

Helen's a woman, and she's my doctor. I guess I might as well make use of what have been useless sessions so far. "Make yourself comfortable," she says excitedly.

I take a seat and plop my feet on her desk which erases the smug grin off her face.

"You said make yourself comfortable," I retort as she pushes my feet off her desk.

"So tell me about her," she says.

"I think you know all there is to know," I say sarcastically.

"I mean, what makes her different than the others? I recall you telling me"—she shuffles through her notebook—"The only thing that interests you in a woman is her bra size and how good she is with her mouth."

I think I did say something like that. Who knew she really was taking notes.

"That was only partly true," I say in my defense.

"So what makes Lauren different?"

"I don't know if she's different."

"Well, there is something about her that is causing you to respond to her differently than you have the others."

"I was just trying to make something right that I messed up for her," I say honestly. She looks at me quizzically. I sit up and explain how everything happened the night I first saw Lauren and how I basically blew up her life as she knew it and only wanted to attempt to repay her for it. After I'm done, she folds her hands on her desk.

"Maybe she reminds you of another part of yourself."

I roll my eyes. "Trust me, it's not that."

"Well, let me ask you something, Cal. I'm assuming you want to see her again or you wouldn't have cared about me offering you the AIC tickets. What happens next?"

That's the million-dollar question. I know what I want to happen next, what usually already happens. I smile at her suggestively.

"So what's the problem? You have no problems with your sexual prowess, so to speak. Or has the medication been affecting you that way?"

"No! No problems there, trust me."

"Well then, what is the issue?" she asks.

"I don't think it'll end there with her. I don't think that's all it could be. If that makes sense," I say, my eyes landing on my lap.

"My, Cal Scott, have you grown a conscience?" she asks whimsically.

I don't say anything because I don't know what the hell is wrong with me.

"Has Lauren expressed to you wanting something more than casual?"

"No, but I can tell she's not the casual type."

"You're inferring, and I've learned that when people infer it could be a reflection of something within themselves that they're projecting onto their situation."

"Are you saying I want her to want something more than casual because that's what I want?" I laugh.

"Is that so ridiculous? You're an adult now. You're not the nineteen-year-old I met so long ago," she says, and I roll my eyes.

"It's okay for you to desire a higher form of intimacy than just sex. It's not something that you have to rule out because you associate it with what Chris would possibly want."

"This isn't about him!" I say, feeling my jaw flex.

"Speaking of Chris—"

"You brought him up," I remind her.

"Have you felt any episodes arising?"

"If I had, I'd tell you," I mumble. I'm getting frustrated with this conversation.

"If you complete my cards, I wouldn't have to ask you these things," she says in a singsong voice that annoys me.

"Can I just get the tickets?" I ask tightly. She smiles, and her hand disappears into her drawer, and she pulls them out, handing them to me.

"Also, you pulled up a ton of information on Lauren. What about Clay?" I ask, and she sighs.

"Not any more than last time. It's a little different to find someone who doesn't want to be on the radar," she explains.

"My patience is running out, Helen," I warn her, walking towards the door.

"You wouldn't be you if it wasn't, Cal," she calls back before I leave.

I always feel lighter when I leave Helen. I joke around with her, but there's more to her than meets the eye. This was just a stop-in with her, but usually she's a griller.

My phone rings, and it's the person I've been waiting on. "Tell me you got something good," I say, trying to cover my annoyance. I've been paying this investigator big bucks, and so far, the trail has been a bunch of dead ends. I know Helen and Dexter have been giving me the run around on Clay, but there's more than one way to skin a cat.

"We think we've spotted him in Ventian."

"Ventian?" I say aloud, to make sure I heard what he said right. Of all the places I've tracked this guy, he ends up right back in the town he ran from? "Do you have someone tailing him?"

"Of course. That's extra, considering what happened last time."

"You guys got it wrong the other time. I hope you don't disappoint me on this one. It won't be good."

I walk to my car thinking of the man who brought me into the world, which probably involved lots of beer and the back seat of some shitty car. Why does he get to walk around after everything he did; not one person has made him pay for any of it. I wonder if he thinks about the kids he left behind, if he's destroyed any more lives, if he knows that one of them is searching for him, that his time is running out and that the one searching for him will be the one to make him pay.

lauren

IT'S MORNING, AND I'm in bed alone, no longer wrapped in the warmth of Cal's arms. I make my way out of bed and prepare myself for another day. What type of day this will be, I can only guess. Today we have to go and get Caylen. Cal will face off with the Scotts and what happens then or after that, I don't know.

I look at the clock on the dresser and see it's not even seven A.M. yet. I take a deep breath and head into the living room of the small house we've nested in for the past day or so. It's cool but foreign, different from our home in Chicago and the Scotts'. It took a while to get used to the Scotts' place, but it eventually became warm and personable. Even though I hated being alone in Chicago, the penthouse was mine, where once Cal and I shared a home. Here, it feels off, like we don't belong. Neither of us.

When I reach the living room, I don't see anyone. I look toward the bathroom and see that it's empty as well. Then I notice the front door is cracked open. I head back into the bedroom and put on warm clothes. Once I'm outside, I see Cal standing in front of the house, his hands clasped on his head.

"Cal, what's wrong?" I ask him as I approach. When he turns around, his expression lost, eyes watery, frustration and confusion evident on his face.

"Oh no," I sigh.

"What happened? Where are we?" he asks painfully. My stomach drops, and I feel my throat tighten. I try to think of what to say to him, how to answer his questions, how to assure him that everything is okay. I need to be strong, but I feel weak. I'm confused myself and overwhelmed. I try to say something but as soon as my mouth opens, I feel as if I'm going to vomit.

"Are you okay?" he says, concern replacing his puzzled expression.

"I—I don't know." I chuckle and begin to laugh as tears fall down my cheeks.

HE DOESN'T REMEMBER anything.

Nothing important at least.

The last thing he remembers is being at the hotel room back in Detroit and talking to me through the bathroom door. Which means he doesn't remember us making love or telling me that he loves me, which makes this entire situation that much more complicated. He's trying to comfort me, but he's shaken himself, and he should be. He's lost and sullen, just like I am, and now I have to explain to him what happened. I don't even know now if it was even him that said those things, or whether it was Cal all along. That thought alone makes my blood boil. If it was Cal then that means that moment between Chris and me hadn't actually been a moment between Chris and me at all and was nothing more than a trick, a test, a sick, twisted game . . .

"I'm so tired of this!" he says grimly. Frustration is radiating from his entire body. I want to comfort him, to tell him everything is going to be okay, but I don't know if *anything* is okay. Cal was just here last night in this house, and now Chris stands before me with not a clue about what's happened. I don't know what to think or how I should feel. I'm at a loss. I feel more lost than before I knew about Cal's . . . or Chris's condition.

"Going back and forth. Why does he do this? Why am *I* doing this?" he says, his voice rising slightly in panic. "How do we do this if he can come and go whenever he feels like it?"

"I—I thought that this would be okay. That everything would be fine, Chris, but I can't even tell you how I feel right now. I don't know how to feel. This is so . . ." My voice breaks. I stand up and try to make my way to the bathroom when Chris stops me, gently touching both my shoulders. My eyes meet his warm, greenish-grey ones, and it makes me feel sick that the man looking at me doesn't remember what he said to me, how he touched me.

"Lauren, what's wrong? I know I missed something. Tell me what," he asks looking me in the eyes.

"It's not important," I say, trying to plaster the fake smile I'd perfected in the weeks prior but am having a hard time even mustering that right now.

"No, it has to be."

I shake my head, denying it. "You should probably call your mom," I say, quickly trying to hold my emotions together as best I can before they pour out of me. Crying in the bathroom has become such a pathetic routine, but routines are comforting and safe.

Once I reach my safe haven I try to catch the breath that keeps trying to escape me. I'm shaking. I have to make myself calm down. This isn't the end of the world. It's just split my world in two, that's all. I have to get it together.

I can't be weak. I don't even have the luxury to choose to be weak. One of us has to be the strong one, and I can't depend on it being Chris or Cal, or anyone besides myself. Everyone can't be a basket case. Someone has to hold it together for Caylen. The thought of her makes anxiety course through my veins. The good thing is that this doesn't affect her yet. She's only one, but what happens when she older? How is she supposed to understand? Understand that Daddy isn't exactly the same daddy every day. How do I get my child to comprehend and understand when Mommy can't?

That's what Raven meant about protecting her from all this. But how do I protect her from the man who helped create her, who loves her. I know for a fact both Cal and Chris love her. It's the one thing they have in common. Cal came back and broke through whatever haze he was in to see her. Chris has fallen in love with her, but how do I not worry? Am I doing the right thing for her? Are they doing the right thing for her? It's like they're both at war, locked in a battle against one another, and it's not helping anyone, not even themselves. It's destroying everyone around them. I can't believe Cal. I wonder if he knew that when he woke up, Chris would be back. I think back to his words. Describing his absences as dreams. It makes me so mad. He gets to go away and dream, leaving me in this nightmare. He's a selfish asshole and a smart one. He had to have known that this was going to happen. That's why he fed me that bullshit last night, barely telling me anything, asking if it could be enough. I should have said 'Fuck no! I need to know everything!' but, of course, Cal plays me like a violin. No, not a violin. I won't even compare this disaster to a classical instrument. He plays me like a three-year-old plays with a toy, without thought or compassion, and I'm the toy without a brain.

chapter 7

A BUST. A fucking bust! Why does everyone I hire have to be such a fucking idiot? It's better to do things yourself than to depend on anyone else. The dunce detectives I hired lost him. How the hell do you lose a fifty-year-old alcoholic with a limp? Fucking dummies. I should have gone as soon as they told me they found him. I should have hopped on the jet and went straight there.

May 10th, 2008

"We'll be landing in five minutes, Mr. Scott," the attendant on the jet tells me, looking at the glass on the floor from one of the bottles I threw across the cabin.

"I will be back in to clean that up for you," she says. I wave her off.

"I'll do it, don't worry about it," I say, frustrated. "Fuck!"

I almost had him. Right in my grasp. I was going to be able to break his fucking neck, and they lose him. I lean back into whatever foreign material seats Dexter probably paid a million fucking dollars for. Thinking of him pisses me off even more. He thinks he's so slick, saying he can't find Clay, to give him time while he sits back twiddling his damn thumbs. It's fine, though. Maybe it's time to twiddle my own thumbs for a while. He thinks he's the only one that can play that game? Fuck Dexter Crestfield. I've been too nice, too calm, too relaxed. I've learned that doesn't get you anywhere. My phone vibrates, and I see it's a text message from my driver, Byron, letting me know they've arrived at the landing site. It surprises me that I feel my anger and frustration dissipating, as I think of the package he's bringing me.

Lauren Brooks, hopefully wrapped in a nice tight little bow, just for me. This definitely *isn't* a good night for me to see her. I'm frustrated and need a release. I haven't had sex in almost three weeks, which is a record for *me* at least, and after this shit today I need a girl I can have climbing walls tonight. I try to push aside the image of how she'd look as I make her cum.

I've never tried this hard to convince myself to *not* have sex with a girl before. She's beautiful, hot as hell, funny, sweet, and smart, but she likes me and that's the problem. Most girls don't like me, they like how I look, the cars that I drive, the money I have, and the places I take them.

Which is cool since I usually just like the way they look, smell, and feel under or on top of me, but she's different. She's dangerous for me. She doesn't even know it. I can't let her know it. I need to get a fucking grip. I'm pulling out the Aston tonight, one of Dex's many toys. I don't even know why, we could have just taken the limo like I planned, but I want her to see it. It worries me that I want to impress her. It's not hard to impress girls, and usually I don't give a shit. The universe didn't give me much, but it gave me looks that make girls wet and usually the more of a dick you are, the more girls like you. Since I've been told I'm naturally a dick, it works out for me, but around her, I don't want to be an ass. I call her, and she's excited, her voice is high, but sometimes in the conversation it'll drop an octave, becoming low and seductive, and I wonder if she knows what it does to me. She seems innocent, which makes me think of how fun it would be to corrupt her, even though I like her just the way she is.

It's a catch 22.

Once I'm off the plane and I can see her, I want to freeze a moment for the first time in my life. She's waiting for me outside the limo, her beauty smacks me in the face. The dress she's wearing reminds me how sexy she is. It isn't tight but short, revealing just enough to make me want to know what's under it. And it's thin enough, so I can rip it off in seconds. The closer I get to her the more adrenaline I feel, my blood already pulsing through my entire body. She smiles at me as I get closer to her, a smile I could see every day. A smile that reminds you of your childhood, fresh baked cookies right out the oven, and as my eyes make my way down her body I feel hungry for anything but food.

"You look," I have to stop myself from saying something that will scare her off. I don't usually censor myself, so who knows what the hell will come flying out of my mouth. I want to stop looking at her, but I can't, and I have to see the full view.

"You've got to do a spin for me." I take every inch of her in. She starts to blush, looking away from me bashfully, and I'm even more turned on.

"Hold that thought." I walk behind her to get a better view. She's a ten from front to back. I have to touch her, but once I do, I don't know if I'll be able to stop. Still I can't help myself. I won't touch her anywhere I want, that's a lie. I want to touch her everywhere and not stop, but I control myself. I'll just touch her waist, her stomach. Those are safe zones. My hands slide across the thin material, and I feel her relax, and I pull her toward me. She feels so good, she smells good, I've got to stop or we won't even make it to this opening.

You need to give her an out.

I can't. Not now, it's too late.

I want her.

For how long?

Long enough.

"I'm glad you could make it," I whisper in her ear, ignoring the voice in my head.

Note to self. Have Helen up my meds.

chris

SOMETHING HAPPENED. I keep trying to think while Lauren has locked herself in the bathroom. Everything has gone so wrong. It's usually what happens after he comes out. He ruins everything. This is the worst I've felt in a long time. Not knowing what the hell is going on, what he did. Why Lauren looked at me with a hint of resentment in her eye, that's when she did look at me. It's like she can't even look at me at all, and how can I expect her to? What the hell did he do? Why am I in Ventian? I want to know everything, but I know this isn't the time to bombard her with questions. She seems about a second away from having a nervous breakdown. I try to pull myself together. I have to fix this. Whatever happened, whatever he did to screw things up, I have to fix. I always fix them. This shouldn't be any different. I hear my phone ring, and I pick it up. It's my mom.

"Hi," she says hesitantly.

"Mom," I say, relieved. No matter how bad things get her voice always gives me hope that they can get better.

"Chris! It's you honey. Thank God. Are you okay, is Lauren okay? William, it's Chris!" she says, going a hundred miles an hour.

"How's Caylen?"

"She's fine, Christopher, but where are you? What happened?" It's my dad's voice on the phone.

"I'm in this place called Ventian. I-I don't know how I got here. Or why I'm here," I say, trying to sound as calm as I can.

"It doesn't matter, son. You just need to come home. Now. The safest place to be is with us," my dad says.

"Is Lauren with you honey?" my mom asks.

"Yeah, she's in the bathroom. She's pretty overwhelmed with all of this. She didn't expect to see me this morning. I'm guessing Cal came back," I admit, feeling my stomach sink. "When she saw me, she seemed confused and upset, but the worst part of all this is that I think she was disappointed that I was here and Cal was gone, but I mean . . . what did I expect?"

"Oh honey. Please don't think that," my mom interrupts me.

"Well, son, that is the problem with you being with Lauren. She's not rooting for you. It's always going to be for Cal," my dad interjects.

"William, you don't know that," my mom says defensively.

"I do know it. We all do. That's why it's best for her to leave once she gets Caylen."

"What!" my mom snaps.

"Look what's happened. He goes away with her alone for a few hours, and Cal takes over. I told you she was the trigger."

"We don't need to talk about this over the phone," my mom says.

"Mom's right. I'll see you guys soon, okay?" I say, hanging up.

I take a deep breath and see that I have several missed calls and voice mails. Aidan's called me almost more times than my mom. That's really not like him. I dial his number, and after a couple of rings, he picks up.

"Where the hell have you been?" he asks angrily.

"Look. I have a lot going on right now, so if this isn't important," I cut him off.

"No it's real important, man," he says, his voice completely somber, which is unlike him, and I feel my heart beat speed up. What else can go wrong?

"What is it?" I ask reluctantly.

"It's not something I think we should talk about over the phone, dude," he says, his voice hushed.

"Just tell me Aidan, I have too much crap on my mind to wonder what's next," I tell him frantically. There's a long pause, which seems like a thousand years.

"Just say it!"

"Look man, Lisa came over here yesterday crying. She's a fucking mess,"

"What are you doing? What the hell are you doing, Aidan!" I hear yelling in the background. It's Lisa. The phone becomes muffled.

"Hey! Hey guys what the hell is going on?" I yell loud enough I hope that they can hear me. After a few seconds, I hang up the phone in frustration. I hear footsteps and see Lauren enter the room.

"Is everything okay?" she asks, looking like the time in the bathroom did her well. Maybe I need to spend a few minutes in there.

"Lisa and Aidan are idiots who are trying to drive me crazy," I say, trying to laugh off how worried I am. The expression on Lauren's face doesn't make me feel less worried.

"Oh Chris," she lets out a deep sigh that worries me even more.

"Lisa called you while . . . while Cal was here, and he blew up on her," she says carefully.

"Oh no," I say aloud.

"What the hell is he a jerk to Lisa for? What did she ever do to him?" I ask angrily, and my phone rings. It's Aidan again.

"Hey Chris." It's Lisa's voice.

"Lisa. I'm so sorry. That w-wasn't me. Whatever he said to you, ignore it . . ."

"Chris. It's okay. I know," she says, reassuring me.

"It's not okay, and I'm sorry," I apologize again.

"Are you okay?" she asks.

"Yeah, I'm fine. Why were you and Aidan fighting?"

"You know me and Aidan. We're always fighting," she laughs, but it's dry and seems forced.

"What's wrong Lisa? Is this about what Cal said to you?" I glance over at Lauren who looks down uncomfortably. It must have been pretty bad to upset Lisa.

"He didn't upset me, Chris. I've been called worse. It's a little strange when it sounds as if it's coming from you, but it was nothing," she says dryly.

"So everything is okay?" I ask unsurely.

"Yeah. Aidan just saw how upset I was and wanted us to talk about it," she says, sounding nervous.

"If you weren't upset over what Cal said to you, what was it?" I ask, sitting down on the couch and preparing for the worst because the way things are going now it has to be bad.

"It can wait. It's not a huge deal with all you have going on now. Just when you get back, let me know so we can talk, that's all." Her voice is calming, that's how she talks to the kids she works with, and that is setting off all kind of alarms.

"Are you sure?" I ask her again.

"Positive. It's nothing that can't wait," she says. I let out a deep sigh and glance over at Lauren who's sitting quietly, listening. If it can wait, I'll let it wait. I have enough on my plate anyway.

"Okay. We're heading back now I think. I'll come over tomorrow morning if that's cool," I say with a shrug.

"Awesome," she says quietly.

"Cool. Does Aidan need to say something to me?"

"No, Aidan's cool. Right Aidan?" she says tightly.

"Yup. I'm all good," he responds dryly.

Whatever.

"Okay. Later then," I say before hanging up the phone.

"Is everything okay?" Lauren says quietly, and I run my hands over my face.

"They say it is, so if they say it's okay, I'm going to let things be okay," I say, exasperated. She nods slowly, and looks down at her lap.

"Is there something you want to tell me?" I ask her. She looks up at me and lets out a breath.

"Lisa knew about Cal when you guys were younger," she says in one breath. I feel my eyebrows shoot up. I definitely didn't expect her to say anything about that. I was thinking more along the lines of what happened with her and Cal.

"No. Lisa would have said something," I tell her, and she starts to squeeze her wrist.

"Did Cal tell you that?"

"No. Lisa did," her voice is barely above a whisper.

"When was this?" I try not to sound annoyed, but I'm not very successful.

"It was about two weeks ago. She asked me to not say anything. I didn't think it was that big of a deal until Cal blew up at her." I shake my head.

"Did she say anything else?" I ask, nervousness in the pit of my stomach.

"No, but she asked me not to tell you for some reason. I didn't want to break her trust, but with everything that's happened, I just don't want to keep secrets anymore, no matter how small," she says, her big hazel eyes sparkling with tears.

"I don't want there to be any secrets between us either," I tell her, and a half smile spreads across her face, and she takes a deep breath, sitting all the way up and facing me.

"Well, in that case, I think you should know that we slept together.

Both you and I and me and Cal."

HER STATEMENT IS like a knockout punch. Her eyes stay on mine and don't drift away. Me and her slept together? Then she slept with Cal? So many emotions are hitting me at once I don't know what to respond to first. She's looking at me for a response, and I know there shouldn't be any secrets between us, but I really wish she could have waited before sharing this with me. I open my mouth to say something, and no words come out.

I slept with her? I'm angry because first, if we did have sex, it's beyond cruel that I can't even remember. Then, if we did, how could she turn around and sleep with Cal. I've only been out of it for two days.

"Please say something," her voice is light, vulnerable, and soothing, and I don't want to be soothed by her after hearing what she just said. I try to think of what to say to not screw this up and to make the gap that's formed between us any wider, but nothing is coming to me.

"I-I don't know what to say, Lauren . . ."

"Whatever you want to say. Just be honest, please," she says, her tone pleading. I feel anger starting to course through me. Bitterness creeps up . . . a jealousy I've never felt before. If I don't say something now, I'm afraid of what will happen. I can't say what I want to say, what I want to say will hurt her. But how could she sleep with him? After everything, how he lied to her, how he left her and Caylen, I wasn't even gone a day, and she sleeps with him?

"I don't remember, maybe Cal tricked you," I say, standing up from the sofa, trying my best not to be bitter.

"Well, the first time at least," I say with a shrug. Her cheeks flush bright red, and she looks away from me. I've embarrassed her. I'm embarrassed for the both of us. I can't believe what I just said to her, I can't believe this has even happened, that I have to say anything and . . . worst of all, how bad it hurts hearing what she just said.

"I'm going to get some air. I think we need to get back to Caylen," I say, heading out the door.

chapter 8

lauren

HONESTY *SHOULD* BE what works, no more secrets or lies. I thought that it would be better to just say it. To get the truth out in the open before another second passed. I didn't know how he'd take it. Whatever he'd say or do, I knew it wouldn't be as bad as facing off with Cal. That's what I *thought*. Turns out this is worse, so much worse. For a brief moment, I thought things would be okay between Chris and me. That he'd tell me everything was going to be okay, and we'd move past it. That he'd say it wasn't my fault and that he was sorry all of this was happening. That he'd maybe tell me how his biggest regret was not remembering. Instead, as soon as the words slipped out, a shell came over him. I saw it as it happened. He hardened toward me, a glint in his eye that for once wasn't indifferent or confused.

He was angry, he was bitter, and for that moment, he couldn't hide it. He tried to hide it, which makes all of it worse, but it was too much for him to even do that. What he said to me made me feel worse than when Cal screamed at me when he found out I slept with Chris. Well, at this point who knows if I slept with Chris, since he doesn't even remember.

It's entirely possible Cal tricked me, slipped in and went for the easy lay. Where he didn't have to answer any questions or put up a fight. We've been driving for an hour, and the tension in the car is suffocating, unable to be ignored. I want to say something, but no words come. I don't know what to say. How do I combat what he said, which was absolutely true? This one man, these *two* men that I love more than any other person besides my daughter. Both cut me deeper than anyone else has been able to, they just use two different knives.

I feel exhausted, my body is rested and energetic, but my mind feels like it's going to either shut down or overload. Chris hasn't said one thing to me since I've gotten in the car. The hardened shell is still on him, and his warm, green eyes stare straight ahead as we slip out of the little town that Cal dropped me into. I wonder what he's thinking, if he hates me. It's hard to think of Chris hating anyone, but the way he's acting, I know he doesn't *like* me right about now. The only thing that gives me some solace is that if he didn't care about me, he wouldn't be this upset. But what good does that do now? My phone rings, and I pull it out of my bag.

"Oh no," I say aloud.

"What's wrong?" his tone is dryer than a dessert, and his eyes don't even glance at me.

"It's Helen. I completely forgot about our meeting," I sigh.

"If there's a good time to talk to her this would probably be as good a time as any," he mutters.

"Helen. Hi, I'm so sorry. There is just so much that has happened over the past two days," I say, trying to stress my sincerity.

"I figured that. Cal called Dexter yesterday," she reveals.

"He did?" I say, trying to not sound completely surprised.

"From the way you're speaking, I take it that Cal is now Chris," she infers.

"We really would love to see you. I-I would. I really could use your help in all of this," I say quietly, wishing I had more privacy than a few inches. It's funny how in just a few days I went from despising Helen and wanting to kick her ass, to wanting to talk to her more than anyone. She's the one person who can help me through this. Because this is not anywhere as easy as I thought it would be.

"Okay. How about I meet you in Michigan tomorrow evening?" she asks, and I let out a sigh of relief.

"That would be so amazing."

"Great. I will call you tomorrow to let you know what time I'll be arriving."

"Sounds good. Thank you. Thank you so much, Helen," I tell her before hanging up the phone.

"Do you think we can trust her now?" He asks, and I look over at him as he briefly glances at me.

"I-I just need someone to talk to. Who understands, who can help me understand," I tell him honestly, fiddling with the phone in my lap.

"I thought that you had a handle on all of this. That you understood," he says quietly, and I can't help but let out a dry chuckle.

"I thought I did, Chris. Even after finding out about you, and Cal not being here, and trying to accept that was doable. But this, it's a completely different thing. You don't understand what it's like for you to be here one day, and he's here the next. In theory I always knew it could happen, but I never really prepared myself for it."

"You hoped for it though. Right?" he asks, with not even a bit of sarcasm under his tone. I take a deep breath and try to think of what to say that won't hurt him, that won't make things worse, but I only have the truth, and I can only be as delicate about it as I can.

"I'm still in love with Cal, Chris. I can't lie to you about that," I say quickly, and his expression doesn't break except for a small twitch in his jaw.

"But, I love you, too, I've fallen for you, and it's hard for me to understand why it seems like loving both of you, who I know as the same man, seems like such a betrayal," I say.

"I never said that I felt betrayed, Lauren. We've been friends, I've started to care about you a lot, but I always knew," he trails off, and the silence is deafening

"You always knew what?"

"If it came down to it . . . who you'd choose," he says quietly. I feel a burning sensation in my throat.

"For you to both hate each other. You have a lot in common. This choice you both bring up. As if it hinges on me . . . it doesn't, you know? It doesn't matter if I picked one of you, what would stop the other from popping up whenever you felt like it?" I say, laughing at the ridiculousness of it all.

"I don't have a choice in this. Why don't you both get that? I love you. That's it, so I'm stuck in this for the long haul, whoever chooses to show up, whichever day," I say angrily. I'm so tired of this. I feel like a fucking volleyball being bounced across a net. I look over at Chris, seething in his quietness. I'm tired of feeling sad, and guilty, and confused. Maybe I should just stay angry. Angry is better than feeling lost, depressed, and hopeless.

"Would you like to know what Cal told me? Why we were in that house, in that town?" I ask him, and he shakes his head.

Really? I'd think he'd want to know that it would be important, but I guess not. But what the hell do I know? I don't even know who the hell I've been sleeping with.

chris

OF COURSE SHE'S still in love with him. I knew she still loved him, it's not like I thought otherwise, but to hear her say it. Even after telling me she slept with him, to hear that she loves him. That hurt, more than I expected it to. But, she did say that she loved *me*.

She's not afraid to say it, or beat around the bush about it . . . but how can she love him and love me? We're so different, and *he's* an asshole. I can't believe I don't remember what happened between us. I said that I think Cal tricked her, pretended to be me, but *I* was being the asshole then. It doesn't seem like his style, and when I was at the hotel with her it was getting harder and harder to be around her and not tell her the truth about how I felt. To not want to touch her and have her in my arms. It's hard now, even with all that's going on. When she's mad, her skin flushes, her eyes gaze in on you, her voice deepens, and to be completely honest, it's absolutely sexy.

How can I not remember anything about being with her? It could have been him, but I want it to have been me, not him. Either way, he still had her after me, right after me apparently. I feel like an idiot, but I can't help but wonder if she liked being with him more than me. He's been with her more and longer. This is stupid! I shouldn't be thinking about any of this, but I can't stop. I have to stop.

There are too many other things for me to be worried about more than who she preferred having sex with. She'd probably slap me if I asked her. Then the thing she said about us both wanting her to choose. I'm sure he does, he's probably sure she'd choose him if it came down to it, but she's right. It doesn't matter what she wants, if she did choose me he just wouldn't decide to go away and never return. If she chose him . . . well I wouldn't even know how to. She's fallen asleep on the last leg of the ride. To be honest, I'm glad, it's hard to pretend to be mad at her, because it's all pretend. How can I be mad at a woman who has decided to put up with someone like me, who when she looks at me, lets me know I've never known true love before her?

I pull up in front of the house. I don't want to disturb her. It seems like she hasn't gotten a lot of sleep in all of this, how could she? She starts to stir and I see her wake. She glances out the window and sees that we're back at my parents' house.

"Great!" she mutters.

"What's wrong?"

"Your fiancé is over there," she says, gesturing towards the house. My heart immediately starts to beat out of my chest when I see Jenna sitting on my porch.

"I know you didn't want to talk about what happened when Cal came back, but it might help you to know that Cal told her that we slept together," she says quietly. Before I can respond, Jenna has come down from the porch and is in front of the steps of the house. Normally dressed so well, she has on jeans and an uncharacteristically oversized hoodie, her hair pulled back.

"Just stay in here while I talk to her," I tell Lauren who sighs and rolls her eyes but complies.

"Jenna, what are you doing here?" I ask, but before I'm even near her, the smell of alcohol nearly knocks me out.

"Really, Chris? It's funny how within just a couple of days, the question of my presence is a necessary one," she says with tears in her eyes, and I feel a sting of guilt.

"I'm sorry, Jenna."

"No! No more apologies or your weak excuses. I am done with you, Christopher Scott," she says poking me in my chest.

"Do you understand what it's been like for me since she arrived," she yells, pointing at Lauren in the car.

"She ruined everything! This wasn't supposed to happen. We were getting married. You loved me!"

"I still love you, Jenna. It's just I can't hold on to you while I figure things out with me. You deserve better than that," I try to explain.

"I'm done talking to you. I didn't come here to talk to you. I want to talk to *her*. She deserves to face me!" she says as she shifts her weight between her feet. Oh no.

"Jenna. I'm taking you home," I say, grabbing her arm as she tries to pull away from me.

"No! This is between me and her," she says, snatching her arm away and heading towards the car where she proceeds to beat on the window, causing the alarm to go off.

"Get out. Get out and defend yourself, you stupid whore," Jenna says as I pull her over to her car.

"What is going on?" My dad comes out of the house, looking confused.

"Jenna's drunk. I've got to get her home," I tell him, even as she continues to tussle in my arms.

"She ruined everything! She doesn't get to just get away with it," Jenna yells.

"Jenna calm down. Stop this—you're better than this!" I tell her firmly.

"Apparently that's not true because I'm still not good enough for you!" she says, pushing me. My dad has made it down the stairs and over to us. Lauren has gotten out of the car at this point and headed inside the house, which sends Jenna into a frenzy.

"You trapped him with your kid. That's the only reason he chose you. Sluuut!" Jenna screams. Lauren stops in her tracks and scowls at her.

"Lauren, don't. She's drunk. Please just go in the house!" I yell over at her.

"Oh please don't, bitch! I'm right here," Jenna continues to taunt her as my dad and I attempt to get her in the car. Lauren stops in her tracks. Thankfully, my mom appears in the doorway and says something I can't hear, and Lauren goes in the house.

"One big happy fucking family, huh Chris?!"

"Jenna. Where are your keys?" my dad asks her firmly, and she slams her hands against the hood of her car.

"Jenna, stop it!" I yell at her. I have never seen her like this before.

"Don't talk to me, Chris. Let your dad take me home. I never want to see you again. Never!" she screams at me before stumbling into the passenger side of her car.

"I'll drive with her. Follow me over," he says before getting into the driver's seat of her car. I make my way over to Lauren's car, and when I look back, Jenna gives me the middle finger. One I have to admit I deserve. Once I'm in the car, I let out a deep breath before resting my head on the steering wheel. Everything Jenna said, I deserved to hear. I should have told her as soon as Lauren got here that we should take a break. I just hoped, I *thought* that things would end differently, that somehow everything would work out in the end, that no one would get hurt and that there would be a happy ending in this for everyone involved. After everything, I thought that we could all get our happy endings, but the longer this goes on, the more it looks like no one's going to get one.

IT ONLY TOOK my dad a few minutes to get Jenna in the house. It seemed like the ride over calmed her down, or the alcohol made her sleepy. I can't believe I'm the one who drove Jenna, a self-respecting, intelligent, beautiful strong woman to get beyond wasted and turn into a person I've never seen before. Is this what I do to people? Break them down, destroy their happiness? Is this what my life has come to? My dad looks relieved once he's out of the house. I see him pause and shake his head before walking to the car and getting in. Once he does, he lets out a deep breath.

"How is she?" I ask, too embarrassed to look at him.

"Jenna will be fine. She's strong . . . she just . . . sometimes you need that moment to crack," he says quietly.

"I know she'll bounce back. I just hate that I'm the one who caused the pain she is in, that I lost a friend."

"Let's get going, Son," he says, and I start the car and drive home. I'm surprised that he's quiet and hasn't mentioned anything about what's happened. I knew I'd get an earful about how he was right, and how Lauren being around is a bad idea, and what I did to Jenna was wrong. I'm sure she told him everything that happened while he was in there. Maybe he's just giving me a break for tonight, one that I'm grateful for. The only thing I want to do right now is sleep.

I turn off the car and start to get out.

"Chris," he says before we're both out of the car. I let out a deep breath. I knew it was coming.

"I was really glad to hear your voice today," he says, patting me on the shoulder.

"Don't worry about everything today, there's always tomorrow for that," he says, before getting out of the car. I start to follow him, and my vision gets blurry.

I'm no longer walking down the driveway to my house but down a street, one that looks familiar, the houses look rundown, the grass is overgrown, and most of them look abandoned. A couple of cars pass by. I make my way up the stairs of one of them. Chipped green paint covers the outside of it. The railing on the stairs is crooked. It's dark out, but the light on the porch flickers like there's a short in its power supply. I knock on the door three times. The reflection on the dirty plastic portion of it reveals that I'm wearing a baseball cap and worn jacket. A deep voice on the other side asks, "Who is it?"

"It's me," he replies.

Cal.

A second later the door cracks before opening. It's a man, a big man, at least 6'3" and about 260 pounds. He lets me in, and I close the door behind me.

"He's downstairs," he tells me.

"Good," I reply as I follow. The house is pretty empty. There's an old dirty couch in the living room only accompanied by a tiny old TV, card table, and a mini fridge. I follow the man to a door revealing a basement.

I follow him down the stairs, the air immediately becoming cooler and stale. When we arrive at the bottom, there's another man, this one skinny in a big set of coveralls and a cap on his head. Then I see him. A man tied up in chair with a black cloth over his head.

"We didn't touch him. He's perfectly intact just like you wanted," the big one says.

"What's the blood on his knee from?" he asks wryly.

"Moving damage," the little guy chuckles. He stops laughing at the look Cal shoots him. He grabs one of the folding chairs, putting it directly in front of the man tied up. Cal removes the black hood from the restrained man's face, revealing a terrified man with tape over his mouth. He steps back, arms folded across his chest. He kneels down so he's at eye level with the man. The man has hooded dark brown eyes and thick, bushy eyebrows with sallow skin, and a small scar on his left cheek.

"So, this is the guy?" he asks dryly.

"That's him," the skinny one says.

"Clay Rice," the big one chimes in.

"Now, I'm going to take this off. If you scream, we're going to have a problem. So you're not going to scream. Right?" Cal says tightly. The man nods frantically.

Cal snatches the tape off the man's face, and he lets out a small yelp.

"What's your name?" he asks.

"Clayton Reece," he stutters, not looking at anyone in the room.

"How old are you Clayton?"

"Thirty. Th-thirty nine, sir," he says as tears pour out of his eyes.

"Do you have any kids Clay?"

"Yes sir. A seven-year-old girl. She's my world, sir."

"Have you ever been to jail, Clay?"

"Yes sir. For a few car robberies when I was younger. Nothing since. I'm straight sir. I-I don't know what I'm doing here," he starts to say in a panic.

"Calm down, Clay. If you start rambling, that's just going to irritate me, and I'm already pretty irritated. Do you have a tattoo on your back?"

"Yes, sir."

"Of what?"

"Of an e-eagle sir," he says, starting to cry. Cal lets out a deep sigh.

"Do you have his wallet?" Cal asks. The smaller guy tosses it to him.

"Okay Clay. I'm going to put this tape back on your mouth and this hood back on your head, but don't worry. These geniuses are going to take you back home, and you're going to forget this ever happened, okay. I'm going to take this just in case," he says, showing the man his ID.

"Wait, what?" the big one exclaims.

"And for your trouble," Cal says, pulling out a stack of hundred dollar bills and stuffing it in the man's shirt, then he puts the tape back on the man's mouth.

"What are you doing? That's our money," the skinny guy says.

"This isn't him," Cal says calmly.

"What do you mean this isn't the guy? He fits the description."

"This isn't the fucking guy!" Cal yells.

"I told you his name was Clay RICE. I told you he has a tattoo of a motorcycle on his back. I told you that he's about 6'4" and this guy can't be over 5'11" you fucking idiots!" Cal roars, and they both look confused and quiet.

"We thought he was lying or changed his name," the big guy says defensively.

"No fucking excuses! Drop this guy back off tonight in his neighborhood, with the money. Then how about you find the *right* Clay!" he shouts, heading up the stairs of the basement.

"Alive!" he adds, before leaving and slamming the door.

"Chris!" It's my mom. Holy shit! What was that?

She runs down the porch stairs and hugs me like I'm five years old again.

"It's okay, Mom," I assure her as she dotes on me like a toddler.

"I was so worried about you. I didn't know when I'd see you again," she says with tears in her eyes.

"I'm not going anywhere, Mom," I tell her with as much confidence as I can, but to be honest I don't know when *it'll* happen, and I'm starting to see things maybe I *don't* want to know about.

"Are you okay, honey?" she says, gripping my face and looking into my eyes.

"Yeah. Just. All of this, you know," I say as calmly as I can. She nods.

"I-I'm sorry about how things have gone with Jenna," she says, and I give her a weak smile.

"Me too," I say as I take her hand, and we walk into the house.

"Are you hungry? I haven't cooked anything since you left," she chuckles.

"I'm sure Dad was thrilled about that," I joke, trying to ease the tension.

"Honey, your dad couldn't eat a bite either. We were so worried after that phone call with Cal," she sighs.

"What phone call?"

"Oh. I thought Lauren might have told you," she says, looking away nervously.

"Ugh. I didn't. I kind of asked her to not talk to me about what happened when he was here," I admit, feeling like an idiot now. She looks at me sympathetically.

"It wasn't a big deal. Just—well Cal being Cal," my mom sighs with a shrug.

"I'm actually going to skip dinner, Mom. I just need to get some sleep," I say, kissing her on the forehead.

"Honey, things are all going to work out just fine. I know it," she says before I leave the kitchen. I give her as much of a smile as I can muster. If only I could believe that. But now, not only do I have to worry about what happens when Cal comes back, but what the hell he did when I wasn't here.

chapter 9

lauren

IT'S GOING TO be a new, wonderful, fantastic day. Well, even if it's not, it can't get any worse than yesterday. The sky would literally have to fall to beat that disaster. I think back over the last year, when it was just Caylen and me, how simple things were then. Except I was lonely, frustrated, and I had a broken heart. The sad thing is not much has changed. Well, now I'm beyond frustrated, confused, and I'm afraid to break someone's heart. I'm afraid that I'm not good enough for one of them, that I'm not strong enough for the other, yet I can't let either of them go. Great, right? At least I got to see Caylen. When I hold her in my arms, her little smile makes all of this seem worth it. Even being called a slut who used my own child to keep the man who nearly has me on the brink of a psychotic break down, is worth her smile.

It took everything in me to not go after Jenna yesterday, but I knew she was drunk, and deep down I can't blame her for being angry. I try to remind myself that my life wasn't the only one disrupted, her life was too. It's just hard to feel sorry for someone who is such a bitch, and how could she call me a whore when I'm the one married to—well *them* I guess.

I'm married to *them*.

It's like the title of a *Jerry Springer* episode.

I'm so hungry, but I've been avoiding the kitchen like the plague. I just can't see the Scotts right now. I can't help but feel it's my fault Cal came back, which to them is like spreading the plague. Then there's being in the middle of Cal's epic tantrum. I know Mr. Scott blames me. Mrs. Scott was so sweet and comforting, yesterday. I know she's going through so much on her own. Not knowing who your son is going to be when he shows up, has to be as bad as not knowing who your husband is going to be. The good thing in all of this is Helen comes today, and I am hoping talking to her will help me to sort this out, to be able to talk honestly without worrying if I'm hurting someone. To tell someone how much I'm hurting. My phone starts to vibrate, and I see it's Lisa. I instantly feel guilty about telling Chris what she told me. I at least should be the one to tell her before he does. I'm not sure if Chris will, but just in case.

"Hey," she says, not sounding like her usually chipper self.

"Hey, Lisa. How are you?" I say, trying to muster up my own chipper tone.

"Okay, I guess. I was hoping you could meet me, so we can talk," she says, her voice almost monotone. Maybe Chris called her or went over there last night, and she's pissed.

"Uhm, did you talk to Chris?"

"Not today. I wanted to talk to you first," she replies.

"Is everything okay?" I ask.

"Okay is relative, isn't it?" she kids, and for a moment she sounds like the Lisa I've come to know.

"I have to meet with a friend later on today . . ."

"Can we meet now?" she interrupts. I look at the clock, it's not even 7:30 am.

"We can get breakfast. There's a diner named Goldman's about five minutes away from you. It's on me."

"Uh, okay. Give me twenty minutes."

"Great. I'll text you the exact address."

"Thanks."

"Oh, and Lauren, can you not mention to Chris that you're meeting me?" she adds, and the twinge of guilt I felt earlier turns into a complete stab.

"Please," she says after my long pause.

"Not a problem," I say hesitantly.

"See you soon."

WHEN I WALK into Goldman's, it's relatively empty. I guess for a Tuesday morning it's expected. I easily spot her in the booth stirring her iced water with a straw. I walk over to the booth and slide in.

"Thanks for coming," she says with a small grin. Her hair is pulled back into a short ponytail. She doesn't have her usual make-up on, none actually. Her blue eyes dart between me and her water.

"You didn't bring Caylen."

"No, Mrs. Scott is going to keep an eye on her until I get back."

"Chris didn't work today?"

"I'm not sure. I'm actually sort of avoiding him," I say with a sigh. Her eyebrow raises.

"You know the whole Cal coming back thing has kind of thrown things off track," I joke, and I notice her smile tighten.

"About Cal. I'm so sorry that he spoke to you that way," I say apologetically.

"Did he say anything about me?" she says abruptly. Other than calling her a lying little cunt . . .

"Not much," I lie. She eyes me, searching my expression as if she's looking for another answer. Or to see if I'm lying.

"I-I have to tell you something," I say hesitantly. Her eyes narrow in on me.

"I told Chris that you knew about Cal from when you were younger," I rattle off quickly. I expect her to become angry, to start screaming at me about how I betrayed her trust, but she doesn't. She laughs and lets out a relieved sigh.

"Oh that's it? It doesn't matter really, not now anyway I guess," she smiles, her blue eyes lighting back up.

"But other than spewing obscenities about me?" she asks with a dry chuckle.

"No, nothing other than that," I say, feeling a little more uncomfortable.

"Why doesn't Cal like you?" I ask her bluntly, and she seems a bit taken aback. "It's just. It seems like there's more to it than you spurning him in high school," I admit.

She looks away from me, her attention going back to the lone lemon in her water glass.

"There are things that Cal knows about me that. That Chris doesn't," she says hesitantly.

"What kind of things?" I ask her, and a sad smile spreads across her face.

" . . . Things that I regret doing," she pauses, and I see tears well in her eyes.

"Things that could hurt a lot of people. Including Chris," she chokes out.

"Cal . . . he knows these things?" I ask her hesitantly. She nods. More secrets.

"Here you go, hon. Are you ready to order?" a waitress asks, interrupting the most awkward conversation ever.

"Whatever she's having. Thank you," I say, and the waitress nods before scurrying away.

"I hope you like egg white omelets," she jokes, while my heart is over here beating like a madwoman.

"If Cal knows whatever these things are, Chris can find out at any time, Lisa. Not only is he starting to remember things, right now there's no way of knowing when Cal will come back. What type of things does he know?" I ask her urgently. "If Cal has something on Chris that can hurt him or put him in danger . . ."

"No, it's nothing like that. It won't put him in any danger or hurt him . . . physically," she says, shaking her head vehemently.

"Lisa, you can tell me," I plead.

"It's better that I don't tell you, Lauren. Trust me. I told Aidan, and he wishes he didn't know," she says, attempting to smile as she quickly wipes away a falling tear.

"I asked you here because I'm going to tell Chris. I was going to tell him before all of this happened, and I chickened out after talking to Cal, and Aidan flipping out like he did . . . Now circumstances have changed where I don't really have a choice. I just have to get my courage back up. I never wanted to hurt anyone. I was stupid . . . so stupid," she says, tears flooding her face.

"Lisa, it can't be that bad. Whatever it is," I say, sitting next to her in the booth and pulling her into a hug.

"We all make mistakes. We all do things that I'm sure we wish we could take back," I say, rubbing her back.

"I didn't ask you here to feel sorry for me," she chokes out. She pulls away from me and takes a deep breath.

"When I tell him, Lauren, Chris is going to need you like he never has before. Promise me you'll be there for him, that you won't let Cal destroy him."

MY HEAD'S POUNDING. Lisa wouldn't budge with any specific information. She's going out of town for the next week to clear her head, and when she comes back, she's going to tell Chris. I can't help but feel like a huge anvil is going to drop, and I don't know how to prepare for it, to prepare Chris for it. We have so much to deal with already. I almost wish that whatever the hell Lisa has to get off her chest she would just swallow it until things return to normal, but I can't ask her to do that. I can't imagine holding something in like she is. So now, I'm standing on Aidan's porch hoping he's home. So far he hasn't answered, so I've proceeded to bang on the door.

"I'm coming. Shit!" I hear him yell. A few seconds later his door swings open, and I feel my eyes widen.

"What the hell?!" he growls.

What the hell is right! He's wearing nothing but a pair of black boxer briefs revealing his five-star sculpted military body. He has two black tattoos wrapping around his large biceps, and I have to tear my eyes away from his hard chest as it's heaving up and down.

"Oh, Lauren. Is everything okay?" he says, his tone going from an angry growl to concerned. I nod, trying to remember why I'm even here as his strikingly blue eyes stare into mine.

God, Aidan is hot! I can't believe this is the first time I noticed how good he looks.

"Can I come in?" I ask, returning to reality.

"Yeah sure," he opens the door for me to come in. Once I'm inside, I notice it's a lot smaller than the Scotts'. Everything is floral patterned and feels really old fashioned, except for the extremely big flat screen television. Then I remember that this is Aidan's grandmother's house. I'd bet the TV is his.

"Feel free to sit anywhere," he says, folding his arms across his chest.

"Sorry about earlier. It's just really fucking early," he says with a yawn. I really am trying not to look, but every way he moves causes his muscles to flex.

"I'm not really in a hurry, if you want to go back and change," I suggest, gluing my eyes to the floor. I hear a dry chuckle escape his mouth.

"Uh. Sure. Give me a sec. I should probably brush my teeth, too, if you're not in a big hurry, so you don't pass out from my morning breath." We both laugh as he disappears down the hall.

A few minutes later he's back, this time in a pair of loose fitting pajama pants and a wife beater. Much better.

"So what's up? Everything okay . . . ?" he asks hesitantly, sitting on the sofa across from me.

"I don't know. You tell me. I just had breakfast with Lisa," I inform him, and his expression sets into a frown. He lets out a deep sigh and claps his hands together in front of him.

"What did she tell you?" he asks, his voice unwavering.

"Basically that she's holding on to a bomb that she's going to drop on my husband, and it's going to have a pretty bad effect. She's not giving me any clues as to what it is. This is going to drive me insane." Aidan groans as he runs his hand through his blonde hair, which is noticeably longer since I first met him.

"I can't tell you, Lauren. It's not my story to tell. I shouldn't even be involved," he says defensively.

"Please, you have to. I'm already a wreck, and this has made things worse," I plead.

"If you know, it's going to make things a hell of a lot worse for you than you not knowing. Trust me, I *really* wish I didn't know," he says, standing up and pacing the room.

"Nothing is worse than the unknown."

"No, there are A LOT of things worse than the unknown, and this is one of them," he says grimly.

"What can I do then? Is there anything I can do to help with the fall-out from this?" The expression on his face tells me this is worse than I've been imagining, and my stomach feels as if it's dropped several floors.

"I'm not sure, but I think what happened is what made him need Cal."

chapter 10

F ATE HAS TO be a prankster. I know this because someone up there has to be laughing his ass off at me. I never thought it'd happen to me, but it has. I've fallen for a girl. A girl I was only supposed to pay back for intervening in her life and fucking it up completely. Now I can't see her not being in mine. I knew once I slept with her things would change, I thought she'd get clingy and want to be around me all the time and not want to share me with other women. Turns out since I met

September 26, 2008

her I can't even think about just screwing around with someone else. Not the way she makes me feel. Her smile makes me feel like everything I thought I had was worthless. I hate it but can't let it go at the same time.

Nothing will make me let her go.

"So you're sure you're ready to up the dosage on this?" Helen asks me for the third time.

"No, I'm not sure. I'm just wasting both of our time because I have nothing better do."

"You said it's safe, right?" I say, irritated with her hesitancy all of a sudden.

"We're still running clinical trials in Russia, and they are a lot more 1. . ."

"Save me the FDA disclaimer, Helen. I want to do this."

"Okay. Okay. Don't let me stop you," she says defensively.

"Not like I would," I give her a wink to let her know I'm an asshole only in fun. She rolls her eyes at me and sighs.

"Remember, the slightest thing happens out of the ordinary, you let me know," she says with a worried grin, one a mom would give her wayward son. I push that thought to the back of my brain where the garbage goes.

"So if I may ask," she starts.

"And you're going to ask anyway . . ."

"Why are you doing this, Cal?"

"Seriously?" I ask her in disbelief.

"I think it's for the girl," she says knowingly.

"The girl's name is Lauren," I correct her.

"I think it's time that we meet Lauren," she says with a wide smile.

"Okay," I say simply, grabbing my jacket, preparing for the crazy Chicago weather that's going to greet me downstairs. Her eyebrows raise.

"That's it. It's that simple?" she's surprised.

"She's been asking questions about meeting my family, and well, you know that wouldn't exactly work out," I say sarcastically.

"I'm shocked. You really care about her!" Helen's way too excited as she steps out from behind her big, intimidating desk and swats me on the chest. I shrug her off, but I can't help the smile I give her. It feels good for it to be out there. That it's been said.

"Have you told her about . . . ?"

"No, and I expect it not to come up in conversation," I warn her.

"Of course. I would never—I sort of have an oath that I'm bound by," she says, gesturing to her wall of a thousand degrees.

"I will be Dexter's beautiful, brilliant wife, and your friend only," she says happily.

"And make sure Dex doesn't make any snide comments, I'd hate to kick his ass in his own house."

"I will handle Dexter. I'll have Luc come and make a fantastic dinner, we will tell her how great you are."

"Well, I'll see you. Email me the details," I say heading out the door.

"Cal," she calls. I knew that was too easy.

"If you really care about her. You should tell her or at least start to prepare her. It's not fair for her to not know," she says solemnly. I pull out the little bottle of pills she gave me earlier.

"If you're as good as you say you are. Soon there won't be anything for her to know."

I WANT TO get Helen's words out of my head. I'm not afraid of much, but the thought of Lauren finding out about me, of her looking at me differently, scares the shit out of me.

I can hear music playing before I open the door.

She stayed.

I've been trying to get her to stay at my house when I go on trips for the past few months, but she always puts up a fight, she's stubborn as hell. I didn't take her for that when I first met her. The only time she really gives in is when I'm inside her, and I can't complain about that.

"You're home early," she squeals, leaning over the railing upstairs. Her smile is always contagious. She bounces down the stairs, wearing a tight t-shirt, squeezing her apple-sized breasts and tiny shorts that she won't have on much longer. She jumps in my arms.

"Ugh, you're cold!" she laughs trying to get away, but I hold her close to me.

"I'm about to warm you up," I tell her, my hand slipping underneath her shirt.

"Your hands aren't," she purrs, kissing me lightly. Just a taste, a tease, she's about to give way more than that.

"You're just in time to watch *The Notebook*," she says excitedly attempting to get out of my grasp.

"The Notebook . . ." I groan.

Hell no.

"And there's popcorn," she giggles, gesturing to it.

Ugh. I want to say no then she gives me her sexy ass little pout face.

I roll my eyes.

"Okay," I give in.

"Yay!" she claps her hands and then helps me take off my coat. I flop on my couch, and a second later she scoots in front of me.

"You used my shampoo."

"I like smelling like you," she admits with a giggle.

"Was it terrible being here?"

"Absolutely, it's too big, too luxurious, and is not up to my standards at all," she says sarcastically.

"My friend Dex. The one I told you about. He and Helen invited us to dinner," I say casually.

"You want me to?" she asks, she sounds surprised.

"Only if you want to go."

"I do," she says quickly.

"Good." A few minutes pass as I try to think of the most discreet way to get her out of these shorts. If her butt didn't look so good in them, I'd beg her to only wear skirts and dresses.

"I was starting to think you were ashamed of me or something," she says playfully, but there's a hint of truth behind her voice. I turn her towards me.

"I'd have to be a fucking lunatic to be ashamed of you," I tell her, and she smiles, the same smile that got me here instead of watching the game, watching *The Notebook*. She kisses me, it's innocent, but enough of an opening for me to pull her lips into mine, her mouth opens partially, and I coax out her tongue as I squeeze her ass. It drives her crazy, and the little sounds she makes try to hide it, make me insane.

"Nooo," she moans into my mouth and breaks away.

"Not until the movie's over," she giggles, quickly turning away from me, but she's close enough I can change her mind. I slip my hands underneath her t-shirt and drag my fingers across her stomach. She takes my hand in hers, stopping my path. I grunt.

"I know what you're trying to do," she giggles. I stop and look at her and think about this moment. I could be like this with her . . . forever. Except forever isn't really an option with me, unless this medicine that Helen's team has been working on actually works. Since

I'm volunteering to be the first guinea pig here, it's all a toss-up, but when I look at her . . . the risk is worth the reward.

You should just tell her.

Helen's voice echoes in my head. I can't just tell her—for one, she probably wouldn't believe me, and if she did, it would change everything.

She's mine, the one good thing in my life, and I'm not going to share her. Everything comes easy for him, life just hands itself over to him, and when it doesn't, he gives up and leaves me to deal with the hard part. I have to fight for what I get, nothing comes easy.

Finding Clay with as much money as I've spent should be easy, but it's been a nightmare, he slips out of my grasp as soon as I have him. He's the last thing I need to put to bed. After he's done, maybe, just maybe, things will be easy, and I can have a chance at something with Lauren. Before her, I never wanted a permanent fixture in my life, now I need it more than anything.

I won't let her go.

lauren

I FEEL LIKE a clock is running, each second that passes causes a crack to appear in an already fragile glass that's barely holding itself together. I hoped coming back to Madison would provide some kind of normalcy, some form of comfort. But right now it feels constricting, like I'm trapped, unable to escape, and everything is closing in on me. My visit with Aidan didn't yield any information, it just made me feel as if I'm standing next to a bomb that's about to blow, but I can't leave because the man I love is strapped in a chair next to it . . .

I hate all of this, secrets and lies. I thought I was moving past that, but I was wrong. I was wrong about Cal opening up to me. I was wrong about thinking Chris would be more understanding of this situation with Cal, and I was wrong to think that I could handle this on my own, that I could make this work. Right now, it seems like nothing is okay.

Everything is on the brink of chaos. My head won't stop pounding, and anxiety is my new best friend. I feel like I'm in a perpetual marathon, but I can't appear that way. I have to appear strong, I have to appear hopeful, like I haven't given up, like things are looking up from here, but in reality I'm barely holding on. There are so many conflicting emotions coursing through me, battling with each other until I'm exhausted. Right now I'm so tired I'm starting to feel numb.

I try to pull myself together as I sit outside the Crestfield mansion. Helen's in there, waiting on me. I was excited about seeing her, someone who could possibly help me to understand the reality of this, but now I feel like I'm going to see a doctor who holds my life in her hands. When I arrive at the door, I'm greeted by one of the housekeepers. She leads me to the second floor, sun seeping through the house, extravagant paintings on the wall. The décor doesn't seem to fit Helen or Dexter at all. It feels as if we've been walking forever through the house—not house, this is a mansion.

When we reach our destination, the housekeeper knocks on the door and introduces me. It's all so formal and a bit intimidating. Helen calls for us to come in. The room is large and, of course, all white and neutral colors. Helen is sitting behind a white desk that stretches out across one corner of the room. Two big, beige arm chairs sit in front of the desk with an adjacent fireplace. The other side of the room seems more for pleasure with a large television mounted on the wall and a matching white sofa sprawled out in front of it. The carpet is white with not one blemish on it. It's modern and completely different from the rest of the house.

"Lauren," she greets me. Her tone is warm and welcoming. She looks different with her hair half up and the rest down. She's wearing a large button-up that falls over her statuesque frame and black tights underneath.

"Could you bring up a pitcher of lemon water, Grace," Helen says, coming from behind her desk.

"Of course, Mrs. Crestfield," the housekeeper says before leaving the room.

"Is it okay if I give you a hug?" she asks cautiously. I feel my cheeks heat up with embarrassment over what happened the last time I saw her. I nod, meeting her half way. Her embrace isn't awkward or stiff, which is how I expected it to be, but warm and comforting. I wonder if the Helen I knew is the real Helen. Cool, calm, collected and sharp. Was that the role she had to play to observe me, to make sure I was a good fit for him? Or is she playing the role now as a kind ear just ready to listen and filled wisdom and knowledge? The thought makes me stiffen up. She pulls back from me, her expression sad and full of sincerity.

"I just want to say how sorry I am, Lauren," she says, holding my hands in hers, "And if someone did to me . . . what I did to you . . . I would have reacted just as you did."

"I know why you did what you did. I don't think it was right, and I really wish that you didn't, but that's in the past. I really need your help in understanding what our future is going to be like," I tell her.

"Right," she nods in understanding and gestures to one of the beige chairs in front of her desk. I take a seat in what feels like a piece of heaven and hope I don't drift off right there.

Grace reappears with a pitcher of lemon water and two glasses, which she pours for both of us.

"Thank you Grace, that will be all, and can you please make sure I have no interruptions?" Grace nods in response before closing the door behind her as she leaves.

"How are you?" she asks, and I start to answer, attempting to tell her that I'm fine and just ready to work on making things right, but the moment my mouth opens, my lip starts to quiver suddenly all my pent-up energy and emotions are unleashed. I cry for what Cal and I had, I cry for not knowing the truth for so long. I cry for the dreams I had for him and I that will never happen, for what Chris and I had seeming so far away, for everything that I have no control over, for the things that I can never fix, what I don't even know needs to be fixed. I cry in her arms for I don't even know how long until I can't cry anymore. When I'm done, she hands me the glass of water, after I use the Kleenex on her desk to clean my face.

"How do you feel now?" she asks, going back around her desk and sitting down. I manage a smirk.

"I feel numb now, which is better than how I felt before I got here," I admit.

"How are things with the Scotts?" she asks, her tone empathetic.

"Mr. Scott hates me," I chuckle.

"He hates you?"

"Yes. He hates me. He hates Cal, and he thinks I trigger Cal, so he in turn hates me."

"He has never been fond of Cal but to project his hate on you . . ."

"Is he right? Do I bring Cal out?" I ask her.

"It's not a bad thing, Lauren." I look at her in disbelief.

"Have you grown to resent him, Lauren?" she asks, and my mouth falls agape.

"Of course not," I say, feeling my defenses rise.

"I don't mean to insult you, and I could see it being a perfectly normal reaction after everything."

"I don't resent Cal. I resent some of the things that he does and how he goes about things but I could never resent him. I love him."

"Good," Helen says with a warm smile.

"You're the only person that seems to think so," I say, resting my head in my hands.

"Do you feel guilty for loving Cal since you've met Chris?" I look up at her, and my eyes drift to the wall full of certificates and degrees, and it hits me that Helen is the real deal. I never knew her this way. I knew she was smart and she used to be a doctor, though I never really thought to ask her what kind, I just had her pegged as this beautiful, trophy wife.

"I do," I admit, and it feels good to be able to say it out loud.

"Since I've met him and his parents and knowing all they've been through, I feel guilty for wanting Cal back. Especially knowing that when he's back they lose their son." She nods as if she understands and leans forward on her desk.

"The hardest thing about treating patients with DID, Dissociative Identity Disorder, is getting them to understand that each and every 'alter' is a side of them. To not look at them differently or as an appendage they want severed."

"I-I still feel really new to this." I let out a deep sigh. "This is just from what I was able to pull off Google, but integration is the final goal?"

"Yes. But it has to be their goal. As long as they still fight one another and can't come to common ground, integration isn't a possibility," she explains sullenly. I run my hands across my face.

"Getting those two to agree to integrate," I chuckle dryly. "It's not going to happen," I say, letting out a deep sigh.

"I will say, Lauren, it's a lot more likely since you've come into their life." I shake my head.

"Neither of them are all that thrilled with me at the moment," I sigh. She looks at me questioningly. "It's really complicated," I mumble, feeling my cheeks heat up.

"Complicated is my specialty," she says with a reassuring smile.

I explain to her all that's happened between Chris and I and how Cal reappeared and was so angry and how Chris says he doesn't remember us sleeping together. It feels so good getting it off my chest I end up telling her about the conversation between Lisa and I and how I don't know what to do to fix things when I'm not sure what needs to be fixed.

"Well that is a bit complicated," she sighs. "First. There is nothing to feel guilty about. You are his wife. We must remember they are the same.

However, you must understand that they think of themselves as separate entities so *they* are not going to be understanding of that fact. It's completely normal for them to see being with the other as an act of infidelity."

"Infidelity. I've never cheated on Cal a day in my life. I was never unfaithful," I say defensively.

"I know that, Lauren, but Cal won't see it that way. In fact you being with Chris may be worse for him than if you were with another man."

My mouth drops open. She can't be serious.

"Bear with me please," she says, being able to tell she's losing me.

"You have to understand that as far as Cal is concerned you're his wife, and in addition to that, he feels as if you belong to him. You are the one thing in his life that didn't belong to Chris. It's one of the many reasons that he never wanted Chris to know about the condition. Why he never told you the truth," she explains, and I feel my stomach twist into knots.

"Is this something that you're inferring or that he told you?" I ask.

"Patient privilege," she says with a weak smile, and I let out a sigh.

"So what I am supposed to do? I don't want to hurt either of them. I don't want me to be the reason they hate each other more than they already do."

"Then don't be that reason. Be the reason they come together."

"I don't understand," I ask, confused.

"My advice is to not be romantically involved with either until they start the process of integration."

"Yeah, well, that will be easy when Cal isn't here," I mumble.

"When he is, Lauren, you can't sleep with him," she says, looking me directly in the eye. I push my hand through my hair.

"That's a lot easier said than done," I admit. I've never had a good track record of turning him down.

"Well you can sleep with both of them, but it will only create division between them and make each of them unwilling to relinquish control to the other, so if you're fine with living like that . . ."

"I get it," I sigh.

"Now this isn't going to be something that Cal will particularly like . . ."

"You think?" He's going to go bat shit.

"But you have to stand your ground. Cal is stubborn and manipulative, but he loves you. That's your biggest weapon."

I nod.

"And as far as whatever Lisa has to tell him. We will deal with the aftermath of that once it happens," she says sullenly.

"Chris's friend Aidan said that what she has to tell him could have been what caused Cal to exist."

I see her eyebrow rise.

"I'm sure whatever she has to tell him isn't the original triggering event," she says skeptically.

"It is possible it is though, right?" I ask her, and for the first time, her eyes glance away from me.

"Of course, anything is possible." And it hits me.

"Do you know what is? What caused this to happen?"

"I can't discuss that with you, Lauren," she says quietly.

"Are you kidding?"

"These things have to be handled delicately."

"Then what did you call me for? If you're not going to help us?"

"I am going to help you, there are just so many things involved with this."

"And why didn't you tell Chris when I had Caylen?" I ask, my anger starting to rush to the surface.

"Can you at least tell me that?" I say sternly. She folds her hands together and looks at them before meeting my gaze.

"Because if we told Chris there was a very strong possibility that Cal would resurface, and at *that* point it wasn't best for anyone."

"What are you talking about? It wouldn't have been best for me to have the father of my child with me during my pregnancy?"

"There are things you don't understand. You don't know all the factors involved in our decision. Please just trust me."

"Trust you?" I ask indignantly. Everyone wants me to trust them while they know everything and I know nothing. Everyone wants me to trust them, but no one wants to trust me," I say, leaving the office. I'm proud of myself that I don't slam the door. I round the corner and swiftly head towards the stairs when I bump into someone else rounding the corner.

"I'm sorry," I say as a hand grips my arm. I look up and see an older man in maybe his early fifties with dark chestnut brown hair, one silver streak through it. He's tall, and his presence is feels intimidating though he hasn't said a word.

"It is always my pleasure to bump into a beautiful woman," he says, his voice smooth, like an expensive cognac, the kind of man that seems like he could buy your life in a moment without thinking twice. He lets go of my arm, a knowing smile spreads across his face, and a cold chill makes its way down my back.

"I was just leaving," I tell him as I try to make my way past him.

"Lauren Brooks . . . or Scott now, isn't it?" I turn back around and see him standing, or positioned is the better word, his hands crossing each other in front of him.

"Have we met before?" I ask. I see Helen appear, walking towards us swiftly, a nervous smile on her face.

"Mr. Crestfield, I didn't know that you'd be in town. Dexter didn't mention anything. Lauren was just leaving."

"Dexter Crestfield, Sr.," he says, extending his hand to me without even acknowledging Helen. I glance back at Helen whose eyes are avoiding mine. I cautiously extend my hand to him.

"Would you mind if we have a little chat?"

"Lauren has somewhere to be, Mr. Crestfield," Helen interrupts.

"I'd only need a few minutes of your time. I think it's about time I meet the granddaughter I've heard so much about," he says coolly.

Dexter Crestfield Sr.—who I remember is my in-law.

DEXTER SR.'S OFFICE is twice the size of the one Helen was in. All dark colors and oak paneling, with little natural light coming in. It feels like the rest of the house, stoic and ridiculously expensive. One thing that seems out of character is that his desk is filled with pictures, some looking like they date back to the early 1900's. Several are of Dexter Jr., and I notice one that looks like a young version of himself with Mr. Scott and . . . Chris.

"I apologize that it's taken us so long to meet. I have been out of town on business," he says as he settles into his leather desk chair. He must have been out of town a lot, seeing as I have never met him the entire time Cal and I were together. I also don't know why he'd feel the need to meet me.

"I can understand why Cal took such an interest in you," he says, his eyes giving me a once over, and I feel more uncomfortable than I already am.

"Christopher is my favorite of the two, I must admit. You always know what you're going to get," he says bluntly.

"Tell me, what is it like to love someone who's so torn?" he asks, and

I wonder why I am even sitting here with this man.

"I'm sorry, Mr. Crestfield, but I'd like to know why you asked me here. I know that you are a man whose time is important, and I'm sure I'm not here just for you to catch up," I say, shifting in my seat. He smiles at me and rests his elbows on the desk.

"Christopher is like William. He's honest, a man that plays by the rules and has values. I suppose you could say he's plagued by his conscience," he chuckles.

"He's not fond of me. He took after his father in that aspect, as well," he continues, as if I hadn't spoken at all.

"Cal, on the other hand. He's unpredictable, stubborn, and calculating. As if he was born from my own loins. He fit right in," he says, picking up a picture of Dexter and surveying it.

"Family is so important. There is absolutely nothing I wouldn't do to protect my family and the ones I love. Even if it is from themselves." The Crestfields are like no other people I have ever met. You never know what to think of them. You can hate and detest them, but they have an air that demands respect.

"I wanted to speak with you personally. Since we've never had a proper introduction," he says, leaning back in his chair and folding his hands over one another.

"Thank you, but this really wasn't necessary," I say, sweeping a stray hair from my face.

"No, actually it is very necessary. Now that you are aware of our little situation," he says, letting out a light breath. Little situation? He can't mean Cal's disorder, there's nothing little about D.I.D.

"Excuse me?"

"I think it is important that you understand the resources that you have available to you, should you need them."

"Resources?"

"Your husband, Cal, held a very important position with my company, and aside from that, he is family, and I like to keep things internal, so to speak." I feel my eyebrows rise. I have no idea what he's talking about.

"Dr. Clemons," he says simply, and then it resonates—she was the woman who Chris saw in Chicago.

"She won't be seeing Christopher as a patient anymore. He's only to see Helen."

"Excuse me?"

"It is in the best interest of the family which you are now a part of. I trust you understand the sensitivity of our predicament, not everyone can know."

"I'm sorry, but you can't be serious? Chris can see whatever doctor he chooses to. This isn't about your company, this is his life," I say, completely taken aback at this man's audacity.

"Helen is the best in her field and has a great team. He couldn't be in better hands," he says simply.

"You can speak to Christopher yourself, but I believe that his choice was made for the very reason you want him to see Helen." He sighs and stands from his desk.

"I apologize, I don't think you understand. Let me clarify things a little further. Your penthouse on Michigan Avenue, is in one of my buildings. The Scott's farm and house is on my property. The land your aunt Raven owns could easily be purchased. Your friend Hillary works at a company that is a subsidiary of—well I'm sure you can infer . . . Just so that you know, *my* best interest is in *your* best interest."

I feel my throat starting to constrict. A chill creeps up my spine. What the hell did Cal do for this man, why would he be blackmailing me?

"I think we have an understanding?" he reiterates.

"Can I go now?"

"You don't need my permission," he laughs. I stand up and get to the door as fast as possible.

"Oh, and Lauren." I stop in my tracks but don't bother to turn around.

"It was a pleasure meeting you."

chapter 11

chris

I'VE NEVER BEEN the type to play games. I never had the time to. When Cal started to take over, I didn't really have the luxury of enjoying life. I didn't date. I was too busy seeing doctors and trying to figure out what was wrong with me. All the sessions and medications left no time for *life*. Everything was put on the back burner: going to college, my music, my dreams . . . The only thing I wanted was to just be normal, to stop losing time. Then, I didn't know about Cal, that he was living life for me, doing God knows what. When I found out about Cal and met Lauren, it was hard knowing that all of these things were happening to me, but it seemed important to know. I was afraid of knowing, but each moment that came back to me I felt a little more connected, I understood him a little more, and I hate it, but what I saw last night didn't make me feel connected or help me understand him, I feel disgusted.

He had a man kidnapped. I don't know what the hell he's been doing or why. Why was he looking for this Clay guy? Did he find him, and what happened if he did? I'm more worried about what exactly he was involved in a lot more than how many women he screwed.

That's what drove me here, back to Chicago, waiting for Dex to come out of his building. I had to wait two hours, but I soon see him emerge in one of his thousand dollar suits, his phone in his hand.

"Dex! I call out as I jog to catch up with him. He glances back at me, he looks bored, like seeing me isn't a surprise.

"What brings you to Chicago?"

"We need to talk," I say adamantly.

"I have a lot to do today, Chris. I don't have time for the soap opera that is the Scotts' lives," he chuckles, but when I grab him by the arm, this time he looks caught off-guard.

"Who is Clay Rice?"

His eyes narrow in on me before he tries to snatch his arm away, but I don't let it go. He needs to see that I'm serious.

"This is a Brioni," he says with derision before pulling away from me and smoothing out the print I left on his suit.

"Is there a problem, Mr. Crestfield?" Two large men have appeared behind me. Dexter sighs.

"No problem, gentlemen. Christopher, I have some time to kill before my next meeting if you'd like," he says, gesturing towards his car. I get in behind him, and once the door is shut, he immediately grabs a bottle of scotch and begins to pour himself some.

"How do you know about Mr. Rice," he says, swishing the liquid in his glass.

"I remembered Dex. And I want to know what the hell did you have me doing for you? Was I some type of henchman?"

"Lower your voice," he snaps.

"Tell me!" I shout.

"I had nothing to do with you and Clay Rice. That was all you, my friend," he says.

"Did he . . . did I hurt someone? Is that what you meant that day you came to my house?" I ask cautiously. Dexter takes a deep breath.

"Don't let your conscience eat you up yet. You have nothing to be guilty over as of now," he says, staring at the glass in his hand.

"What do you mean, 'now?' Who was that guy?" He pauses a moment before taking a deep breath.

"Clay Rice was the man who was with your mother when she was killed." The word sounds foreign to me. *My mother*, the mother I think of is Gwen Scott with long red hair and a smile that melts your problems away. The woman who took care of me for as long as I can remember, who's back home in Madison with my daughter. But after a moment, the thought creeps in, one that rarely creeps in much with me. That though Gwen's my mother, she's not my biological parent, and the fact that my name wasn't always Scott. It was Rice, a fact that should stick with me, but never has. I remember the day when I was ten years old that my parents sat down with me and showed me my birth certificate and asked if I had any questions, if I wanted to talk about my feelings.

I didn't.

I had no feelings about it. They were all I knew, all that I remembered. No one else was important, the past wasn't important, and just like whatever happened before it, I buried it deep down in no man's land.

"Killed. She was murdered?" I ask, my voice a ghost of itself. Every emotion in me seems to be on pause. I'd thought that my heart would speed up, that my breath would catch, but I feel nothing.

Numb.

"She was shot," he says simply.

"By Clay Rice," I infer, putting the pieces together.

"That's what Cal believes," he replies.

"Was he ever convicted? Did he go to jail?"

"There wasn't enough evidence."

"So what happened to him?"

"After the charges were dropped he disappeared," he explains and reaches into his brief case and pulls out a flash drive.

"This is all the information that I have about the case, information about both of your parents." He is holding it out for me to take. My eyes stare at the little black drive that holds a key to my past, to a world I never knew about, or wanted to know for that matter.

"I don't want it," I tell him sternly.

"Do you think it's wise for you not to have it?" he asks smugly.

"Tell me whatever I need to know." I'm sure nothing is in there that he wouldn't want me to know anyway. I don't trust the Crestfields as far as I can throw them.

"Well Christopher," he says, a little annoyed. "You should know that Cal is pretty set on killing Clay Rice, and he's coming dangerously close to doing it,"

"What?" I ask, not able to hide my anger or surprise.

"I have done my absolute best at trying to prevent that from happening. However, since Cal has not been working for me, I'm unaware who his contacts are, and the fact that he told me to go fuck myself during his last excursion, it will be more difficult than it has in the past to keep him from doing so."

This is a bad dream. This is all a bad dream. He wants to kill someone. He wants to add murderer to the list with asshole and jerk-off?

He can't do this.

"I can't let this happen. I won't let this happen . . ." I let out a long grunt.

"What is wrong with him? Does he not care about going to jail, or ruining his life?" I ask in disbelief.

"He doesn't think that he'll get caught of course, Christopher."

"Right because he doesn't *think*. He just acts!"

"Do you not think that someone who has committed murder deserves to face some means of punishment?" he asks quizzically.

"It's not my job to punish people. He's not the judge and the jury. He doesn't even know if this guy killed her."

"That's what he remembers, Chris." I look up at him, confused.

"Remembers. He remembers?" I ask.

"He remembers quite a lot apparently."

"I have to stop him. He can't do this," I say quietly.

"I need your help," I say, forcing the words up from my throat. It tastes bitter to even say them aloud.

"With my help comes inconvenience, as you may know."

"I don't care about the inconvenience. If he does this, I won't be able to deal with it. If he's able to make this happen . . ." I say honestly.

"I can have someone tail you."

"Follow me?"

"Just in case."

"He's resourceful. I think you need to tell Lauren what's going on."

With all that has happened, and all she has worried about, I don't want to put that type of stress on her. Telling her that he . . . that I'm intent on killing someone—my biological father. That's not something she needs to know.

"I'd rather this stay between us. She has enough to deal with."

"Your choice, my friend."

"My people are very discreet. It will be like they're not even there."

"It has to be. I don't want her to think we're being followed. I want things to be as normal as possible."

"Thank you, Dexter," I tell him, before reaching for the door.

"There may be another way, where you don't have to live like this," he says casually.

"What other way?"

"It would come with some risks . . ."

cal

SAME DREAM ALMOST every night, one I wish I could get away from. The woman's pale white skin contrasts against the pool of red blood surrounding her, soaking her clothes and mine. The little boy, who cried for hours before someone found him. I used to wake up in a cold sweat, my heart pounding as adrenaline coursed through me. But now I've grown immune to it, at least that's what I've tried to convince myself. I tell myself I'm not affected, that this dream isn't as terrifying as it used to be. But how can I forget the woman and child when I'm still tormented by my own cries, and panic nearly suffocates me?

April 16th, 2011

Something has changed. I look at the woman lying beside me, and everything is better. So why do I feel worse? Before her, I never wanted kids or a family, to be so close to someone that their loss would feel worse than this recurring dream. I love her, and love interferes with my only cure. This wasn't supposed to happen. I wasn't supposed to love anyone but myself. The only feeling I ever wanted was revenge. Revenge and pleasure—nothing more, nothing less. For me they are one and the same, an obsession that became an addiction. But this—her arms wrapped around me, and her breath on my skin—feels like peace. Peace and vengeance don't work well together, having one sacrifices the other.

She'll graduate soon, go onto the next chapter in her life. I feel like the book is about to be closed on me. She's not sure what she wants to do after school. She talks about getting a job, but she's hated every place she's interviewed. She's about to jump into the cycle I loathe—work for pennies, buy a house you really never liked, and just get older and more miserable as each year passes. She should travel, see the world, draw it on that sketchpad of hers. I want her to see the places I was able to see once I broke free. Paris, Rome, the Alps, I've been around the world and back. She deserves the same; she deserves everything she wants. The problem is she wants *me,* and I want her more than anything I have ever wanted. But she doesn't really know what having me means.

I went to the jeweler Dexter uses and bought one of the most expensive rings they had, but I haven't given it to her, what's stopping me is the fact that I love her, and I know her. I know that she wants marriage, but not the kind that I can give her. She wants children. She wants someone who she can grow old with. A normal guy, and normal is just not me.

Then why do you have the ring?

"Good morning," she says, running her hand through my hair, her eyes barely open.

"You still have two hours to sleep."

"What's wrong?" she asks, cupping my face.

"Nothing," I tell her playfully, before rolling on top of her. She laughs.

"It looks like your mind is somewhere else," she says, looking at me earnestly.

"Just thinking about how I want to take you to Europe," I tell her, and she rolls her eyes playfully.

"Yeah right." She doesn't believe me, but when I tilt my head and look into her hypnotizing eyes, they widen.

"Are you serious?" she asks, and I feel her excitement growing by the second.

"Your graduation present," I tell her, and she pushes me off her.

"I-I can't go to Europe with you," she says, and I have to hide how much her words sting. They're stern and like a kick in the nuts. I try to think of something to say to brush it off.

"You'd rather have fun here, hanging out at Navy Pier?" I joke, nudging her in the side. She sighs and looks back at me, her eyes big and sad.

"Sometimes I wonder if this is all real," she says quietly.

"What do you mean?" I ask, getting up and sitting next to her.

"I know I've already told you this, but you're not like anyone I've ever met before."

"I'm one of a kind." I wink at her, and a small smile appears on her face.

"You are, and that's what's so scary about this. What do I do after you, how do I get over Cal Scott?" she says, looking me right in the eye and a wave of sadness passes through me. Get over me. What is she talking about? Is she breaking up with me? Fuck! Am I being dumped?

"What are you talking about, Lauren?" I feel my voice becoming tense, anger starting to course through every part of my body. She gets out of bed and starts putting on her clothing.

This could be your easy break. If you love her, you'll let her go.

"We're in two different worlds, Cal. I live in the real world, and you live in the perfect world . . . for you," she says looking away from me.

"I feel like my stay's only temporary. Things are so great, and I'm just waiting for the other shoe to drop, when you'll wake up and realize that you're suffocated, or this isn't what you want . . . that I'm not what you want," she says, and I hear her voice choke up. I get off the bed and pull her towards me.

"Hey. You're the greatest thing that has ever happened to me," I tell her, her eyes still downcast.

"I'm not the prize. You are," I tell her, cupping her face in my hands. I hate that there are tears in her eyes. This is the first time I've ever seen her cry up close, but I think of all the tears she'll shed if I don't let her go.

What am I doing?

"I graduate next week, Cal. I'm going to get a real job and really be an adult. I have to start figuring things out."

I feel myself getting mad, disappointment taking over, and I can't let it boil over, not in front of her. I stand up and walk to the other side of the room.

This could be for the best. She deserves more than this.

"There are things I want, but I don't know if we both want the same things," she says sullenly.

This is your chance. If you love her, you'll let her go. Take the ring back to the store and set her free.

"I don't know if what I want is going to be good enough, or exciting enough for you."

She wants normal, and you sure as hell can't give her that.

"What do you want Cal?" she asks.

"To be happy," I say with a chuckle.

"Me too," she says quietly. She grabs her little overnight bag she brings whenever she comes. I'm tired of her bringing that shitty bag. It reminds me that she's only here temporarily. She walks past me to the bathroom. I head out of the room and go downstairs. In the kitchen, I pull out my medication vial from behind the cups in the cabinet and look at the little yellow pills in them. Helen's voice echoes in my head.

There's no guarantee that this will work, Cal.

This isn't even considered trial stage yet.

There are a lot of risks for you to consider.

"Sometimes the reward is worth the risk," I tell myself, before popping my second one for the day in my mouth and washing it down with water.

A half hour later she's downstairs, fully dressed, with her bag on her shoulder.

"I'm going to get out of here," she says, grabbing all her hair and putting it at the top of her head. I get off the couch and walk in front of her. Her eyes avoid mine. I put my hands on her waist and pull her towards me.

"You're coming to Europe with me," I tell her simply, and she rolls her eyes.

"How many times do we have to talk about you asking and not telling," she says, a small smirk on her lips. She says she wants me to ask her whenever I do something, but I know she likes it when I tell her what to do.

"This is an exception, you told me no, so now I'm telling you that you're coming with me to Europe, because you work hard and deserve it, and I want to have you on every beach I step foot on," I whisper in her ear. She giggles and sighs.

"No, no, no," she says, stepping away from me.

"You're not going to convince me like that," she says playfully.

"Then I'll convince you another way," I tell her, picking her up and carrying her over to the couch.

"You're hot," she says in between pants.

"I'm always in heat," I tell her with a wink.

"I think only female mammals go in heat," she giggles. She's such a nerd. Then her face scrunches up.

"No your skin is really hot," she says, in a panic. I put her down, and she puts her hand on my head.

"Do you have a thermometer? You feel really warm," she says worriedly.

"No I'm fine," I wave her off. I don't feel hot, but when I put my hand on my head, I do feel hot, I think.

"I'm good, Lauren. You need to get to your class right?" I remind her.

"It can wait. I'll go to the store and get you a thermometer," she says, simultaneously grabbing a bottle of water out the fridge.

"Don't do that. I can go, you think about what we were about to negotiate," I tell her, and she frowns, thrusting the water at me.

"If I drink this and promise to go get a thermometer, will you go to class?"

"What if something's wrong, and I leave, and you die while I'm in school," she says dramatically.

"You're not getting rid of me that easily," I tell her, squeezing her on the butt before pulling her towards the door. She stands there in protest.

"I'm going to go throw on some clothes, and I'll head to the drug store, and if I even feel a little bit abnormal, I'll call you on the way to the ER, okay?" I tell her, and she looks slightly appeased.

"You promise? Because if you don't, I'm headed back here," she warns me.

"Cross my heart and hope to die," I tell her and that gets her to give me a little smile.

"Don't say that," she pouts, and I kiss her, but she pulls away with a worried expression.

"If you stay any longer the clothes are coming off, since it's hot and all," I tease her, reaching for the button on her pants, and she swats me away.

"Okay. Don't forget," she says heading out the door.

"See you, gorgeous," I tell her as I watch her walk down the hall to the elevator. Once she's inside, I close my door, grab my cellphone, and dial Helen's number.

"You didn't mention one of the side effects was over heating!"

chapter 12

lauren

IT'S BEEN ALMOST a day since I've seen Chris, really seen him. I think with everything that has happened over the past few days, we're avoiding one another. Things have changed so much. Things were never simple or easy even between Chris and me. But now, it's like the tension and awkwardness between us has multiplied. We at least had easy moments, sweet moments, and *one* intense one, which he doesn't remember, and it's best for me to not even think about it. So many things are weighing on my mind. It's been hard to sleep, hard for me to even think. This whole thing with Lisa, and then Mr. Crestfield threatening or blackmailing me, I'm not sure which. I'm not sure who I can even talk to about this. The one person I feel like may be able to help me is Cal and, well, there isn't even a point in thinking what a conundrum that is.

How did things get so messy? Why are things so terrible? Why can't they just get better for once?

"Hey," his voice wakes me from my trance. I'm not even sure if it's real or imagined until he steps inside my room and shuts the door behind him. The sad part in all of this is, with as much as I have to be worried and stressed out about things, the sight of him and the sound of his voice make my whole body tingle. I feel myself flushed, my hormones obviously did not get the memo that there will be no relief. In fact, I've been forbidden to, like a child.

"Caylen's sleeping," I say absentmindedly.

"Yeah, I see her," he sort of chuckles. Of course he sees her, he's not blind.

"I wanted us to talk," he says, sitting on the far side of the bed. I nod, banishing the thoughts of the last time we were both on a bed together.

"Things have been weird since Cal came back," he says apprehensively.

"Yeah they have," I admit with a laugh.

"I haven't been avoiding you," he says quietly.

It seems exactly like that.

"I wouldn't blame you so much if you have," I tell him, because in all honesty I've been avoiding him. I'm still trying to wrap my mind around all the information I've received today, creating more questions and hardly any answers.

"I put in for leave at work today."

I want to tell him he shouldn't have, that he loves his job and should keep it, but I'm sure with all that has happened he has good reasons.

"I'm sorry. I know you liked your job."

"They said I can come back whenever I'm ready," he says, giving me a small smile. "I'm thinking of trying to get back into my music," he continues. As a smile begins to spread across his face, his eyes practically light up.

"That's great! You should. You're really good, Chris," I say, sharing his enthusiasm.

"I'm okay," he shrugs.

"You're a little better than okay. You can sing a girl right out of her clothes." The words slip out of my mouth before I can stop them. I expect awkwardness to float in, but it doesn't, he just smiles wider and laughs, and I do too.

"Maybe a shirt, not sure about the whole outfit," he jokes, and I'm so thankful. Thankful, that at least right now, things have gone back to how they were *before* everything changed. Well, that's relative since everything is constantly changing with us, a freakin' swinging pendulum.

"I'm sorry about Jenna yesterday," he blurts out.

It's funny. So much has happened that Jenna's little outburst is the least of my worries. I'm reminded that I'm not sure what their status is. Before everything happened, I knew things were rocky, and after we slept together, I was sure things would be ending, but since Chris has no recollection of that happening . . . my headache is getting worse now.

"Cal was an ass to her. I won't play naive, her actions weren't exactly unwarranted," I say with a shrug. He nods as silence settles between us.

"I'm sorry I don't remember what happened between us," he says sincerely. His eyes are soft and expression apologetic in the way only Chris can be.

"And . . . I was immature with how I responded to you telling me about you and Cal," he continues, his eyes on his hands.

"I understand . . . sort of," I add with a laugh, and he looks up at me with a smile.

" . . . and when I said or implied that maybe it was Cal pretending to be me to sleep with you . . . I was full of it," he says, folding his arms. "For one I thing, I think Cal is too full of himself to even consider pretending to be me." I can't help but laugh at that statement. "Because, the way I was feeling before the blackout happened, I'm not entirely surprised that what happened, happened," he says, letting out a long sigh. With those words, I feel a smile begin to spread across my face, and it takes everything in me to keep it small.

"I want you to know that I ended things with Jenna before we left for Chicago."

Butterflies are starting to flutter in my stomach.

"It wasn't fair to be with her and lead her on. Especially with the feelings I have for you," he continues, and my breathing starts to slow down. He stands and walks over in front of me.

"I want to remember this," he says and just like that, his lips are on mine. His hands slide across my back, and he pulls me into his arms. He's so warm. His kiss is tender but firm, causing all my stress and worry to melt away. Just being close to him, his body against mine . . . my lips immediately respond, it's what they know how to do. I feel high, like he's a drug, and it feels so good, he feels so good, he smells so good. I stop and wonder if I'm dreaming, but I really don't want to know. Because if I am dreaming, it means I'm not doing anything wrong. There is no guilt to be associated with this, as his hands slide underneath my shirt, and I have no reason to feel bad as my hands slide under his shirt to feel the skin I want against mine.

I just want a little relief, is that so wrong? Will it be damaging? Each soft kiss he plants on my neck, makes the past few hours seem so distant and as the shirt I have on goes over my head, the problems we're facing are being thrown over the bridge, and it feels good.

Really good.

but this feels familiar. All too familiar, his lips have trailed down my stomach, and there's the feeling of being swept away. The rush I feel reminds me of the intensity between us, the things this man can do to my body, how this feeling kept us tied together when everything was pulling us apart. This feeling covered up secrets, and lies . . . this pattern is starting itself again.

"Chris," I moan. It shouldn't be a moan. It should be a stern exclamation.

"This, we shouldn't," I say between pants.

"You're right, Caylen's . . ." he says as we both clamor for air. In a few swift movements, we're out the door, and he's pulling me up the stairs. It's so hectic, I was supposed to be protesting this, stopping what's about to happen, but I haven't. We make it to his room without bumping into either of the Scotts, but my adrenaline is so high I probably wouldn't have cared. When the door shuts behind us, I'm back to reality, the contrast of this space against where Cal and I last made love. The fact that if I sleep with Chris, Cal will be hurt, and if I don't sleep with Chris, Chris is going be hurt. I lose either way. Helen's words about not being the one to divide them but unite them, echo in my mind. How do I do that? I can feel him behind me, his energy so different from Cal's.

"Are you okay?" he asks, his eyes searching mine. I nod as his hands rest on my waist. I can do this. It's only once technically, he doesn't remember the last time, so it should be fine.

"Tell me what you want," he whispers in my ear, and I immediately step away from him.

"What did you say?"

""I asked what you want. Anything, and I'll give it to you," he says, bringing my hands to his chest.

"I love you. I didn't know it then, but the moment I saw you I loved you. I didn't know what it was because I'd never felt that way about anyone before. And getting to know you, I know why he fell in love with you, because I'm in love with you, too," he says, and the resistance I planned on applying to his chest to push myself away from him is gone. I kiss him with all I have.

chris

IT'S STILL ME.

I'd be lying if I didn't say a small, well a pretty big part of me, thought that after I slept with Lauren I'd wake up days later, but as I open my eyes, and the sun is shining in on us, and she's lying next to me, I feel like the happiest man alive. She's so beautiful, so amazing. I didn't expect what happened to happen when I went in her room last night. I intended to tell her what happened earlier that day with Dexter, not all of it, but at least some. I didn't want any more secrets between us, but when I saw her, everything changed. I'm different with her. I can't pretend or hide my feelings. They take over, and I'm not so sure it's a bad thing. Something that feels this good can't be bad. Last night was greater than I ever imagined it being. She's perfect, every inch of her. I wouldn't change one thing about her. Having her next to me, in my arms, makes all of this not seem so bad; everything that's hanging in the air over us isn't so bad when she's with me. We can do this. Together.

Do what? Get rid of Cal because she's definitely not going to help you do that.

She could, it's not as ridiculous as it sounds. I just have to show her that I'm the better man, it should be obvious. I'd be the better father for Caylen, not him. He's a future murderer heading for prison. Having him gone is best for everyone. Except she doesn't know about his plans, or what he's done. If I can remember what he's done . . . but then again . . . he is me. I've been trying to think of that more and more, trying not to see us as two different people, he's a side of me. I have to tell her, but what is telling her going to do other than worry her? She has enough to be worried about. Why am I even thinking about this right now?

I've got to learn to live in the moment. I have a woman who I'm crazy about lying right next to me, in my arms. She's beautiful, smart, funny, and already my wife. This makes things easier, no more worrying about how to make my family work. It's all fixed. Things are going to be okay. God this feels good, having her here, right next to me. I kiss the back of her neck, and she starts to stir.

"Good morning," I tell her. She turns to face me, and she looks at me as if she's observing me as she touches my face.

"It's me, Chris," I say jokingly, and for a slight moment I panic, what if she doesn't want it to be me? What if she's disappointed?

"Good morning, Chris," she says, a wide smile spreading across her face.

"What time is it?" she asks quietly. I glance at the clock on my desk.

"It's a little after six," I tell her.

"Your parents are probably already up. I should get back down stairs," she says, sitting up in bed.

"Stay. Just a little longer," I say, surprising myself. I know my parents bumping into Lauren coming from my room isn't the best way to announce we're together, but right now I don't care. This . . . it feels right. She cups my face, leans over, and kisses me. It's light, and soft but intense. I don't want it to end. I slide my hand across her back and pull her onto me.

"If we do this we're going to get caught," she laughs as I bury my face in her neck, trailing kisses across her shoulder. She lets out a soft whimper, and I have to have her. I've never wanted a woman so badly in my life.

"Just a little while," I promise her. What have I been missing?

"Just a little while?" she mumbles, our lips pressed against one another.

"Chris, I need . . ." I practically jump out of my skin. By the time I turn around the door is closing.

"Oh my God, was that your dad?" Lauren says, covering her face.

"Pretty sure it was," I groan, getting out of the bed.

"Great," she says, hiding under the covers.

"This is going to be a great way to start the morning," she laughs, as she peeks at me from under the covers, her hazel eyes sparkling in the sunlight. It makes the awkward and uncomfortable conversation I'm about to have with my parents worth it.

"I'll go down and handle it," I tell her, searching for my clothes.

"No I can't let you do that alone," she protests, getting out of the bed and searching for her things. She's completely naked, and it stops me in my tracks. Last night I didn't take time to really see her. It was dark, but right here in the morning light she looks amazing. She catches me staring at her, and she blushes.

"We better hurry. I know they're waiting on us," she says, pulling her shirt over her head.

"You're beautiful," I can't help but tell her, and she laughs.

"Thank you," she says bashfully.

"You're not so bad yourself," she says with a wink and heads to the door. Before she opens it, I take her hand.

"Are you sure you want to do this with me? I have no idea what might be said down there," I warn her. She lets out a deep breath.

"We're in this together," she says, taking my other hand. I can't help but kiss her again.

"I mean how bad can it be? We're adults, we have a child, and we're married. I . . . it's going to be fine."

WHEN WE MAKE it down stairs, my mom is at the stove frying sausage, and my dad is at the table, his arms folded. They both look up as we enter. My mom with a grin on her face, and my dad with the biggest scowl I've ever seen.

"Good morning, you two," my mom greets us.

"Morning, Mom," I say, glancing over at Lauren who's smiling nervously.

"Are you two ready for breakfast?"

"Yes," Lauren says quickly.

"Come on, you both sit down," my mom says cheerfully. I wonder if my dad told her. I can't tell. I know she's happy for us to be home and everything is relatively normal again, but if she knew, she definitely wouldn't take it how my dad is taking it. He's like a spoiled kid.

"Is Caylen awake?" Lauren asks before sitting down.

"You'd know that if you were down here with her," my dad mumbles.

"William," my mom scolds.

"Wow," Lauren sighs in disbelief.

"Well, I guess we better just get this out the way. Mom, Lauren and I had sex last night," I blurt out, almost surprising myself. My mom's mouth drops open a little. Lauren looks down at her plate, but I can see a small smirk on her face.

"I gathered that," my dad spouts.

"And there should be nothing wrong with it. We have a daughter, we're together, and we're married," I continue.

"There isn't a problem with it at all," my mom adds quickly.

"Really, Gwen. You don't see an issue with this?" my dad says sardonically.

"No, I do not, William. Have you ended things with Jenna, Chris?" she asks.

"Yes I have," I add quickly.

"Well, what is the problem, William?" she asks simply.

"I'll tell you all what the problem is. The problem is the elephant in the room," he says, and I let out a deep breath.

"Lauren, would you care to enlighten them on the conversation that we had about this exact problem?"

"Your dad thinks I'm a trigger for Cal," she says quietly.

"That's ridiculous," I say defensively.

"Oh is it, Son? Because it's been less than a month since she's been here, and all of a sudden he reemerges," he states sarcastically.

"You don't know if that's true!"

"Well, I do know that any relationship that causes that man to come to the surface shouldn't exist, period," he says stubbornly.

"William, stop it," my mom says.

"And any person that is okay or even welcomes Cal reemerging whenever he feels like it, isn't welcome in my home," he says, staring directly at Lauren.

"Are you kidding?" I ask him in disbelief.

"No, he's not kidding Chris," Lauren adds, getting up from the table.

"Lauren, please. Let's just wait a minute," my mom interrupts.

"No, Mrs. Scott. It has been blatantly obvious that he hasn't wanted me here since we arrived. I appreciate him being so forthcoming this morning."

"This isn't just William's house, this is my house too, Lauren," my mom says quickly.

"Why do you hate him so much?" Lauren asks, staring directly at my father.

"We've been over this before. The same reasons you should hate him, and just to make it clear, I am not the only person in this room who wishes Cal never existed," he spits.

"Son, I only say this because I love you. You're not who she wants; you're the consolation prize, the compromise. You said it yourself, she loves Cal, and everyday she's going to wish you were him!"

It feels like someone has squeezed my insides when those words leave his mouth, but before I have a chance to react, Lauren has slapped my dad right across the face.

"How dare you! How dare you pit your son against—against himself! Chris has a condition, a sickness, but you've brainwashed him into believing that he's two different people. The belief that Cal isn't a part of him is doing more damage than anything I ever could," she says turning to my mom. "I love your son. Every part of him. Being with him on a good day, a bad day, when he calls himself whoever is okay with me! I think you understand that," she says, looking at my mom hopefully. Then she looks at me.

"I hope that you and Cal can understand that one day," Lauren says to me with a sigh. "I think it is time for me to leave," she continues with a forced smile.

"Impulsive, violent, rash. Who does that remind you of?" my dad says smugly.

"You deserved that. How could you speak to your son that way?" my mom scolds him. "I don't know what the problem is. But you're letting this turn you into someone I don't like very much. Grow up William," she says before standing up and following Lauren. For a moment, my dad looks like he's just realized what a jackass he's been.

"If she leaves, I'm going with her. Wherever she goes," I tell him, getting up from the table.

"Chris. I don't want to hurt you, but what I said is the truth. We both know it. You deserve better than that," he says. I walk closer to him and lean down in his face so that he understands that I mean every word I'm about to say.

"I suggest you get on the good side of my wife and the mother of your grandchild. I'd really like my daughter to know the man I grew up with and loved. Until he comes back, stay away."

lauren

"I AM SO sorry for William's behavior, honey. He's just afraid," Mrs. Scott explains, holding Caylen while I frantically gather our things. Our welcome has officially been worn out. Well, mine at least. I'm pretty sure Caylen is welcome to stay as long as she likes.

"I'm sorry for that out there. I shouldn't have hit him," I say apologetically. Am I sorry for hitting William? No. I am sorry for disrespecting Gwen's house.

"He deserved it," she says with a sigh. "He shouldn't have said those things to you or Chris," she continues, sitting down on the bed. "I–I just wish that he didn't have so much malice in his heart for Cal," she adds sullenly.

"Me too," I add, taking a moment from tossing the clothes into my suitcase and sitting beside her.

"Do you hate Cal, Mrs. Scott?" I ask her genuinely. She's so sweet, she could very well hate him and just do a good job hiding it.

"Oh honey, no," she says with a laugh. "To be quite honest with you, I don't see them as being different at all. I differentiated the two because it was easier for William to see Cal as the 'bad part' of Chris. I've never seen him that way," she says, giving me a squeeze on the leg.

"The first time we *officially* met Cal as an adult, when I saw him, and he spoke to us, I didn't see him as this other person. I saw my son, whatever he chooses to call himself. As a parent, you don't stop loving your children when they don't follow the plan you have for them, or go a little off course," she explains then sighs. "Well you shouldn't," she adds.

"I hope I can be half the mom to Caylen you are to Chris, Mrs. Scott," I tell her honestly. She pulls me into a hug with Caylen sandwiched between us, so we release quickly. But thinking back to the first day I arrived with Caylen in her kitchen, wondering what it would be like to hug her, it's everything I thought it would be. For a moment, it seems like everything is going to be okay. Like the world isn't off its axis, like my husband isn't torn in two.

"Everything will be okay, sweetie," she says, squeezing my hand. "I really wish you'd consider staying," she pleads.

"I think it's time," I say with a tight smile.

"I guess it is," she says with a sigh.

"It is," Chris says, standing in the doorway. My heart jumps when I see him.

"I'll give you guys a minute," she says, standing with Caylen. "I'm going to enjoy every second I can with her before you leave," she says to me as she carries her out.

"I'm going to work on your father, Chris. He's stubborn, but he loves you so much." Chris nods and gives both her and Caylen a kiss before they leave the room, and she shuts the door behind her.

"My mom really likes you," he says before sitting on the bed next to me.

"She's been nothing but kind to me since I've arrived and is the best grandmother Caylen could ever ask for," I tell him.

"So did that go as good as you hoped it would?" I ask with a laugh, trying to lighten the mood.

"Much better," he jokes, and we sit quietly, tension starting to swirl around the room.

"About what your dad said," I start, and he takes my hand.

"I get it. I do. And how you feel about Cal, I'm trying to . . . I can get past that," he says. "I know how much you love him, and I know it will take more time than it has for you to love me like that, but I'll wait. As long as it takes," he says, looking into my eyes and holding my hand. I should be thrilled about his declaration, it's selfless and so Chris-like, but that's not what I want. I need them to see past this. It's not some type of contest or tug of war. They are the same.

"Chris. I already love you like that. This is a disorder that makes you feel different, but you are one and the same to me. Don't think of it as me wanting one side of you more than the other. I want all of you," I tell him, and he looks disappointed, letting go of my hand. My stomach drops. Maybe it was too soon, but when is soon going to be soon enough. Especially after everything Helen told me. I did the exact opposite of what I was supposed to do. I'm not going to coddle them anymore, He is *one* man, one man that I love, and they need to understand that not me. When I woke up next to Chris this morning, guilt tried to trickle in. It tried to steal the joy of the moment from me, but when I really think about it—why should I not feel good about sleeping with my husband? He's my husband officially. The Jenna thing is completely done with. There is no way I'm going to alienate him and push him back to her. It felt right . . . well it did feel a little wrong, too . . . but it mostly felt right. I need him to know that it's right, whenever we do it.

"I've been trying to make an appointment with my doctor," he says, putting his head in his hands. I feel a sting of guilt lance through me. The conversation with Dexter Sr. comes up in my mind. "Her secretary called and left me a message saying she'd be out of the office all month. Then when I called back to make an appointment her secretary said she wasn't out of the office, but when I told her my name she said she didn't have openings for the next six months," he says, frustrated.

Oh my God, Dexter Sr. has had Chris blacklisted. Isn't that against some type of medical ethics?

"I really want to try to grasp this. It's just really hard," he groans.

"I know," I say, interlacing my hand with his.

"But I'm here. We're in this together," I say, giving him a little smile.

"I'm thinking about just seeing Helen again, when we go back to Chicago."

My heart skips a beat.

"You're coming with me?" I ask him. I mean it makes sense, but I don't know if he's really ready.

"Why wouldn't I? We're in this together, right?" he says, giving me a smile that makes me hug him. Maybe all of this won't be so bad. Maybe everything will be okay. After everything that's happened, we deserve a break. Maybe now we'll get one.

chapter 13

IT CAN'T BE her. It can't fucking be her! But as soon as I
make it downstairs and turn the
corner, there she is, standing at
the desk. When she sees me, her
eyes light up but just for a minute
before worry starts to show in
her face.

"I'll handle it from here
Lamar," I tell the concierge at the
desk. I put my hand around her
back and usher her towards the
front doors.

November 7th, 2010

"What are you doing here?" I
ask through gritted teeth.

"I came to speak to your soon to be wife," she says simply. As soon
as we're out the door, the time for playing nice is over.

"How could you do this, Cal? How could you do something as major as this? Does that poor girl know about your disorder? How could
you marry someone and not even tell us?" she says, her voice breaking.
For a moment, I feel a slight tinge of guilt.

"How dare you come here? The night of my engagement party, and
tell her what? The man you're marrying isn't fucking real!"

"I was going to tell her the truth."

"Your version of the truth. It's always the version that you and
William think up, isn't it?" I ask her.

"Cal, you cannot do this. Do you understand what you're doing?"
she says, her tone pleading.

"I know exactly what I'm doing," I tell her.

"No you don't. I don't know how you've pulled this off so far, but what are you going to do when you marry her and she wakes up in bed with Chris!" she exclaims.

"That is never going to happen!"

"You don't know that. She deserves to know," she pleads.

"You just don't want me to be happy."

"That's not true," she says pleadingly.

"Of course it's true. You don't give a shit about me. All you want is Christopher back."

"That's not true, Cal! I love both of you," she interjects.

"He's not coming back, Gwen! I'm on medication that will get rid of him completely!"

"W-what are you talking about? You're taking drugs? What are you taking, Cal? Are they safe?"

"It doesn't matter, but you and Will can get it through your heads that your mild mannered little farm boy is never coming back."

"What medication, there isn't any medication that's a cure, Cal. Integration is the only way . . . are you taking something illegal?" she says, frantically grabbing my arm.

"It's not your concern," I tell her simply, snatching my arm away.

"It is my concern. You're my son, and I love you!" she says, and for a moment I almost believe her, but she doesn't care about me, only the person that I keep at bay.

"Cal, please!" she says, grabbing my arm again as I turn away from her.

"How can you love her when you shut love out? How can you know what love is?" she asks, looking directly in my eyes.

"She's love! I love her more than anything. If you screw this up for me, I'll disappear, and you'll never see Chris again," I say, before snatching away from her. I turn around and see Lauren heading my way.

Fuck!

"Leave. Now," I tell Gwen before heading back to the building. Before I can enter, Lauren's come outside, and we meet right at the door. My heart is about to blow the fuck up. She looks down the street right at

Gwen, who thankfully is walking in the opposite direction.

"What was that about? Who was she?" she asks, eyeing me suspiciously. I shrug, trying to be as casual as possible. If she only knew how fast my heart was going. My palms are sweaty; I have to calm down.

"Nothing," I tell her, walking back through the entrance of our building and waiting for her to come in. I hate lying to her, I try to never do it, this isn't exactly a lie, but it makes me feel like shit. She looks back at me and then back in Gwen's direction, and my throat feels like it's about to close up. Gwen's stopped walking.

Shit! What the fuck am I going to do?

I glance at Gwen, and her eyes connect with mine. The only thing I can do is shake my head.

Fuck it.

I mouth *please* to her. I've never asked anyone for much. I regret little, but right now I wish I could go back in time and get on my fucking knees and beg Gwen not to say anything. She nods slightly. It's subtle, and even Lauren won't notice it, but it's enough to make my heart stop slamming into my chest.

"Are you coming?" I ask Lauren impatiently. She looks over at me, but she doesn't move, instead she glances back in Gwen's direction again, but she's gone by that time. Her eyes narrow in on mine. She's pissed. I can deal with pissed, after what I could be dealing with, pissed is welcome.

"Nothing," she says bitterly as she walks past me into the lobby.

"I took care of it. She didn't want anything important," I say casually, my heart rate returning to normal. I sit down in one of the big chairs in the lobby. I've never needed to sit down as much as I do right now.

"Well, what happened? What did she want with me?" she asks anxiously.

I'm going to have to tell another fucking lie.

"She really wasn't making any sense. She seemed hopped up on something. I told her to leave." I pull out my cellphone so I don't have to look at her. I can't look her right in the eye and lie to her.

"Well, maybe you should have let me talk to her," she says, nudging me. She does it again until I look directly at her. Her hazel eyes won't let go of mine. I don't want to lie to her again, but I can't lose her. If I told her now I'd lose her.

"Look. She wasn't making any sense. She probably pulled your name off an article of some event we've been to with Dexter. You have to be careful about just anyone trying to see you. When you're associated with the Crestfields, people see dollar signs and will sell you any sob story thinking you can write them a check. Most people have some type of agenda, and I'm sure she did, but she won't be back. You can't just trust anybody now, okay?" I feel like shit. A crock of bullshit. It sounds like it makes sense, but she knows me, and she's not buying it. I grab her hand, and she sighs and nods just a little bit. She wants to believe me, but she's not stupid.

"Okay," she says simply, but it's forced and hesitant, and she pulls her hands from mine and folds them in her lap. She's thinking. She knows this doesn't add up.

"Mr. Scott, your car is here," one of the car attendants informs us.

"Thanks," I tell him, standing. I wait for Lauren to do the same, but she doesn't.

"You're coming, right?" I say jokingly, but in all honesty, I don't know if she's coming. She glares at me and rolls her eyes before following the attendant.

This is going to be a long fucking night.

Engagement Party Checklist

✓ Ridiculously large banquet hall
✓ Overly expensive food
✓ Hundreds of people you don't give a shit about telling you congratulations
✓ Pissed off and annoyed fiancé,

She knows something is up. She wouldn't talk to me in the car. She keeps moving when I try to touch her, and it's killing me. My gratefulness for Gwen has expired. Why the fuck would she come here? How dare she show up at my house, threatening to tell my fiance about my past? It's the past. Our future doesn't include them. Nothing before her matters.

Fucking Dexter had to have told her I was engaged, and to show up the day of my engagement party? If Gwen had talked to Lauren, everything would be ruined. My life would be ruined. She's never looked at me the way she is now. With . . . distrust, like she's seeing me for another person. I don't want her to look at me like, like I'm the villain, she's never done that before.

Since we've been here, she's been distant and quiet. This is the first time I've ever had to flat-out tell her a lie.

We both plastered smiles on our faces as we greeted a bunch of people we don't even fucking know. This was all Helen and Dexter's idea. We shouldn't even be here, but Lauren lit up at the idea of a big engagement party. Dex didn't spare any expense, taking the title of best man and running with it. I can't wait until I get to talk to him about his little game, sending Gwen the day of my engagement party.

"A toast, to an invaluable part of Crestfield Industries, my friend who I consider my family. Cal Scott and his beautiful future wife Lauren." Everyone raises their glasses and toasts to us. She looks over at me, and we kiss, but it's different. There's always been something behind it, pushing its way out of both of us, but right now it seems like she's pulling instead of pushing. The applause roars throughout the room as glasses clink and pictures are taken. I don't give a shit about any of it if Lauren isn't feeling it. I lean over and whisper in her ear.

"Love you, babe." She smiles at me, but it's weak.

"I love you, too." It's dry and half-hearted.

Before I can call her on it, Lauren's aunt Raven and her best friends are near us.

"You look so beautiful, honey," her aunt says. "Cal, extremely dashing as always," she adds, squeezing my shoulder. I wink at her, and she blushes. If I didn't know any better, I'd swear this lady had a crush on me.

"How much did they drop on this? I feel like if I drop a plate I'd be out of a car," Angela teases.

"What's wrong, L?" Hillary asks, eyeing me suspiciously. Hillary and I didn't get off on the right foot, but I like her now. She really loves Lauren and is protective of her; I can't fault her for that even if she acts like a whore.

"Nothing, everything's fine," she replies meekly. Everything isn't fine, and I know exactly who's to blame.

"I'm going to go talk to Dex," I say, excusing myself and heading over to Dexter and Helen. I didn't get a chance to really talk to him since Lauren and I arrived almost thirty minutes into the dinner.

"Excuse me," Dex says to a flock of buzzards who are only here for a stab at his wallet. I throw my arm over his shoulder as a friendly gesture when I want to pull him into a choke-hold.

"Talk to Gwen lately?" I ask, once we're far enough away from the crowd.

"I did," he says simply.

"What'd you tell her?" I ask, smiling tightly.

"I may have mentioned that I was attending your engagement dinner today."

"What the fuck is your problem?" I say, crossing my arms to keep from punching him in the face.

"I didn't know your engagement was confidential," he retorts smugly.

"She could have told Lauren everything Dex, and now she thinks something is up. She's distant at our fucking engagement party."

"Well it's about time," he adds with a grin. I scowl at him.

"Tell her the truth," he says, looking me squarely in the eye, "I don't want this blowing up in our faces later."

"Nothing's going to blow up if you let me handle it. Helen and I are handling it, stop running your fucking mouth," I warn him.

"I think you should consider whom you're talking to Cal," he says, adjusting his cufflinks.

"The great Dexter Crestfield. I don't give a shit. You're supposed to be my friend, you're not my mentor or my daddy."

"Then stop acting like a child!" he says, stepping closer to me. I'm a little surprised.

"This can go very badly for all of us. You know who is going to get involved then. I'm trying to keep him out of it,"

"I'm not afraid of your father," I laugh.

"Well you should be."

"Why would he care about who the hell I marry?"

"Because you're adding another person to the equation who you have to trust."

"She doesn't know anything," I retort.

"Which means that you don't think that you can trust her. So, if you can't trust her to even tell her the truth about yourself, can you trust her with anything else?"

"It's not that I don't trust her," I sigh, running my hands over my face.

"I want her to love me for me," I say quietly. "Not for who I was. Not for who everyone thinks I should be."

"I don't want her to look at me like I'm some broken man, the way everyone else does."

"If she loves you, really loves you, she'll understand," he tells me, squeezing my shoulder.

"If you don't tell her, this is going to go bad, and I'm not going to fix any of it. You're on your own."

"The medicine's working," I tell him adamantly.

"So that's what you're placing all your cards on. A medicine that's still under trial, that *you're* the test subject for?" he asks.

"You bet on Helen, I'm betting on her, too," I retort. He shakes his head.

"Starting your marriage based on secrets and lies doesn't make for the most stable foundation," he sighs.

"So that's not what your and Helen's marriage is based on?" I laugh, and he scoffs like he's offended.

"Of course not. We have tons of secrets between us, but they are not ours, only other people's," he says, squeezing my shoulder before walking away from me and back into the crowd.

I let out a deep groan. I don't drink, but I've never wanted a stiff drink more than I do right now. I glance at my watch. This is fucking boring. My life almost just fell apart, and I need something to distract me, I need something to intoxicate me. It won't be anything in a bottle, but a slinky little grey dress. I work my way through the crowd, avoiding meaningless conversations with people I don't even like. It takes me about twenty minutes before I bump into Angela who's wobbling a bit having had a few too many drinks herself. She grabs my arm and pulls me into a dance.

"You and I need to talk, mister," she says, her words a bit slurred.

"How can I help you?" I joke back. Angela's one of the few people I like. She's smart, funny and straightforward, and I know she'd go to war for Lauren which makes her okay in my book.

"L really loves you," she says sternly.

"Well I'd hope she does," I kid with her.

"No. I'm serious," she pouts. "She's never loved a guy how she loves you. You've changed her." She says the last part off-handedly.

"What do you mean?" I ask as she pulls my arm for me to spin her around.

"She's grown up, not the same naïve girl who got off the bus from Michigan," she says, stopping her dance and motioning for me to follow her away from the dance floor. Once we are, we sit down at an empty table. "You know we didn't know what to think of you and her at first. I will admit I didn't think you could give her what she wanted," she continues, and I wonder if this girl is a mind reader.

"I want to give her everything she wants," I say simply.

"Good. Because she deserves it," she says, the slur almost gone from her voice.

"A guy like you could break a girl's heart," she says, standing up before she squeezes my shoulder. "But you wouldn't do that, right?" she says in my ear before gliding back onto the dance floor.

I wouldn't do that. I can't do that.

I maneuver throughout the hall and spot Lauren grabbing a glass of champagne and heading up the stairs to the second level. I quicken my pace to catch up with her. The second floor is virtually empty. Since everyone is on the main floor, I know she must be as over this as I am. She walks to the end of the hall where it's dimly lit and sits at a table alone. I take a deep breath and walk toward her.

"Drinking alone isn't good," I wink at her.

"Well, it's a good thing you're here then," she says sarcastically.

"To you," she says, lifting her glass briefly before downing the champagne. She stands as I near the table and starts to walk past me. I grab her wrist, and she lets out a deep sigh.

"Really Lauren? You're going to act like this at our engagement party?" I ask.

"How should I be acting, Cal?" she asks, wryly. I step closer to her and whisper in her ear.

"Like the sight of me makes you wet."

"You are disgusting," she says, but I can hear the slightest amusement in her voice.

"I have to know if I'm right," I tell her pressing her up against the wall. She stops my hand as it starts to creep under her dress.

"Am I really enough for you, Cal? Just me, one woman for the rest of your life?" she asks me. I can hear the sincerity in her voice, her eyes revealing everything, and it hits me. She thinks that Gwen could have been another woman. I have to lean down so we're face to face. She's in her come fuck me pumps. They're tall, but she still only comes to my chest.

"You're it for me. Right now, tomorrow, always," I tell her, and her smile is back, the distance is gone, and she's mine again. She kisses me like she missed me. She moans in my ear as I push her underwear to the side and slip my finger inside of her.

"We're going to get caught," she pants.

"You want to be more discreet I take it?" She nods her head while licking her lips. I grab her hand and pull her to the table she was sitting at before and her eyebrow raises.

"Have a seat, Ms. Brooks," I say, gesturing to the chair she was sitting in. She eyes me suspiciously with a smirk but sits down. I walk behind her and push her chair underneath the table.

"What are you up to?" she laughs. I wink at her and take off my jacket and hand it to her before lifting the thick grey tablecloth and climbing underneath it.

"Should I climb under there with you?" she giggles.

"Nope, just sit back and relax," I tell her as I move her legs apart.

"Cal, no!" she says trying to shut them.

"Have a drink, Lauren. I'm about to," I tell her as my tongue slides up her thigh.

"Oh my God," she says nervously. I see her hands making sure the tablecloth covers her lap as I tug her underwear down.

"Cal, this is so bad," she purrs, as my tongue finds its way inside her. "What if someone . . ." she says tightly as she melts around me. She doesn't finish her sentence as her hands grip my hair.

I start to go faster and glance at my watch. I can usually get her off in about five minutes tops if I really want to, it only takes longer if I want to tease her, but since I know she's scared as hell of getting caught, I won't do that right now.

"Cal," she pants out, trying to be quiet. The little whimpering sounds she's making have me thinking that pulling her under the table might not be such a bad idea.

"Shit," she says as her legs start to get tighter around my neck, and I know she's almost there.

I hear her phone vibrating on the table.

"It's Helen. They're probably looking for us," she cries.

"They're probably c-coming," she says digging into my shoulder, her legs start to shake, and her body goes limp. I climb out from under the table and take a seat next to her. Her eyes are closed, but the smile on her face is priceless.

"I owe you," she says, leaning her head on my shoulder.

"You've got time to pay me back," I tell her, running my hand through her hair.

"How much time?" she asks with a giggle.

"Forever."

chris

I'M GOING TO Chicago. When the words came out of my mouth, I heard them, they felt right to say, but really what the hell am I thinking? Chicago? Chicago isn't me. I don't know anyone there, I don't have a job there, and Cal has home field advantage. But Dr. Lyce and Dex can keep an eye on me if Cal comes back. Most importantly, I'll be with my family, Lauren and Caylen, and that's how it should be. They're what's important, right?

A new start.

It could be good. It's going to be good. It's all going to be great.

I'm excited, big city, new relationship, sort of. If I can quit thinking about the fact that Cal is a potential murderer, hell-bent on killing my biological father, it would be a lot easier, but since I can't, then we'll just have to deal with it. The fact that Cal remembers things from my childhood and I don't isn't comforting either. To know my dad, the person who brought me into this world, could be a cold-blooded killer, and Cal wants us to follow right in his footsteps, is more than a little disconcerting.

"Hey!" Aidan knocks on the door to my bedroom twice.

"What's the occasion? Since when do you knock?" I laugh at him. He shrugs.

"What's all this?" he asks, gesturing to the bags and boxes I have scattered around the room.

"Lauren's going to Chicago, and I'm going with her."

"Dude, you're taking enough stuff to move," he chuckles, and I grin at him.

"I am moving," I tell him, and his eyes widen in disbelief.

"Wait a minute, get the fuck out," he laughs. I spend the next fifteen minutes catching him up on everything that's happened between me and Lauren, Dexter, Jenna, and my dad. Afterwards, he lets out a deep breath.

"Whoa. I think I need a minute to process all of this," he laughs. "I don't know where to even start. Just to make sure I got all of this—you're moving to Chicago because you ended it with Jenna, and you can see your doctor whose husband is having people follow you around because your alter ego wants to kill your real dad because he thinks he killed your mom," he asks, and I nod.

"Yeah you've kind of got it all down . . . I think." He shakes his head in disbelief.

"And your parents are cool with you moving?"

"They're not thrilled. My mom doesn't want me to go, but she knows we can't stay here with my dad acting like a jerk," I say, sitting next to him.

"So as far as your murderous alter ego goes," he says, covering up a laugh, "Lauren doesn't know about this, or about you having people follow you?"

"She has enough to deal with," I say, standing up and starting to pack my things.

"You think it's better for her not to know?" he asks, frowning. I shrug.

"It's not that I'm hiding things from her. It's just . . . yeah, I think it's better that she doesn't know," I admit.

"If the roles were reversed, you wouldn't want to know?"

"No. Sometimes ignorance is bliss," I shrug, and he begins to laugh.

"What?"

"I'm just surprised, you know, seeing how upset you were about your parents hiding everything from you," he says sarcastically.

"That was different," I say defensively.

"How was that different?" he says smugly. I have no defense. He's right. I should tell her. She has every right to know, but it's all been so much on her. I wish we could get a day, just one day, without disaster rearing its ugly head. I sit down on my bed and pull a Snickers out of my pocket to eat.

"I mean it could even give you an edge up on this thing." Aidan shrugs.

"What do you mean?"

"I doubt she'd be hoping for Cal to come back if he wants to kill someone," he laughs.

"I don't want her to not want him back because of that. I want her to not want him back because she loves me, who I am. I don't want to win by default."

"Chris, this isn't a game, man," he lets out a frustrated groan, and I'm caught off guard.

"This is your life. In all seriousness, you have got to stop looking at this as a competition," he says, and it sounds like he's scolding me.

"I'm sorry, when did you become my dad?" I ask, trying to hold in a laugh, but the expression on his face is anything but jovial.

"Do you really think Lauren just wants *Cal* back?"

"I-I don't know," I shrug.

"That girl wants all of you. Not just you or him. She wants her daughter to have a father, for her to have a possibility of a normal life. I have to tell you the worst thing in the world is not you having DID. Life comes with a shitload of problems, and you really need to get yourself together because whenever something goes bad, you guys can't keep flipping the switch.

"What's going on?" I ask him suspiciously.

"What do you mean? I'm giving you advice as your friend. As your best friend!" he exclaims. I stand up and look at him.

"What are you not telling me?" I ask him, crossing my arms. He looks caught off guard.

"Nothing. I'm just trying to help you!" he says defensively.

"You've never been a good liar, and you rarely take your head out of your own butt long enough to care about what's going on around you. Something's up. What's going on?" I demand.

"So that's what you really think of me? I'm a self-absorbed jerk-off who doesn't care about the people I love. Real nice, Chris," he says angrily.

"No, don't flip this. What the hell is going on?" I demand, and he looks down at the floor guiltily.

"When are you leaving for Chicago?" he asks quietly.

"What does that have to do with anything?" I ask him impatiently.

"It's not for me to tell you, man, but there are some things you need to know before you leave," he says, crossing his arms.

"What things?" I ask, and he just looks down at the floor. "Oh, so you can bring it up but not say anything?"

"I didn't bring it up. You brought it up!"

"Okay, whatever it is, just say it," I urge him.

"I can't!" he says throwing up his hands.

"You know what's worse than knowing there's a monster under your bed?"

"Knowing there's one under your bed but not knowing what it looks like," I laugh angrily.

"It doesn't involve me. I told her to tell you, she needs time."

"Who? Lauren?"

"No, Lisa," he says. I remember her calling me, and Lauren mentioning it, but so much has happened, it slipped my mind.

"What would something with Lisa have to do with me?" I say, feeling my anger cool some. There isn't really anything Lisa can tell me that will knock my world off its axis. Now I'm more worried about her than anything. I grab my cellphone and dial her number.

"She hasn't been answering, she left town . . ."

"Hello," Lisa says.

"Hey," I reply and see Aidan's stunned expression.

"Is there something you need?" she asks sheepishly, and I look at my phone in disbelief.

"What do you mean is there something I need?" I laugh.

"It's just been a really—I have a lot going on, Chris," she stutters, and I glance at Aidan whose gaze won't leave his feet.

"Look, I'm going to Chicago with Lauren, and Aidan thinks there's something important you have to tell me. I don't want anything hanging over my head before I leave. My mom wants to have dinner tonight, but since our record with those haven't been great, I'd rather not," I chuckle. There's a long pause.

"When are you leaving?" she asks quietly.

"Why does it matter? Are you home?" I ask, feeling my annoyance grow.

"Yeah, but I have . . ." she stutters.

"Cool, I'll see you in about an hour," I say, before hanging up the phone.

"Are you coming with me?" I ask him, and he only nods.

"You know what, you're being really weird . . . maybe you should stay here," I laugh, leaving him in my bedroom. I head down the stairs and see my dad standing there.

"Can I talk to you?" he asks, and I let out a sigh.

"Did you think about what I said this morning?"

"I did," he says quietly.

"I want to speak with both you and Lauren."

chapter 14

lauren

HE'S COMING WITH me.

Chris and I are going back to Chicago. This time there isn't a question of his motive. He's told me that he loves me, that he wants to be with me and raise Caylen together. I should be ecstatic, everything is coming together—but on what type of foundation? Secrets and lies? This doesn't feel right. I can't shake Dexter Crestfield's smarmy smile from my thoughts. I keep trying to get Lisa's looming secret out of my mind. Helen's instructions, which I basically threw out the window, are making me rethink everything. I keep thinking that going back to Chicago may not be the right move, but whenever I think about Chris's dad I can't imagine us staying here another day.

If we leave we can avoid the entire Lisa ordeal until . . . I don't know, until . . . If things somehow become perfect and she ruins it with whatever she has to tell Chris. It's selfish and stupid, but I really just wish she wouldn't. If it's not life and death and it will hurt him, I wish she'd just keep it to herself, but then again, whatever it is Aidan thinks it could be the cause of Chris creating Cal. What could Lisa have to do with something so big? But if she tells him, could that be the key to them integrating? I have to know that Chris is committed to that before doing a re-run of what I did last night with him.

"Hey," I turn and see him standing there, a nervous smile on his face, and it instantly makes me feel better.

"How is the packing going?" I ask, letting out a pent-up breath.

"It was good until Aidan interrupted me," he sighs.

"Aidan's here?"

"He just left," he says, rubbing the back of his head.

"Did he want anything in particular?"

"Other than to irritate me," he chuckles, and I smile, relieved. Aidan didn't budge on telling me anything about what Lisa told him, but he's a very straightforward guy and doesn't seem like the type who'd be able to keep a secret in plain sight.

"We sort of had an argument, but he's going to meet me at Lisa's later." He shrugs, and my heart speeds up.

"Lisa's," I can't help but repeat.

"Yeah. He said she has something important to tell me. I want to get it out of the way before we leave," he says, sitting down on the bed I have been sharing with Caylen during this visit.

"Are you okay?" he asks, concerned. I swallow the lump in my throat.

"Of course, why would you ask that?"

"Well you've folded that shirt over almost three times since I've been in here," he chuckles. I toss the stupid shirt on the bed.

"I'll admit my nerves are a little on edge," I sigh, and he does the same.

"This probably isn't going to help, but my dad wants to talk to us."

"Really? He hasn't dished out enough verbal abuse yet?" I ask sarcastically, grabbing another shirt.

"He says he wants to apologize to you and doesn't want us to leave on a bad note," he adds. I look at Chris in disbelief.

"I know my dad's been a real prick lately," he laughs, and I nod. He's been more than a prick.

"But that's not the man he usually is. That's not the dad I know. It's just . . . I think this Cal thing . . ."

"If you want us to talk to him Chris, I can do that, but the moment he says anything negative or remotely insulting, I'll be exiting the conversation," I shrug and he smiles, relieved.

"Okay. Are you ready now?" he asks.

As ready as I'm going to be.

"Yeah, let's get this over with."

I follow Chris into the dining room. Mr. Scott is sitting at the head of the table, his hands folded but his face relatively relaxed, and the hardened frown I've become accustomed to is absent. When he sees us, he even smiles, and that shocks the hell out of me. Since I've met the man, he's never smiled at me once. I don't know what Chris said to him after our conversation this morning, but it really must have been something. When we're seated, he takes a deep breath, and shifts his body weight towards me.

"First, I'd like to apologize to you Lauren," he says without a hint of bitterness or anger hidden beneath his tone. I nearly fall out of my chair.

"I have been extremely inhospitable to you since you've arrived," he continues. "Just a plain jerk," he adds with a chuckle.

Yeah you have.

"I blamed you for things that were not your fault. I used you as someone to take my anger out on since they weren't here for it, and I am truly sorry for how I have behaved towards you."

Has hell just frozen over? Who is this man sitting in front of me?

"Christopher, what you told me this morning really was a wake-up call for me. You did exactly as you should have and stood up for your wife, for her respect, and I couldn't be more proud of you," he says putting his hand on Chris's. I can't help but note how pleased Chris looks, how much stress seems to have lifted off him just in these few minutes.

"I want you both to know that, if you choose to stay, it will be different around here on my end. I will be here to support whatever decisions you make, but both Gwen and I would be thrilled if you chose to stay."

So that's what this is about. He wants Chris to stay, God forbid he steps out from under papa's wing.

"Well Dad that's . . ."

"You don't have to answer me now. I'll give you both time to talk about it. I just know that one of the main reasons you're leaving is because of the way I have been acting, and I couldn't sleep tonight if I knew that I was breaking up our family," he says, and I can't believe my eyes when I see that Mr. Scott is actually tearing up. What in the world has just happened? He turns towards me.

"Lauren, do you accept my apology?" he asks and takes my hand in his. I can't believe this is happening. I glance over at Chris who looks like he's about to tear up as well.

This man has been nothing but mean, nasty, and cruel to me since I've known him, but this guy in front of me seems to not even be the same person. If Chris was his biological son, I'd swear that DID runs in their family.

"I-I," I don't know what to say. I glance back at Chris who has this pleading expression on his face. How can I not give him what he wants? His happy family. If William can stop being a jerk, or at least pretend, then I can move forward, I guess.

"Of course," I tell him, and before I know it, he's stood up and pulled me into a bear hug.

Am I dreaming? After he releases me, he does the same to Chris, but Chris's return embrace is genuine.

"Thanks, Dad," he says, beaming. Mrs. Scott appears in the doorway and soon everyone is hugging. I don't know what to say or what to think. They're happy so I should be happy. This could mean things are going to go really well. We deserve a break after everything that's happened. Chris deserves a break. Then my thoughts drift to . . . what happens after?

cal

"I CAN'T SAY I'm not surprised, because nothing about you surprises me. But you—successfully married and happy? I didn't exactly see that in your future. I am very proud of you," Helen beams at me like a gold digger who's just spotted a dying, single billionaire.

"Why thank you, Mother. I knew you'd be proud," I say, just as sarcastically.

"Even remembering your two month anniversary. I am very impressed," she says, handing me the box with Lauren's present in

February 7th, 2011

it.

"These are the Dorothy shoes?" I ask, looking at the box. Helen has it wrapped in black paper with a big red bow.

"The correct name is limited edition Loubuitons," she corrects me.

"The Dorothy shoes that fine ass Jessica Alba had on?" I ask.

"Yes Cal. The 'Dorothy' shoes," she says dryly and takes a seat on the couch next to me.

"Dex only remembered our anniversary because his assistant reminded him."

"I know I don't say it a lot, but thank you—for everything," I tell her with a shrug.

"You deserve to be happy, Cal. I'm glad you've finally allowed yourself to be," she says, patting my shoulder.

"Well, I'll be happy once you get the final okay on the meds," I tell her, handing her my empty pill bottle. She can't give me a refill until she receives some final results.

"I'm headed to the team right after I leave here. Besides, I better get going, before I ruin your surprise," she says, standing from her seat.

"Let me know what Lauren says once she sees the shoes. I had trouble parting with them," she says before I head out the door.

I look at the clock. Lauren won't be expecting me for a while. I've worked out for two hours. I can't wait until I get home and get to see the look on her face when she sees them. Especially since I'm going to pretend not to remember what today is. Everything has been so fucking good. I've never been this happy in my whole life. I never thought I could feel like this about someone. I took all that I wanted out of life. Everything I have, I had to take or fight for. With Lauren it's not like that, for once the universe is cutting me a break. Me, the black sheep, the prodigal son, happily married to a beautiful, amazing woman who loves me. Not for who she thinks I am or wants me to be, just me. There's really no better feeling than that. I wouldn't trade it for the world on a platter.

I KNEW SHE'D be pissed when she thought I forgot our anniversary. She's so sexy when she's pissed. It's cute that she tried to hide that she was upset at first. She was obviously disappointed, but with a little prodding, she let it out. I hate when she doesn't say what she feels. I don't want her to hide any part of herself from me. That's why my favorite look on her face is right when she comes. You can't hide that at all.

"You're mad," I sigh, trying to keep from laughing as I put down my suitcase.

"No. Well, yeah, I am. I can give you a pass for forgetting our anniversary, even though it was only two months ago, but if you think I'm going to give you a pass for every holiday because you think it's 'cliché' or 'arbitrary' . . ." she trails off as I pull out the shoes Helen had wrapped. I set the box on her lap and laugh at myself for the big cheesy grin that's on my face.

"You were saying, Mrs. Scott?"

A huge smile spreads across her face, and she rolls her eyes at me.

"You're a jerk, you know that?" she jokes, untying the bow on the box.

I sit next to her and kiss her neck. She's so careful taking it apart.

"Come on babe, tear into it!"

"Okay, okay. It's just so pretty," she squeals, removing the paper, and when she sees the box, she freezes. She looks over at me, her eyes wide and bright.

"You didn't!" she says excitedly. She opens the box to see the pair of Dorothy shoes she talked about for a week straight.

"Oh my gosh, Cal!" she says, her eyes tearing up.

"Read the card," I say, pointing to it tucked in between the shoes. She picks it up.

These shoes look like they're straight out of 'The Wizard of Oz,' but since sometimes I'm like the tornado that blew you into Oz, I guess you can wear Dorothy's red slippers. And if I'm gone and seem lost, maybe you can do a little click, and I'll find my way home.

"It's corny, isn't it?" I ask, feeling a little embarrassed.

She nods and climbs on my lap.

"As corny as you being my Prince Charming," she says, kissing me softly. I want more of her. I wrap my arms around her waist and press her down on my lap so she can feel how much I want her. She giggles.

"Are you going to wear them for me?"

"I have the perfect white dress for them," she says, running her hands through my hair.

"No dress. Just them," I say, watching her skin turn red.

"Later," she promises. "I have to run and pick up your gift," she says hopping off me. She runs to the console table and grabs her purse.

"No, my gift can be you," I whine. She cannot leave me with a full hard-on.

"It will be. Tonight," she promises, reaching the door. I give her the saddest face I can muster.

"Don't look at me like that." She giggles, and I make my way closer to her. "No. Five feet," she laughs threateningly, her hand on the doorknob.

"I hope you've gotten a lot of sleep since you've been gone. Because you're going to be up all night," she says, giving me a faux-warning, and my body perks up at the thought.

"Plenty," I say with a wink before she slips out the door.

MY WORK-OUT THIS morning must have really kicked my ass. I usually never take naps. When the phone rings, I almost put it back down until I see it's Dexter, and he's called twice.

"What's up, Dex?" I ask groggily.

"We have a problem," he says solemnly. His tone causes me to sit up in the bed.

"What type of problem?" I ask him anxiously.

"Helen's talked to her team. The medication hasn't been

recommended for further trial . . ." I heard what he just said, but he can't have just said what I think he's just said.

"Can you run that by me again?" I ask, hoping that I heard him wrong, that I'm still asleep, and my brain isn't functioning right.

"I'm sorry, Cal," he says quietly. He's sorry? No, no fucking way.

"I don't give a shit what the eggheads are saying. Have Helen bring me the rest of what she has," I say simply.

"Cal, she can't. The medication has shown dangerous side effects. They are going to do further testing but as of now, it's all being decimated."

"You're kidding me. You're fucking kidding me!" I yell. Fuck controlling my temper or trying not to be mad. This, this can't—they can't just stop it.

"It's been working, Dex. Other than the damn hot flashes, it's working. You know it is," I say, feeling myself start to panic.

"Helen can tell you the medical specifics, but if you have any more, flush it. You have to stop taking it."

"Bullshit!" I yell into the phone. I want to throw it into the wall.

"I know you're mad, Cal,"

"Mad? I'm fucking furious! I can't stop taking it. What the hell am I going to do? You told me you were sure before I did this. This changes everything!"

Fuck me. Fuck me. Fuck me!

"I'm not going to stop!"

"Cal, this is Helen. Listen to me, everything is going to be okay. I promise you, we'll make this work," she says, trying to calm me down. I'm so mad there are tears in my eyes.

"I-am-not-going-to-stop!"

"If you don't, you're dead, Cal. You understand, this could kill you," Dexter says as if he's talking to a fucking kid.

"I might as well be Dex! How the fuck am I supposed to explain this?"

"Lauren loves you. She will understand. We just tell her the truth," Helen says. The truth. *Yeah the truth, after we're already married. Tell her she's trapped in a marriage with two different people?* I won't do that to her. I can't. There has to be another way.

"I won't. I can't take her through that shit,"

"Let me see what I can do, Cal. Let me figure things out," Helen interjects.

"Well, figure it out fast," I say and hang up the phone. My throat is burning, there's a stinging in my chest. I want the feeling gone now, fast. I throw my phone down and next thing I know I've punched through the fucking wall. It hurts, but it distracts me from what's wrong . . . what is about to go terribly wrong.

Shit, I'm bleeding. I barge through my door, and I see her there. Her eyes wide, completely still. I'm going to lose her. This is going to be the end of us.

"Cal, what's wrong? You look upset," her voice is wavering, and she's squeezing her wrist. She only does that when something's wrong

"Um . . ." What do I tell her? I have to tell her something. I run my hands over my face.

She rushes up the stairs to me and takes my wrist in her hand looking at my swollen knuckles.

"Cal, what did you do?" she asks frantically, leading me to the guest bathroom where she starts running water over it.

"Don't be mad, but I punched a hole in our wall," I say trying to downplay that I just busted one of our fucking walls like a psycho.

Her head snaps towards me.

"Why did you do that?" she asks, grabbing our first-aid kit and pulling out the antibiotic wipes.

"Dex really pissed me off," I say, sitting on the edge of the bathtub while she cleans my hand.

She nods as if she understands.

"I kind of heard you talking to him," she admits, looking up at me guiltily. What the hell did she hear? I can't even say anything.

"Did it have something to do with me?" she asks, sitting on my lap. I wrap my arms around her and rest my chin on her shoulder, and she starts to rub my hair. I don't deserve her. That's why I'm going to lose her. Fate was drunk off its ass when it let me have her, and now it realized it fucked up.

"I'm-I'm going to be gone a little more than I thought I was," I can't even look at her as I say it. She lets out a breath she was holding in. She's relieved. If only she knew. She smiles widely at me, and I wish I could feel the relief she's feeling right now, but I'm suffocating, like walls are closing in on me.

"That's okay. I mean, it's not okay, but it's nothing to go punching holes in the wall over," she teases. "I'm a big girl," she adds quietly.

I try to smile, but I can't.

"I'm not feeling too good, babe. Would it be really fucked up if we didn't go out tonight?" I try to see how bad this sucks for her, but she's good at hiding it and gives me a pageant girl smile

"No, babe. If you're not feeling well it's nothing we can't do another day."

"Are you sure? Because we can if you still want to do something, I can just lie down." I cup her face in my hand and look into her eyes. If she's really disappointed, she's doing a hell of a job at hiding it.

"No, get some rest. It's your first day back home, and you're proba-bly jet-lagged. It's fine," she says, before giving me a soft kiss on the lips.

"I'm going to make it up to you," I promise her.

"And you don't have to sit here with me. You should call your girls and go out." I try to sound excited for her. She should go out. I'll have to get used to not having her. I walk into the bedroom and lie across the bed.

"I'm not going to spend our anniversary out with them. As long as I'm with you, that's what's important," she says, lying next to me.

I wrap one of my arms around her and hold her close.

"You know that I love you, right?" I try to sound upbeat, but I just can't muster it.

"Of course I do," she says, looking back at me curiously.

"No, seriously." I turn her body around towards me, so she's facing me completely.

"No matter what. Whatever happens—if anything were to hap-pen—nothing, under any circumstances," I take her hand and place it on my chest and hold it there, "will ever take you from here. Even if it doesn't seem like it, always know how much I love you. I've never loved anyone as much as I love you, and even if I screw it up . . ."

She cups my face in her hand

"Cal, you're scaring me. Is everything okay?" she asks, sitting up and staring at me. No, it isn't, but I won't think about that now. She's here, and I have her.

"Yeah, just trying to get laid," I say, trying to kill the terrible vibe in the room. She continues searching my face.

"You can tell me anything. Nothing would change the way I feel about you. You'll always be my Cal." I wish what that were true, but my situation is the outlier to any situation she can imagine.

"I know. That's why I love you," I tell her, pulling her towards me and kissing her long and soft, how she likes it. I don't do anything else. I don't deserve anything else. We have a problem, the clock has just started on our happy ending, and it's turning backwards. She's about to find out I'm not her fucking prince charming, not even close.

chapter 15

chris

THIS MORNING IF you'd told me that my dad and Lauren would be able to talk without scowling at each other, I wouldn't have believed you. That Lauren would actually agree to stay until the end of the month in my parents' house, I would have laughed in your face. It's funny how so much can change in the span of a few hours. I don't know what prompted my dad's change of heart. I wonder if it was the threat of kicking him out of my life that did it. Who ever said you win more flies with honey never met my dad. I look forward to living in a house that isn't a warzone. I'm glad to have him back to himself again and not this angry ticked-off guy he's become since Lauren arrived. At first I didn't think she would accept his apology, but she did, and I know it was because of me. Because she thinks I needed her to. Maybe I did.

I just can't help but want some things to be more familiar, like they were before all of this chaos happened. Getting things back on track is a huge step in the right direction. It reminds me that everything that's gone wrong could possibly be fixed. Nothing is unfixable. That's what makes me feel better as I walk to Lisa's door. I don't know what it is she has to tell me, but whatever it is we can fix. With Lisa, you never know what the problem could be. We've been friends since elementary school. She's always been the person I could talk to. She's always had a way of making me feel better when things seemed hopeless, when we were young anyway. Now the things that seemed hopeless then would be a cake walk now.

I know she's going to be happy to hear that Lauren and I are making it official. Well, I guess it doesn't get any more official than being married. I ring her doorbell and wait for her to answer. After a few minutes, she still hasn't come to the door, so I ring it again and knock harder at the door. Her car's outside, so I know she's home.

"Come on, Lisa," I mutter to myself. Before I start to knock on the door again, she's opened it.

"Hey, Chris," she says, avoiding eye contact.

"Hey. What's going on with you?" I ask, walking past her into her house. I'm surprised it's clean. Ridiculously clean. Lisa's never been filthy, but she always has stuff everywhere—clothes, old containers of food— but today it looks like my mom has been here and cleaned up for her.

"I've just been busy," she says as she walks past me and sits on her sofa, her hands clasped together in front of her.

"How are you?" she asks dryly. I chuckle.

"I'm good, and you ma'am?" I ask sarcastically. That causes her to smile a little.

"What's up? What's been going on with you?" I ask, sitting next to her on the couch. She sighs and runs her hands through her hair.

"I-I have a lot on my mind," she chuckles.

"Did you get fired? Are you going to jail, what's up?" I joke, nudging her, and she stands up and crosses her arms.

"You changed your hair," I say, surprised. I didn't notice it until now, but the red streak is gone, and she's back to her normal blonde color. Her nose ring is out, too.

"Yeah. It's time for a change," she says quietly.

"So, you're going to Chicago?"

"Eventually. Right now we decided to stay," I tell her happily. Her eyebrows rise, and a smile spreads across her own face.

"We?" she giggles. I nod.

"Me and Lauren and Caylen," I tell her, and her eyes widen, and the dark cloud that's been over her head since I walked in has disappeared briefly.

"So you guys are . . . Did you break things off with Jenna?" she asks excitedly.

"Yeah. We're going to try to make this thing work," I tell her, and she runs over and gives me a big hug.

"That's so great Chris. It's about time you listened to me," she says, patting me on the back.

"Thank you. For being there, for listening, for being you, and never judging. I don't tell you enough, but you're a great friend. I don't know what I'd do without you." I expect her to joke and give me one of her sloppy kisses on my forehead when she gets emotional, but instead her whole body stiffens. I step back from her and I see tears in her eyes.

"Lisa, what's wrong?" I ask, starting to feel nervous. I've only seen Lisa cry once in my whole life and that was when her mother missed her graduation because she was too drunk to remember to show up.

"I'm so glad you're happy, Chris," she says, her voice wavering as she turns away from me.

"Lisa, what is going on?" I ask, starting to become anxious.

"I don't want to be the one to ruin it. I didn't want to do this. I swear to God I never meant to hurt you," I turn her around, and she's crying so hard her body is shaking. I pull her to me.

"Lisa, what is it?"

"Why are you crying, Lisa?" a small voice says from behind us. I turn around and see a little girl of maybe seven or eight, with long blonde hair and bright blue eyes.

"Everything's fine. Go back in my room, okay?" Lisa says trying to pull herself together.

"Who are you?" the little girl asks me.

"I'm Chris, Lisa's friend," I tell her, looking back over at Lisa.

"What's your name?" I ask, kneeling down so we're at eye level. She gives me a shy smile.

"I'm Willa," she tells me.

"Please go back in my room, sweetie," Lisa says, ushering her half way. When the little girl leaves, I look at Lisa for an explanation.

"Is that one of your students? You didn't kidnap someone's kid, did you?" I say half-jokingly. Lisa has a big heart, and I wouldn't be surprised what she'd do to help a kid, even if it wasn't exactly legal. She sighs, it seems like it lasts forever, and then she wipes her face.

"No. She was staying with my aunt. But now my aunt's really sick, and she can't take care of her anymore," she says quietly.

"You're adopting your cousin?" I ask her, sitting back down her couch. I'm not surprised, Lisa loves kids, but to actually take care of one, to be a parent, I don't know if she's ready for that yet. She shakes her head.

"She isn't my cousin. She's my daughter," she says quickly. So quickly I know I haven't heard her right.

"Wait. What?" I ask her in disbelief.

"I had her when I was nineteen," she says, tears coming back to her eyes. I feel like I should say something, but I'm at a loss for words. Lisa has a kid, and she never told me. How could I not know this?

"I-I don't know what to say," I say, letting out a deep breath. "Wow, Lisa," is all I can come up with. We both sit in silence, and then my heart starts to beat faster, and I remember why I'm here.

Oh no. Oh NO!

"She. She isn't mine is she Lisa? You and Cal didn't . . ." I say, feeling like I'm about to throw up. That son of a bitch. That son of a bitch! She stands up and turns away from me.

"Lisa, tell me. Say something now," I say, my own voice shaking. She turns back around, her lips quivering and her hands shaking.

"She's not your daughter. She's your sister."

WHEN MY MOM told me she had cancer, everything changed. Everything seemed sharper, faster, so fast that nothing really mattered. It all blurred together as time sped up. My world shifted off its axis, my life couldn't be the same.

When Lisa said those words, the exact opposite happened. For a moment everything around me froze, time moved in slow motion. I can only describe it as when you get really drunk and you move around lazily, everything's foggy. Your mind is like a swamp, your thoughts float around, and everything is sticky. Not sticky, muddy, muddy is the word I'm looking for. When what you hear is so far-fetched, so catastrophically bad that your brain doesn't compute it. It can't compute it. It's so ridiculous your thoughts won't process it.

Like a glitch.

I don't know how long Lisa's been standing in front of me, but I know she could not have just said what I think she just said. It's impossible, I can't even respond to it, because if I responded I'd be just as ridiculous as she is. I don't even think I'm here right now. I'm in a nightmare, a constructed dream. Cal is fucking with me. This is all an illusion so he can break me down, mentally fuck me so badly that I can't come back from it, but I know this isn't real. My best friend isn't standing in front of me, with a kid I just met in the other room, telling me she's my sister.

It's implausible, because in order for that to be true that would mean she would have had to screw my dad. My father, who would never do anything as disgusting as sleep with my best friend.

He wouldn't betray my mother like that. Because if he slept with my best friend that would make him . . . *a hypocrite, a filthy piece of shit?*

It would mean that everything he taught me about values and being a good person *was bullshit*. That everything I believed in *was a fucking lie.*

"Christopher," she squeaks out meekly. It snaps me from my trance.

"Say something. Please." I look up at her standing in front of me, tears streaming down her face and I feel a switch about to go off. Like a bomb about to explode, and it's taking everything in me not to. So much that I'm afraid to move because the slightest thing could set me the fuck off.

"Say that again," I ask simply, and she shakes her head. "How is she my sister?" I say, cocking my head trying to understand. Hoping against hope there is some reasonable explanation for this. She looks away from me, and I take a deep breath. "Did he rape you?" I ask, cringing at the word. Her eyes look up at me.

"No," she says quietly.

"So you willingly fucked my dad?" I ask her bluntly. She seems caught off-guard, surprised I guess that *I'd* use that type of language.

"It wasn't supposed to happen," she says, crying again. I want to get up and leave, leave her right here crying, but my body won't move. My mind has too many questions, and it won't let any of my limbs budge until I have answers.

"Yeah, I don't think fucking your best friend's dad is ever supposed to happen," I say quietly.

Nice one, Chris.

"Chris, please," she begs.

Bitch, fucking slut, don't believe her tears.

"Chris please, what? What Lisa, would you like me to do or say? You're telling me that kid in there is my dad's—My FUCKING Dad's— Lisa! She's what, seven or eight? Which would mean," I stand up, my legs finally gaining strength, "You slept with him when we were in high school?" I feel like I'm about to vomit.

"We made a mistake!" she says through tears. So many tears.

"How many times?" I ask, holding my head.

"Please, it doesn't matter," she whimpers.

"How many times?" I roar.

"A lot! I loved him. We loved each other," she says. Now I'm going to throw up right here.

"You sat in our house. My mother's house," I say disgusted.

She's a fucking cunt . . . what do you expect?

"Shut up!" I shout. Both to her and to the fucking voice in my head. It's him and he won't shut up. He knew.

"Cal knew. He knew didn't he?" I ask her, walking closer to her, so close she backs into a wall.

"He—I—we thought it was you at first," she whimpers, looking down. She's guilty.

"He caught us. Or you did, but after that, you began to act strange. That was the first time you disappeared for days. We thought when you came back . . . we just knew that you were going to tell your mom." She shakes her head. "But you didn't, you weren't even mad. We eventually realized it was because you didn't remember. After that, you started call-ing yourself Cal, and whenever you did you were so mean and hateful towards us. We didn't know then," her voice is shaky.

"It was our fault. We made you this way," she says, breaking down. I shake my head, I feel energy in me coming from everywhere. I walk towards her, looking at the girl I'd trusted, who was my friend, who for a brief time, I had a crush on. I cover my face and then slam my fists on the wall on both sides of her. She screams before sliding down to the floor. The little girl comes out, runs over to her, and hugs her.

"Leave her alone!" she yells, and I try to slow down my breathing. This rage is growing within me and I don't know how to handle it.

"Does he know?" I ask her, trying to calm my tone. She shakes her head.

"Great. I'll deliver the happy news," I say, before heading out the door.

cal

March 12th, 2011

YOU CAN'T OUTSMART the universe. It doesn't make mistakes. It catches up with you. Sooner or later, if you're meant to be fucked, you will be. It's like those plane movies when the kids think they've outsmarted death, but at the end of the movie, they get decapitated or burned alive. The universe remembered that Cal Scott doesn't get to be happy. That my life was never supposed to be anything other than what it was, pointless, meaningless, and insignificant.

"Cal." Helens voice interrupts my pity party. She and Dexter sit across from me at their huge ass conference table. Her voice is sympathetic, Dexter looks like he cares, and it makes me want to throw up. I don't want their sympathy. I don't want them to give a shit. No one should give a shit.

"Are you sure you want to do this?" she asks me for the third fucking time.

"I don't have a choice, Helen," I say, trying to keep my voice dry and even.

"You could tell her the truth. Let her decide. That's what I'd want," she says. I look over at Dexter who's holding her hand. They don't know how lucky they are. To be able to love each other without any interference or handicap. The biggest of their problems is agreeing on where they want to vacation.

"I can't do that do her. I made a mistake when I married her. She doesn't deserve the life she'd be stuck in with me."

"Shouldn't that be her choice?" Dexter asks, sipping from his glass of brandy. I'm contemplating asking him for one even though I never drink.

"I have to make the right one for her. She'll get over me and meet a nice normal guy," I say, more to myself than them.

"You're really going to let her go? Just like that?" Dexter asks suspiciously.

"Trust me, it's not 'just like that'," I say defensively.

"I think you're making a mistake. I think you should tell her, and she will understand. She'll stand by you," Helen says, pleading.

"I didn't come here for you guys to convince me not to do this. If you don't have the medicine to fix me, if you don't have a solution to this problem, I don't want to hear any alternatives or suggestions!" I tell them.

"Okay," Dexter says simply, Helen nods. Dexter slides the folder over to me. I review the terms of what we discussed. The financial details at least. I want to make sure Lauren's taken care of the rest of her life. She shouldn't have to want for anything. I flip through to the final page in the folder—divorce papers. I look away quickly, grab the pen on the table, and sign it. When she's ready to move on completely, I don't want anything to stop her. I don't want her to be stuck, even though it feels like a knife cutting through me as I sign my name. Once I'm done, I slide the papers across the table to him. He takes the folder and stands up.

"Well, I think I'm done here," he says, heading towards the door of their office.

"Dex . . ." He stops mid-step.

"Remember, she's not to know under any circumstances about Chris. No matter what," I tell him. He turns back towards me.

"None?" he asks. I can't think of a reason that would be important for her to ever need to know.

"None. Promise me—on your name," I tell him. If it's one thing that's important to them, it's their name.

"Done," he says quietly before leaving the room.

"I'm sorry about Gwen, Cal," Helen says solemnly. "I'm sorry about everything," she says, her voice cracking.

"Come on, Helen. You have to keep up the façade that you don't have a heart." I wink at her, and she smirks.

"Be careful, I'm going to start thinking *you* have one," she says as we both stand.

"I have a heart. It's just not all that big," I tease her. She walks over and gives me a hug. For the first time ever, I really hug her back.

"I know you want her to hate you when you tell her goodbye. Just try to remember, that could be the last time she sees you. Leave her with something to know how much you love her," she says, looking me in the eye.

"Take care of my girl for me," I tell her as she walks me to the door.

"Absolutely," she promises as I enter their private elevator to take me to the exit. She waves, and I give her a little salute.

WHEN I WALK into the house, it's dark except the light in the hall near our bedroom. I close my eyes and take a deep breath before I head up the stairs. This is the first time since I've known her that I don't want to see her. That I wish I didn't have to because I know what I'm going to tell her is going to hurt her. I never wanted to hurt her, now it seems like all I've done is hurt her. I think back to that night when I first saw her, how I was trying to save her from that douchebag Michael. I wonder if she would have been better off with him. When I walk in the room, she's sprawled across the bed. Her long dark hair covers the sheets. She's beautiful, and she seems at peace. Even with all the chaos I've brought her, she still sleeps peacefully.

I want to touch her, to kiss her, but I won't do that. I don't deserve that. I deserve to walk out of here and never hear her voice, or feel her touch again. I leave the room and walk around the house. The only place I've ever felt at home.

She made my house a home. She's my home.

I sit down on the couch and think of all the things I've done to her. How good I've made her feel, how bad I've made her feel.

After they stopped the medication trial, things just started to crumble. Chris started to come back more frequently, and our transition began taking a lot less time. I had to be gone more often. I even had to stop working. I couldn't tell her why, so I started to 'omit' the truth. I guess that's what liars tell themselves to feel better, but in reality, it's all a big fabrication. She started to be suspicious, but she's way off base. She thinks I cheat on her. That I have all of these women. I tell her I'd never cheat on her, but she doesn't believe me because there's no other plausible explanation. The real explanation is the opposite of plausible. She started to resent me. I saw her change.

She built a persona around herself, one that she puts on to not give a damn, but I see it in her eyes how much it hurts her, and I hate myself for it. She thinks I hate her and that makes everything worse. I try to show her I love her the only way I know how without lying. The only time I can see behind her walls she's built up is when I'm inside her, literally. I'm turning her into someone I never wanted her to be. I liked that she spoke her mind, now she only tells half-truths. She's angry, and I know it's because she's hurting. This is going to hurt her, but she's strong. She'll get over me, move on. She can have the life she always wanted. Someone she can know, whose family she can meet, where her biggest decision is where to go on vacation.

I've been down here awhile. I head back upstairs. Before I go into our bedroom for probably the last time, I ready myself for this. Ready to take the role of villain, to make her see me as someone I never wanted her to see me as. That's one of the reasons I loved her so much because even in all our fights and arguments she never looked at me like that.

Today she has to.

"You're finally up," I say, turning on the light.

"How long have you been here?" she asks, covering the yawn escaping from her mouth.

"About an hour," I say, sitting in a chair across from the bed so we're face to face. She glances at me, her eyebrow arched.

"So what did you want to talk to me about?" I pull my chair closer to her and sit back down. She looks at me curiously, I can't look her in the eye.

"Cal," she says softly, reminding me of the girl I fell in love with. Not the pissed off angry woman she's been the past few months.

"What's wrong?" she whispers, like she's afraid to hear the answer. I wish more than anything I didn't have to, but I can't let her know that. Anger is what she'll want to hold on to, it's what she needs.

"I've never lied to you," I say, steadying my voice. "And I'm not going to start now," I drop my head down, run my hands through my hair. *How am I supposed to do this?* My heart rate picks up.

"Just say it," she commands.

I take her hand. I won't have the strength to do it if I don't remind myself how much I love her, more than myself.

"I-I have to leave." The words are bitter as they come up from my throat.

Her expression hardens, and she pulls her hand away. "You called me back for this?" She's sighs, obviously frustrated and annoyed, and stands up. I take her hand and pull her back down.

"Look, this is different," I tell her.

"Everything is different with you, Cal. If you weren't so different, maybe I wouldn't feel so screwed up right now," she snaps at me. She's pissed, and I deserve it, because she's right. If I wasn't different, we wouldn't be here right now. I wouldn't have to do this if I wasn't different. She could be happy. I could make her happy, but things aren't different, they're the same, and I have to let her go.

"I don't know *if* I'll be back."

"What?" She looks confused. "Would you mind repeating yourself?" she says sharply.

"I'm going to make sure that you're taken of. I put sixty thousand in your personal account . . ."

"What? You don't know if you'll be back?" She's frantic, and I try to stay still, calm. "Why does it sound like you're saying that you're leaving me?"

"I have to," I tell her, trying to remain indifferent . . . cold, but it's the hardest thing I've ever done.

"Is this about me, how I've been acting? Is this some kind of revenge thing?" she asks, her voice starting to waver.

"This has nothing to do with you," I force the words out.

"Exactly, Cal! Look what you're saying—I'm your wife—and your decision to leave has nothing to do with me?"

"I don't have a choice."

"What are you talking about? Cal! Talk to me, please," she says frantically. "Look at me!" she pleads.

I can't look at her.

"What is wrong with you? Why are you acting like this?" Tears fill her eyes, and I feel like I'm being punched in the chest.

"Tell me what the hell is going on! Tell me what's going on with you for once!" she begs, and I just want her to stop crying, to stop pleading. I want her to yell at me and hit me and punch me . . . not this.

"I can't!" I yell at her.

"This isn't about me," I say, walking away from her. I don't know how much longer I can keep this up.

"Then who is it about?"

I can't answer her.

"You won't tell me that either, huh?" she says quietly.

"What am I supposed to say, Cal? What?" she yells. "Am I just supposed to accept you leaving? No explanations except 'you have to.' Not that I've ever gotten one from you. This won't be any different except who knows when you'll come back? If you come back."

"My stock dividends from the company will still be deposited into the account . . ." I try to focus on what I'm supposed to tell her and nothing else.

"I don't care about the fucking money! I never cared about any of this—the trips, this house—I never needed this! All I wanted . . ." she's screaming now. "All I wanted was you, can't you see that?" I close my eyes to stop what feels like tears about to start. I can't cry in front of her.

"Say something," she whispers.

"Is there someone else?" she asks.

"I told you I've never cheated on you," I say, using anger as my weapon.

"Then why? People just don't decide to leave out of nowhere. There has to be a reason, tell me you're in love with someone else; that this isn't working; that you're in trouble; just tell me something!"

"There's nothing I can tell you," I say quickly.

"What am I supposed to do?" she asks, her voice so light it's like it'll shatter.

"Helen and Dex will take care of anything you need . . ."

"Helen and Dexter? They know about this? How long have you known that you were leaving me? Have you gotten bored with me, or is this just a spur of the moment thing?"

She can't think that. She has to know that's not what this is.

"It's not like that," I tell her, walking towards her.

She steps away from me. She won't let me touch her. "Then what? Tell me what it's like. Tell me something. Tell me why!" she begs. "I can't believe you're doing this to me!" she screams, and I don't know how much longer I can do this. She walks over to the bed and covers her head with her arms. She's crying so hard that she's shaking. This wasn't supposed to happen like this. She's breaking right in front of me. I'm breaking her down, and it wasn't supposed to happen like this. I reach out to her, and she snatches away from me, but I grab her and pull her close.

"Why? Why are you doing this to me?" she whimpers.

"I'm sorry," I tell her, holding back my own tears.

"No, you aren't," she cries.

"Yes, I am," I whisper in her ear.

Then she wraps her arms around me and she looks up at me. "Don't make me ask you to stay." She begins to cry harder. I look away from her.

"I wish I could," I tell her. I shouldn't have said that. I'm confusing her. I'm confusing myself. I can't stay. This will hurt her, but she'll come back from this.

"Don't! Don't you dare make this seem as if it's out of your control. If you wanted to stay, you would!"

I put my hands on her waist and bring my lips to hers. I don't kiss her, and she doesn't kiss me back, and I can't blame her. I kiss her cheek then rest my cheek against hers.

"You'll get through this, you'll have to." I tell her. This isn't how things were supposed to go. I don't know how they were supposed to go now.

"If you're leaving, go!" She pushes me. "Leave." I hate you! I hate you, you fucking bastard!" She hits me, and pushes me and screams and cries. I stand there and take it, take it all. I deserve it. When she's done, she rests her head briefly on my chest then takes a deep breath.

"Just go," she whispers as she sits on the floor, tucking her head in between her knees. I want to tell her that I love her, that it's fucking killing me to leave her, but that would only make things worse. I start to walk towards her, but I know me touching her isn't what she needs right now. I leave the room and shut the door behind me and let go completely. I hit the wall. I kick it until I can't anymore.

I hate myself. I sit next to the door and cry. I cry for her. I cry for myself for the first time in my life.

I'm losing the best thing I ever had.

chapter 16

lauren

"I KNEW I loved Gwen the first time she made me smothered pork chops and mashed potatoes," Mr. Scott laughs, holding Caylen as Mrs. Scott sets the table for dinner.

"He fell in love with my cooking, Lauren," she says happily.

"Her looks had a little something to do with it, too," he chuckles. I laugh, taking a sip of iced tea. Gosh, this guy is so different from how he's been over the past couple of weeks. He's actually funny, dare I say charming, and not a total prick. He's been telling stories and jokes for the past hour while Mrs. Scott cooked. I actually didn't notice Chris had been gone as long as he had until I got a text from Lisa saying to call her ASAP.

"Excuse me," I say, getting up from the table, but as I do, Chris walks into the kitchen.

"Now we can eat!" his dad laughs. Chris smiles widely, but it's forced.

"I made your dad's favorite. Pork chops and mashed potatoes," Gwen says happily.

"Great," he says, kissing her on the forehead. He heads to the kitchen, and I follow him.

"So . . ." I ask, watching him wash his hands.

"What's up?" he asks shortly.

"How did things go with Lisa?" He glances at me, and I notice his eye twitches a bit.

"Did Lisa talk to you about what she needed to tell me?" he asks as he continues to wash his hands.

"Uh, no. I tried to get her to tell me, but she wouldn't," I tell him, and he only nods.

"What happened?" I ask, noticing he's still washing his hands.

"Oh, we'll all talk about it after dinner. I think that's best," he says, continuing to scrub his hands.

"I think your hands are clean enough," I chuckle, but he continues washing them, his eyes don't leave his hands.

"Chris," I say and notice he's not even paying attention to me.

"Chris!" I say firmer and nudge him. His head snaps up at me.

"My bad," he says turning off the water. He turns towards me and kisses me on the lips. It's soft and sweet at first, but then he starts grabbing my ass and backs me against the counter and lifts me onto it. I push him away.

"Cal!?" I ask him frantically, and he scoffs at me.

"Nope. I just always wanted to make out in the kitchen," he shrugs.

"Your parents are right in the other room with our daughter," I laugh, and he grins at me, leaving me on the counter top extremely confused. I try to gather my thoughts when Aidan knocks at the kitchen door. I jump off the counter and open it. He's standing there with his hands on his knees as if he ran all the way here.

"Are you okay?" I ask him, and he nods catching his breath.

"I-is Chris here yet?" he manages to pant out.

"Yeah, what's going on?" I ask him hesitantly.

"She told him. Has he gone crazy yet?" he asks.

"Uh no. He's sitting at the table with his parents," I tell him, and Aidan's eyes widen.

"What happened?" I ask him firmly. Before he can reply, Mrs. Scott enters the room.

"Aidan sweetie. You're just in time for dinner. Come join us," she gestures toward the dining room. "Come on before the food gets cold," she says adamantly. We follow her from the kitchen. I glance back at Aidan for some type of hint about what is happening, but he doesn't give me any. His anxious energy gives me a bad feeling.

"Aidan, I'm so glad you're here. I know you wouldn't want to miss this," Chris says playfully, but something is off.

Really off.

"Can I talk to you a minute, Chris?"

"Sure. After dinner," he says.

Dinner started weird, but as it goes on, everything seems fine, perfect actually. The food is great, as always. Chris and his parents tell us stories about them over the years. Except whenever they pull Aidan into a conversation, his answers are short, and he stays unusually quiet.

"Is everyone done? I'll gather the plates. Would anyone like some wine?" Mrs. Scott says, standing up from her seat.

"Oh no, Mom, sit down for a minute. I've got a story everyone is going to love. We'll see if you all remember it," Chris says happily. I can't help but notice Aidan's put his head down.

"Here we go," Aidan mutters.

"So this was about . . . I can't even say how many years ago. I think about nine or ten actually. God, doesn't time fly?" he starts, and I can't help but notice how animated he is.

"Well, anyway. You went out of town to visit Aunt Clara," he says, turning towards his mom, "and I was staying at Shawn Clarkson's house to help him set up for his sister's sweet sixteen. I kind of had a crush on her back then." He laughs, and Gwen does the same, but I notice Mr. Scott is sitting perfectly still, the color has almost drained from his face.

"I had come home because Shawn's stereo went out, and I came to get mine, and I walked in on Dad fucking Lisa."

Oh SHIT!

The room is silent. Dead silent while everyone processes what the hell Chris just said. Is this a joke?

"What?" Gwen says breaking the silence. Chris begins to laugh.

"What did you just say, Chris?" she says, grabbing his arm.

"Oh yeah, Mom. I completely forgot about it. It just so happened around that time is when Cal came about," he turns his body towards his dad.

"What do you think, Dad? You think there's a correlation between me walking in on you banging my best friend in our house and me dissociating?" he asks sarcastically.

"Chris. I can explain," Mr. Scott says.

"Yes, let's explain," he laughs. "I think this is your answer as to why dad hates Cal so fucking much. Because he held information that could potentially destroy this family," he says matter-of-factly.

"William, tell me this isn't true," Mrs. Scott demands. She's not crying or upset, she seems in complete shock.

"Lauren and Aidan, could you please excuse us?" Mr. Scott says, and Aidan and I practically jump out of our seats.

"NO!" Chris roars.

"No more secrets, no more lies. Let's put it all out there for everyone to see. I haven't even gotten to the best part of the story yet," he says angrily.

"Explain how fucking selfish you were for delaying or really sabotaging my treatment because you were too fucking scared that if I integrated, I'd remember everything!" Chris says angrily. I look over to Mrs. Scott who now has tears streaming from her eyes.

"William, how could you?" Mrs. Scott whimpers.

"It wasn't like that, Gwen. I swear to you," Mr. Scott says, standing up. He tries to walk towards her, but Chris jumps between them.

"No, don't go near my mom!" Chris says, blocking him. "Tell her how many times you fucked her. That it wasn't just a one-time deal, that you screwed her enough to knock her up!"

"Oh my God," I can't help but mutter. Everyone in the room, including Mr. Scott, looks caught off-guard by that.

"What!" Mr. Scott says, confused.

"Yup, I guess you kept on screwing her long after I found out because she had your kid when she was nineteen. You have a fucking seven-year-old daughter and her name's Willa. How sweet is that?" he says viciously. I look over at Mrs. Scott who has stood from her seat and run out of the room. Mr. Scott pushes past Chris and follows her.

"Our dinners are always the best, aren't they?" Chris laughs, and Aidan shakes his head.

"That wasn't the way to do that, man," Aidan replies disdainfully.

"Oh, well, tell me, Aidan. How should I have confronted my dad about screwing my best friend?" he asks him angrily.

"Who are you? Because if you are Chris that was a real jackass thing to do," Aidan says leaving.

"How has this turned into my fault?" he shouts angrily. I pick up Caylen and walk over to him.

"I know you're hurting right now. I can't imagine how you must feel. But how you handled this. It doesn't seem like you," I tell him, and he frowns.

"I'm not hurting I'm mad. I'm angry, I'm fucking furious! He deserved that!" he says, his expression hard and cold. I nod.

"I'm not saying that he didn't. But you were so busy trying to stick it to him, you didn't notice how you were hurting your mother. Each jab you made at him cut through her," I say, trying to get through to him. He doesn't look at me.

"When you really need someone to talk about this. I'm here," I tell him, handing him Caylen. I'm not sure if he's Cal or Chris, but whoever he is, he won't disappear if he has her with him, and after that, I need to sleep. This was just too much.

I WAKE UP and glance at my phone. It's 2:30 am. I head upstairs to Chris's room to make sure he's okay with Caylen. Once I make it upstairs, I see Mr. Scott sitting outside of his bedroom door, his head in his hands. I turn back around to head downstairs.

"Lauren," he calls to me. I stop and walk back towards him. He looks terrible. Dry tear stains run down his cheeks. His hair's a mess. I can't help that a part of me feels sorry for him.

"I know you must think I'm the lowest person on earth, after how I treated you and hearing about all this," he says. I stand quietly, not knowing what to say.

"I am the dumbest man on the planet," he laughs at himself and starts to cry. I don't know what to do. I wasn't expecting to run into him.

"She's never going to forgive me," he whimpers. Oh this is so awkward.

"It could be worse. Cal could be back," I joke, trying to cheer him up. He chuckles.

"That's the worst part about this. That was Chris in there today. I made *Chris* like that," he says shaking his head.

"I destroyed my family, more than Cal ever could," he continues.

"I blamed him for my own stupidity. For the mistakes I made. I took it out on him. I hated him because he saw what I did and held it over me, and I was too much of a coward to tell my wife the truth," he continues.

"Can you talk to her?" he says desperately.

"I-I—she probably needs time alone," I tell him.

"No, she shouldn't be alone. She won't speak to me. This has to be eating her up!" He stands up and takes my hand.

"Tell her how sorry I am and how much I love her. That Lisa and I was the biggest mistake of my life, and I was going through a crazy mid-life crisis. I never loved anyone as much as I love Gwen. Please tell her," he begs me, ushering me to the door.

"But how would I get in," I ask him frantically.

"It's not locked. She says she doesn't want to see me, and I'm respecting her wishes. I can hear her crying. She's not asleep. Please be there for her." I nod, I'm willing to do anything to get away from him. His despair and desperation is heavy in the air. I reluctantly turn the knob of their bedroom, and it opens like he says. I give a weak smile as I go in and close the door behind me.

"Mrs. Scott," I call quietly. I see the light in their master bathroom on. I walk in and see Mrs. Scott sitting on the floor, her back resting up against their tub. She's not crying, but she looks dazed.

"I-I hope I'm not bothering you," I say. She glances up at me and gives me a small smile.

"William asked you to come in here, didn't he?" she asks. Her voice is dry and scratchy. She must have been crying for hours.

"Yeah," I say, not knowing if I should smile or cry with her. She looks so different—like she's aged five years.

"I-I could go if you want to be alone," I say quietly, and she shakes her head, so I sit down on the toilet top. She's quiet for a long time.

"I spent so much time in this bathroom when I was sick," she says after a couple of minutes. "The chemo made me feel so terrible," she continues. "I came in here to try to hide how sick it made me. I knew how much it hurt them to see me hurting," she says, clearing her throat. "I literally wanted to die. I really did. Every single day, I was so sick of being sick," she says tightly holding her head. "But I held on. I fought, and I fought because I knew if I did die they would never be the same, that they couldn't handle life without me then. I didn't want to leave my family in disarray. I asked God to just make me stronger and better even if it was just long enough to make Chris love his dad again, how he used to," she says, and her voice shatters at the last part. "I know when the affair started," she shakes her head. "William, he was happy. Happier than he had been in such a long time," she laughs, but she's bitter and looks like she's hurts her. "He had been going through some type of—the only thing I could call it is a mid-life crisis. He hadn't been himself. Kind of withdrawn, he kept saying he didn't feel accomplished. He wasn't happy, and I tried everything to get him to be happy, but I couldn't break through the wall he put up. He had been like that for months, and then one day out of the blue the funk was over. He was back to the man I knew and loved," she sighs, and tears fill her eyes again.

"I thought it was because of something I had done. That he had fallen in love with me again and all along he was happy because he was sleeping with someone the same age as our son," she starts to cry. "It makes me sick. They did it in our house. Our house, Lauren. How could they do that?" she says, crying harder.

"I let her sleep in my home, I taught her how to cook. Oh God, she asked me for advice about boys." She shakes her head. "How stupid have I been? All of that time she was wearing her little shorts and tiny tops I thought she was flaunting herself to get Chris's attention, and she was after my husband. She had an affair with my husband," she says, hitting her lap. I down and hug her—tight and long—she hugs me back.

"I couldn't have children, Lauren. I could never give him a child," she cries into my shoulder.

"They broke my baby, Lauren, and made their own. I can't forgive them for that. I can't," she says, squeezing me harder.

chapter 17

lauren

WE LEFT THE day after the bomb was dropped. Mrs. Scott left before us, headed to her sister's. She's not sure what she's ultimately going to do, but she says she can't stay in that house with Mr. Scott any longer. We offered for her to come to Chicago with us whenever she wants. She says she will take us up on the offer. Well, it wasn't really *us* that made the offer to be honest. It was me.

Chris.

I don't even feel right calling him Chris anymore, because he's different. The night he found out everything from Lisa, he was so angry and acted completely out of character, but I'd prefer that to whoever he is now. He's withdrawn, quiet, and moody.

Just a shell of himself.

When I heard Lisa's secret, I knew things were about to get bad, but the moment the words left his mouth, that he has a little sister, I knew it was going to be an uphill battle, and we were already stationed so far underground. How he's been acting . . . that I didn't expect. We've been in Chicago for three weeks, and he hasn't cried, he doesn't laugh, he barely speaks. He's like a droid drained of any personality whatsoever. The only time I see a hint of him is when he plays with Caylen. I see a flicker of joy, a moment of happiness every now and then, but besides that, nothing. He doesn't want to talk to anyone, not even his mom. She calls every day to check on him and he just sits on the phone giving one or two word answers. Everyone else he's shut out completely.

It's expected that he wouldn't speak to his dad or Lisa. They *both* call several times a day. Not together, well as far as I know. I told his dad he needs time. Probably a whole lot of time. Lisa, well I don't know what to say to her. I don't think that's a relationship that's ever going to be the way it was. He won't speak to Aidan either, and he barely speaks to me. The only familiar thing he does is play his guitar. But now he stays on my iPad, which is a little strange since he's never really been into electronics. Every single day he's on that thing for hours, it's beyond annoying.

"He's been like a zombie, and I have no idea what to do. I can't tell him I know how he feels, that everything will be okay. His dad cheated on his mother with his best friend, who she has a secret child by. Is that something you can get over? His family is destroyed. Now when I look at him, I don't see Chris or Cal," I tell Helen. She's been out of town since I arrived back in Chicago, and it feels so good to be able to talk to her now.

" . . . and this may sound crazy, but whenever I leave the house I get this weird feeling that I'm being followed," I tell her, laughing at the absurdity of it. "I think I may be starting to lose my mind," I say, taking a sip of my coffee from the bistro in our building lobby.

"You're not going crazy, Lauren. You have been under a lot of pressure, and I commend you for holding up so well," she says, squeezing my hand.

"What's wrong with him? If Cal is his alter and helps him when these things happen, where is he?" I ask frantically.

"I believe that Christopher has shut himself down emotionally. He has dissociated himself from reality entirely. He's locked Cal out. This is what I say when I mean that Cal and Chris are one. Even when Cal isn't at the forefront of his conscious state, he is always with Chris subconsciously. There cannot be a Chris without Cal, Cal without Chris. They both make up the man that you know and love," she explains, and I let out a deep breath.

"So what do we do? How do we fix them? He can't be like this forever can he?" I ask anxiously.

"I need to see how far gone he is," she replies.

"He told me he didn't want to see or talk to anyone," I tell her.

"If he's not exhibiting any emotions then he won't exhibit anger, annoyance, or frustration," Helen retorts.

WHEN WE WALK in Chris barely glances up us. His eyes remain on the TV that's been stationed to Nick Jr. since I left.

"Hey babe," I say cheerfully. He doesn't say anything, as usual, only slightly nodding.

"Christopher, it's so good to see you," Helen says enthusiastically. When he doesn't reply, she picks up Caylen.

"Hi beautiful. I've missed you so much." She kisses Caylen on the cheek.

"She looks so much like you, Christopher," Helen says, standing in front of him. He doesn't say anything.

"I am sorry about what happened with your parents," she offers, sitting next to him. He glances over at me before staring back at the television.

"I told you I don't want to talk to anyone," he says, his tone the same monotone it's been since we stepped foot in our house. It hasn't lowered or risen since.

"Lauren told me that, but I knew that you'd make an exception for me," Helen says playfully.

"What do you want, Dr. Lyce," he asks stoically.

"I came to see how you're doing. If there was anything I could do to help you."

"I don't need any help. I've never felt better. I'm completely fine," he says, grabbing the remote beside him and turning the channel. The patience I've been holding on to these past two weeks is starting to wear thin.

"You're not fine, Chris!" I interject. Frustration outweighs the patience I've been holding on to by a thread since he started acting like this. He briefly glances at me but doesn't say anything. Helen shoots me a warning glare and I let out a sigh as I sit on the couch opposite from them.

"How do you like Chicago?" she asks, changing the subject.

"It's fine," he says.

"Is there anything that you miss about being home?"

"This is my home now," he says without missing a beat.

"Are you happy, Chris? Does being with Lauren and Caylen make you happy?" she asks, and this is one question I'd love to hear the answer to.

"I don't want to talk about them with you," he says, getting up from the couch and walking to the kitchen, and I follow him.

"Well, talk to me about it. Are you happy here, with us?" I ask him as he searches through the refrigerator almost like I'm not there. Since that night, he has treated me like a piece of furniture or something.

"I'm here," he says casually.

"Are you?" I ask him, looking into his eyes. I wave a hand in front of him, and he just steps around me and heads back to his seat in front of the television with his soda in hand. I shake my head and laugh at myself.

"Helen, I'm not going to talk to you. You can go ahead and leave whenever you're ready," he says in that same indifferent tone that is making me want to scream.

"I'd like for her stay," I say, annoyed.

"Whatever," he says and takes a swig of his drink. He then sits next to Caylen on the floor and starts playing with blocks.

"Lauren, I need to be going, but I'm going to run and grab something from my car I have for you first," she says, getting up and walking to the door.

"Do you want me to come with you?" I ask her with a sigh.

"No it'll only take a minute," she says before leaving. I sit down on the couch, my arms folded as I watch him live in a world that no one else is a part of—he won't let me be a part of—at least he interacts with Caylen.

"I wish that you would talk to me," I say aloud.

"I do talk to you," he answers promptly. Which he makes sure to do, but he only answers when I ask him something, it's like trying to bounce a stone off a brick wall.

"You respond to me. You don't talk."

"I didn't know there was a difference," he says, his attention on the wall he's building with the little blocks Caylen plays with. He has enough walls up, if she wasn't over there, I'd kick it down. I've tried being patient, understanding, and meek, but I am at the end of my freakin' rope with him. He can't think that I'm going to live like this, with a robot, that's what he's acting like. He gets up he showers, eats, cooks, plays with Caylen, watches TV and plays his guitar, which he won't even play in front of me. He goes in the guest room and plays and plays. He goes to sleep in the same bed with me, but he doesn't touch me. We're in a humongous king-sized bed, but we might as well have those little twins they show on the old TV shows—that's how far apart we are. I could live with Chris, I could live with Cal, but whoever this is, I can't do this. I thought Helen could help, but how can she help if he refuses to talk to her? A few minutes later, my phone vibrates. Helen says to meet her down at the café.

"I'll be back," I tell him, grabbing my keys.

"Yup," is his only response, he doesn't even look up at me. I'm not surprised but it still makes me want to scream. When I make it down to the lobby café, I see Helen standing there.

"You see what I'm talking about?" I say when I reach her.

"I do. It's not completely unexpected with everything that's happened. He doesn't talk to you at all?" she asks.

"About as much as you saw up there. He's shut me out completely," I shrug, trying to hide how much it hurts me.

"You have to understand that Chris had a strong moral compass that he anchored based on his family. He and his father had a very close relationship. He was his role model, his values, his beliefs all stemmed from that relationship. The person he built himself to be was on that foundation and now, that structure has crumbled. Everything he knows or once believed is questionable for him," she explains.

"So everything he believed about, family, loyalty . . . love, he doesn't believe in anymore?" I ask, commanding myself not to cry. Helen gives me a sympathetic smile.

"It's just all questionable for him right now. However, he is here, with you and Caylen. That says a lot," she says squeezing my shoulder.

I let out a deep sigh.

"So what do I do?" I ask, in need of some sort of direction because right now I don't know which way to turn.

"What have you been doing since he's been like this?"

"I-I haven't done anything. I've been trying to give him time. I thought after a while he'd just snap out of it, but next week will make a month of him being like this. I just didn't want to make things worse."

"We need Chris to feel again. For him to let his emotions back in."

"And how do I do that?"

"You were able to get Chris and Cal to fall in love with you once. It shouldn't be hard to make them remember why," she says, giving me a reassuring smile. I chuckle.

"Yeah, I don't know if I'm really up for that again," I tell her honestly.

"Emotions are intertwined, happiness, joy, sadness, anger. Make him feel one, the others will follow through."

WHEN I GET back upstairs to our apartment, nothing's changed of course. Not that I expected something would, but in my life recently things could flip in the blink of an eye. *Make him feel something*, she says.

Yeah that's going to be easy.

"I was thinking we could go to dinner tonight. There are so many amazing restaurants here," I tell him. He glances over at me.

"Whatever you want," he shrugs. I let out a deep, frustrated breath and head into my bedroom. I pick up my phone and call Angela. Last week she finished her thesis and went on vacation to the Bahamas to celebrate.

"Hey, hon!" she says enthusiastically.

"Hi. What are you up to?" I ask her innocently.

"Nothing much, I've been watching a marathon of *Snapped* mostly," she chuckles.

"A whole marathon? Isn't that kind of depressing?"

"Yeah, I guess it is," she admits.

"Well, I have the perfect way to bring some sunshine into your life,"

I laugh.

"And how would you do that?" she says cautiously.

"By getting Caylen for the weekend," I say optimistically.

"Really? Of course I can. What do you have planned . . . how are things, is he still acting like he's from the *Walking Dead?*"

"Pretty much. I talked to Helen though and she says that I should try to snap him out of it in so many words,"

"And how are you supposed to do that?" she chuckles.

"I have a couple of ideas, but as long as Caylen is here, I don't know how well I can implement them," I admit.

"Hmmm. You must tell me how this goes," she chuckles. "Anywho, yeah I'm in for the weekend. You can bring her whenever you're ready."

"Great. I'll be over in about an hour and a half if that's okay."

AFTER I'VE PACKED up Caylen's things for the weekend, I scoop her up into my arms off the living room floor. Chris looks at me curiously as I get her dressed, but doesn't say anything.

"Are you excited to stay with Aunt Angie this weekend, Princess?" I ask Caylen. I glance over at Chris. He rises from his seat and walks toward us. He kisses Caylen on the forehead and heads upstairs. I don't even have to guess. When I get back, he'll be in the guest room playing his guitar with the door shut. It only takes me about fifteen minutes to make it over to Angela's. When we arrive, she quickly buzzes us in, and I make the trek up the stairs to her apartment.

"Hi princess!!" she squeals in excitement, taking Caylen from my arms.

"What's up, mama?" she says, all of her attention on Caylen.

"I need to start working out again. Your stairs almost killed me," I say, catching my breath.

"Are you ready for fun with Auntie Angie?" she coos, taking off Caylen's coat.

"She should be asleep in the next hour or so," I tell her.

"No worries, if she's not I have a whole night of fun things planned for us. Now what about you and the hubby?" she asks playfully.

"I am going to try to break him out of this trance that he's fallen into," I shrug.

"I really miss him. I miss *both* of them as crazy as it sounds," I chuckle.

"They or he . . . he's in there, Lauren. If he wasn't he wouldn't be sitting at home with you and Caylen," she says, taking a seat on her sofa and patting the cushion next to her. I plop down next to her and watch as she switches the television from Lifetime to Nick Jr.

"I thought for some reason knowing whatever happened that caused his condition would make things better, but instead it made things worse."

"One of the things that's interesting about DID is that it's a mechanism for coping with tragedy, pain, loss. When you think about it, we all dissociate when we don't want to feel. We deflect. Now we don't necessarily do it to the extent of those who have the disorder, but when you think about it, we're all searching for a form of it, whether it's drinking, using drugs, or even shopping."

"I guess you're right," I say, mulling over her words.

WHEN I MAKE it home, the living room is as empty as I expected it to be. As I head up the stairs, sure enough I can hear the sound of the guitar being played. I stand next to the door and listen for a couple of minutes, trying to figure out my next move.

"Make him feel something," I say softly, reminding myself of Helen's words. I have been doing the exact opposite since we arrived. I open the door and he stops playing.

"You don't have to stop on my account," I tell him playfully.

"I was finishing up anyway," he says as he starts to put the guitar away.

"I wish you wouldn't treat me like this," I tell him, stepping in front of him.

"How am I treating you?" he asks, closing his guitar case.

"Like I'm a stranger, or a roommate you tolerate. I know you're hurting, I just wish you'd let me help you. That you'd let me in," I tell him, grabbing his hand.

"I'm not hurting. Everything is fi . . ."

"Everything is not fine! Stop saying that. You are walking around like a zombie! I don't even know who you are anymore," I plead with him.

"Well, that makes two of us," he says, walking past me and heading downstairs.

I follow him.

"So that's it. You're going to be like this forever? Not talking, keeping everything bottled up, acting like I don't exist?" I ask him angrily. "You're going to let him ruin everything? Stop living your life based on a mistake *he* made. How can you let anyone have that much power over you?" I shout at him, and he stops in his tracks and turns to face me.

She said to make him feel something.

Well . . . here goes.

"Cal would never let him do that. He'd never let anyone else's actions dictate his life or the decisions that he makes," I say tightly, meeting his stare, which has gone from indifferent to intense in the span of a sentence. His eyes squint at me.

"You don't think he would, do you?" he says, a smug grin on his face.

"No," I tell him adamantly.

He chuckles as if he's in on a joke I'm not aware of.

"So you laugh now?" I ask him sarcastically.

"As much as he's done, you still think he's noble, that he can do no wrong," he says, shaking his head.

"Don't you get it? He's not the hero in this. He doesn't come out to save us," he says dismissively.

"Well, right now, you for sure aren't the hero," I retort. I see his eye twitch, and he turns away from me.

Is it working? I don't know, but at least his tone and the stoic expression that's been on his face for the past month has changed. He turns back around, his arms crossed against his chest.

"Do you want to know why he was in Ventian?" he asks, stepping closer to me.

"He told me that his biological parents lived in the area," I say quietly.

"Did he tell you that he was looking for Clayton?" he asks sarcastically.

"If that's his dad, why wouldn't he want to find him?" I respond.

"Did he tell you he wants to kill him?" he says casually, making my heart drop into my stomach.

"W—what?"

"And when I say that, I don't mean like an arbitrary threat. I mean he's hired people to track him down. That he's kidnapped men he thought were him, and he is dead set on finding and murdering him," he says tightly. "So you see when I sit here quietly and appear to be in my thoughts, it's not just because William had sexual intercourse with my best friend. It's not because I want to appear anti-social, it's because I am trying my absolute hardest, to maintain control in one of the most trying times of my life so your *beloved* Cal doesn't come out and kill someone and get me sent prison!"

His words keep echoing in my head, blood is rushing through my ears. Is it true? Is this for real?

"Cal wants to kill someone?" I ask him in disbelief. He scoffs at me. Since when does Chris scoff at me? He laughs dismissively and walks into our bedroom. I try to collect my thoughts. I think back to when Cal and I were in bed together and how he talked about his mom and dad, but he didn't say he wanted to kill his dad. I feel like I'm about to throw up. I go into the bathroom, splash water on my face, and take a deep breath. I gather my nerves and go into our bedroom. He's sitting there, the television is on the news.

"You're not Chris, are you?" I ask him hesitantly.

He looks towards the ceiling.

"How intuitive of you," he says dryly. My heart starts to beat faster. The moment he started referring to his dad as William, I knew something was off.

Another one? A fucking other one?

I hold my head in my hand and sit on the bed. This is crazy—so crazy. I remember reading that most people who have DID have more than one alter.

"And who are you exactly?" I mumble, rubbing my temples.

"You don't have to give me a name, but if you must, you can refer to me as Collin. I'm not an attention whore like my counterpart Cal is," he says, his posture changing in the span of his sentence. He's sitting upright and even has a slightly different accent.

"How long have you been here?" I ask him.

"It depends on what you mean," he says simply. Then he turns towards me.

"I am always here. I have been transitioning in and out when Chris needed me since he spoke to Lisa. However, if you mean when I came to the forefront completely would be just a few minutes ago when you tried to trigger Calvin," he answers.

"However, in actuality, I am always there. We all are."

"We? Oh Jesus," I say, covering my face in my hands.

"How many are there of you?" I ask, almost afraid to hear the answer.

"I won't worry you with those details," he says, walking over to our closet. He opens it and sighs.

"Calvin isn't one of my favorite people, but I must say I prefer his style of dress to Christopher's. If you don't mind, since you're aware of the situation, can I be free from these off the rack jeans and department store t-shirts?" he asks.

"I don't care what you put on. Why did you come instead of Cal?" I ask, watching him as he sifts through the boxes of Cal's clothes packed in the closets.

"Calvin is the most dominant part of us. He can execute more control in *most* cases. Christopher lets him do so. However, with Christopher having checked out, so to speak, and you goading him as you just did, Cal was very close to gaining control, which at this moment is not in the best interest of any of us," he says

"We can peacefully co-exist if all of our agendas are aligned," he says.

"What do you mean . . . integration"?

"If that's what you'd like to call it. Prior to Christopher falling in love, their agenda's clashed. You have made it where they share a commonality. Christopher finding out about William sent him into a bit of a shock, which would have allowed Calvin to transition as you all like to call it. However, Calvin's urge to kill Clayton will not work for any of us. It would destroy Christopher, and none of us are interested in seeing if prison is like what they show on TV."

I look at him, his mannerism, his expression, everything about him is so different. He seems to be a lot more sophisticated than Chris and Cal. He actually reminds me a little of Dexter.

"Would you like a glass of wine, Lauren?" he asks, with a knowing grin.

"How much do you remember?" I ask him, skeptically.

"I know everything," he says with a quick smile.

"Everything?" I ask him.

"Everything," he says with a wide smile.

"Chris doesn't know everything. Does Cal?"

"Calvin thinks he does, there-in lies the problem," he says once he's completely dressed. He's wearing a suit of Cal's, but it looks so different on him the way he put everything together.

"And are you going to tell me everything?" I ask him hesitantly. He walks towards me and smiles.

"I am going to help you, Lauren. However, there are a few things I'll need you to assist me with, and tonight it will require a nice dress and your hair to be a tad more presentable," he says before heading into our bathroom.

"Oh, and if you can go into the guestroom and get those pills Christopher has in his guitar case and toss them out, that would be fantastic."

"Pills?" I ask in disbelief.

"Yes, some experimental drug that Dexter convinced Christopher would get rid of Calvin. All it does is make us queasy, and it's hard to sleep,"

"Dexter gave Chris pills? Why would he do that? I thought . . ."

"Remember Lauren, everyone has an agenda. No matter how much they pretend not to," he says before closing the bathroom door.

Is this really happening?

WHEN WE PULL up to a valet with half a million dollar cars in front of us, I wonder where exactly Collin has taken me and if maybe I should text someone and let them know what's going on. I don't know anything about this side of my husband, a side that grooms his hair perfectly. He seems harmless enough and has been more forthcoming than Cal ever has, but he hasn't told me where we are or why we're here. We walk into the beautiful, completely filled lounge, and the maître de greets us.

"Do you have a reservation?" she asks.

"I am a party of Dexter Crestfield's," he says confidently. She takes a moment to look at her screen, and in a moment she smiles brightly. She calls to another waitress.

"Can you show them to Mr. Crestfield's area," she says. We follow the waitress, and Collin puts his hand behind my back, ushering me forward.

"What are we doing here?" I ask him. This place doesn't look like Dexter and Helen's style. When we've dined with them, it's been at more modern, exclusive places. This place, while very upscale, seems a bit mature for them. When we reach the private area, my knees almost buckle.

Dexter Crestfield Sr. He looks over at us curiously before a wide smile spreads across his face, and he gives a signal for the very two intimidating security guards to let us in. Collin starts to move forward, but my legs won't budge.

"What's wrong?" he asks simply.

"I—I don't like being around this guy. What are we doing here?" I say tightly.

"If you want me to help you, you help me," he says, pulling me forward.

"Lauren, how nice to see you again," he says, standing as the man seated with him at his table does the same.

"Senator Garvin, these are my grandchildren," he says enthusiastically.

"She is quite stunning," the senator says, looking at me as if I was brought in on a tray for dessert. His date, who looks young enough to be my little sister, shifts in her seat as she glances over at me.

Relax, I am not your competition.

I haven't been in a dress in a while, and I pull down the short white cocktail dress Collin insisted I wear.

"Senator, if it's not too much of an inconvenience, can you and your guest excuse us? We have an immediate private family matter that we need to discuss," Collin interjects. Mr. Crestfield's eyebrow rises as he eyes Collin, but without missing a beat, he turns to the senator and his companion.

"If you could excuse us for just a few moments?"

"Of course," the senator says as he and his date leave the table.

"Now, who is it accompanying you tonight?" Mr. Crestfield says, eyeing me.

"Honey, take a seat," Collin says, pulling out my seat. I take it, and Collin does the same.

"We haven't met before, how would you like me to refer to you. Mr. Crestfield?" Collin says sarcastically.

"Is this a joke?" he says, looking at me. I focus my eyes on the table.

"No, this isn't farce. My name is Collin and, unlike Christopher and Calvin, I remember *everything*," he says smugly. Mr. Crestfield takes a sip of what looks like brandy and sets it down, appearing unfazed even though my stomach is doing flips.

"What is it that you want?" he asks.

"I want what's owed to us. A third of Crestfield Corporation," he says, folding his hands calmly.

"What?" I ask him, confused.

"I am sorry and what makes you think that you're owed anything that I have?" Mr. Crestfield asks, amused.

"Would you really like to get into those details? Because I, for one, prefer not to repeat myself. Maybe we should have a reporter present for the conversation so everything is on record and there are no misunderstandings," Collin says easily. He and Mr. Crestfield stare each other down for what seems like forever, all while my heart tries to jump out of my chest and make a run for it. I know that something that this is important and that I have no idea what they are talking about, and the way Collin just strode in and asked for a third of Crestfield Corporation makes me realize that he knows something he isn't supposed to. Finally, Mr. Crestfield laughs. I glance over at Collin, whose face is like stone.

"I like you, Collin. You remind me of a younger version of myself," he says, taking another sip of his drink.

"I too took a lot of risks when I was younger, against men that were more powerful, richer and supposedly a lot smarter," he says.

"Are you sure you want to travel down this rabbit hole with him. Mrs. Scott?" he says, his eyes now on me.

No, I don't want to go down any freakin' rabbit hole! Even though it doesn't matter now since my name might as well be Alice at this point.

"You talk to me, only me," Collin interrupts him.

"Okay Collin," Mr. Crestfield says calmly. He makes a signal, and a moment later a woman approaches the table.

"Could you bring me a pen and paper, please," he asks her.

"Right away, Mr. Crestfield." She's back in an instant, handing Mr. Crestfield the items he requested and disappears right after.

"Would you like a drink, darling? You look so nervous," Mr. Crestfield chuckles.

"She's fine. You have," Collin looks at his watch, "about two minutes to give me your answer."

Mr. Crestfield just smiles, scribbles something on the pape,r and then holds it out to Collin.

"What is this?" he asks, irritated as he looks at it. I look at it, too. It's an address.

"You may not be very interested in it, but Cal is," he says, smiling so widely you'd think he'd just won the lottery. A look of realization comes over Collin's face. He stands up abruptly.

"Let's go, Lauren," he says, grabbing my arm, almost pulling me out of my chair and dragging me across the floor.

"What the hell is going on?" I ask him, tired of being clueless in all of this.

"It's Clayton Rice's address," Mr. Crestfield calls out. I look back at Mr. Crestfield, my eyes widening in horror. The grip Collin had on me has completely loosened. I look at his face, the taut expression that he'd worn before gone, relaxed, and a smirk replaces it.

"Hey, gorgeous, you look especially sexy tonight."

"Cal?" I ask, hesitantly afraid to hear the answer. Out of all the times for me to want him here, now is not one of them. He walks back over to the table where Mr. Crestfield sits, looking especially pleased with himself.

"It's been a while, Cal," he says, a grin on his face.

"Yes it has. You are a lot easier to do business with than your son," Cal says, happily snatching up the address on the table. I rush over to Cal and grab his arms.

"You cannot do this," I tell him tightly. He rolls his eyes and sighs as he continues walking away from me.

"Melissa, can you make sure that Mr. Scott's car is brought around ASAP," I hear Mr. Crestfield say.

"Cal, this will destroy you. You cannot do this. Cal!" I plead with him. He lifts me off my feet and kisses me, and puts me down

"It's going to be fine. Don't worry," he says simply and gives me a wink. I try to keep up with him, but it's hard in these five-inch heels. I stop to take them off as we're near the entrance and as his luck may have it, our car is pulling up. He walks to the driver's side and hops in. When I run to open the door, it's locked. He lets the window down.

"I've got to do this, babe. It's all going to work out. I promise," he says and pulls away. I throw my shoe on the ground and rush back into the restaurant to where Mr. Crestfield is.

"Tell me that was a fake address!" I say desperately.

"I have a dinner to finish, if you don't mind my dear," he says dismissively as his companions approach the table.

"You're welcome to join us. However, I think you have more

pressing matters to attend to," he says condescendingly. How dare he. How fucking dare he. Every ounce of intimidation I felt, gone out the window. I pick up the glass of water in front of me and toss it in his face before quickly heading to the exit.

I don't know what to do. I don't know what the hell to do! I don't know who to call, who I can trust. Dexter's father just gave him the exact location of the man he wants to kill. I don't know who can help me. I settle on calling his mom, who doesn't pick up. I groan and call Mr. Scott.

"Lauren. I'm so glad you called," he says hopefully. It's funny how much he's changed.

"Mr. Scott. Do you know anything about Cal's birth parents?" I ask him desperately.

"What. Why are you asking that?" he stutters.

"Collin told me that Cal wants to kill his dad, Clayton because he thinks he killed his mother, and we ended up meeting Mr. Crestfield and Collin asked for a third of his company, and somehow Mr. Crestfield knew how to trigger Cal, and I think he gave Cal this Clayton guy's address, and I'm pretty sure he's on his way there to kill him," I ramble without a single pause.

"Wait, what? And who is Collin?"

chapter 18

cal

I'VE BEEN WAITING on this day for a long time. Dex never came through. I feel stupid that I never went directly to the real source . . . Dexter Sr.

When Chris pissed all over himself after finding out his daddy was screwing his so-called best friend, I knew my time was coming to take over, but when she told him she had a kid that was his sister, even I couldn't believe that shit, and good ol' Chris just couldn't take that blow. Unfortunately, other greedy pussies stepped in, trying to keep me from claiming what's mine.

I thought Collin was smarter than that. Asking for a third of Dexter Crestfield's company. Fucking greedy dumbass. Chris's weakness is his feelings. Collin's is that he thinks he's so much smarter than everyone else. My weakness is this mother fucker's existence sitting tied up in front of me which I'm about to eliminate very soon. I like watching him squirm. I'm enjoying it a whole lot actually.

All of the time I spent looking for him, and he was right under my nose. He lived just a few blocks from the house in Ventian. I knew I was close, I just didn't know how close, and I really want to ring those fucking PI's necks. I'm waiting for him to wake from the blow to the back of the head I gave him. When I saw him, I couldn't believe it. The man who caused the same fucking nightmare for me again and again. It's all going to be over soon though. He'll be dead, the little boy in my dream can have peace, and the fucker that shot my mother right in front of me will be wiped off the earth.

Then I can live in peace with Lauren and Caylen, and all will be well with the world.

After a long ass hour, the bitch finally starts to stir. I pull off the bag on his head, and his eyes widen, and the small thread of uncertainty that I grabbed the wrong guy is gone. I'll never forget his eyes. I see them in my dream every night.

"What's up, Pops? Remember me?" I laugh at him. I still have the tape on his mouth so he can't speak, but he shakes his head as if the more he shakes it the better his chances are to make it out of here alive, too bad for him. I don't give a shit how he answers my questions—the only way he's leaving this house is post-mortem.

"I know you had a thousand little bastards running around, but see me, I'm special. You remember my mother, Isabella?" I ask him sarcastically. The expression on his face now is priceless. He looks at me more closely, and I can see the horror in his face as he recognizes he's met his undertaker.

"Yeah. I think you do," I nod.

"I bet you never expected to see me again, did you?" I ask him. "Then I was a helpless little boy, left crying in the pool of blood after you shot his fucking mother right in front of his face," I growl at him. He shakes his head again, and I can hear him straining to talk.

"Oh, oh it didn't happen like that? You're not the right guy?" I ask, laughing, and I hit him right on the mouth with the back of my 9 mm.

"Fucking liar. I relive what happened every night. Every single night. I will *never* forget your face," I growl at him, disgusted as I see him crying. I stick the gun right between his eyes.

"Don't you fucking let one more tear drop, or I will start by blowing off your fucking dick."

"Cal!" I turn around and look back to see Lauren and fucking Will Scott coming down the stairs. Stupid Chris and Dex, I forgot he was having me followed, traitor.

I point the gun at William. Lauren gasps.

"Cal, what are you doing?"

"You know, as much as I can't stand Chris, I really do owe the guy. Maybe I should just do him a favor and kill your ass, too," I joke, but neither of them laughs.

"Cal, put the gun down," she pleads, tears streaming from her eyes.

"Why the hell are you crying, Lauren? This is going to fix everything!"

"He's not going to shoot me, Lauren," William says, way too calmly.

"Oh I won't?" I laugh, aiming at his knee.

"No!" Lauren screams. Ugh. She's ruining everything.

"Both of you . . . get the fuck out!"

"You're not going to shoot me or that guy in the chair because if you do your wife, the woman that you love, will never look at you the same."

Oh, cue the violins.

"If anyone knows that, it's me, son. Gwen will never ever look at me how she did before this happened," he pleads. I glance over at Lauren who's crying and is looking at me like I'm the worst person in the world. I go over to Clay and smack him with the gun again.

"This is all your fault!"

"Cal! What do you remember from that night?" William yells.

"I don't have to explain anything to you!" I shout at him.

"Don't explain it to me. Explain it to Lauren," he says. "Get her to understand why you have to do this." I wonder what type of two-bit reverse psychology he thinks he's using. I really should shoot him in the fucking knee.

"Think, Cal. What do you really remember?" she says, crying. I let out a groan.

"He shot my mother, Lauren. Right in front of me, he left me there until someone found me," I tell her.

"Who found you?" she asks. I start to answer her, but I can't. I don't remember.

"Does it matter who found me?" I ask, frustrated with all of this.

"How clear do you remember that day? Cal, you were five," she pleads.

"When your mother gets shot in the fucking face in front of you, that's not something you forget!" I shout back.

"Is that really what happened?" she asks quietly. Her voice has a way of taking my anger down, and I hate it.

"I talked to Helen while we were on our way here," she says, slowly approaching me.

"Lauren, stay over there," I tell her, but she continues approaching me.

"That is not how Chris or any of the other alters remember it," she says.

"Why don't you like to drink?" she says.

"What does that have to do with anything?" I tell her.

"You, the one who lives on the edge, and indulges in all of life's pleasures doesn't like to drink?" she says, and I feel myself growing impatient.

"Your mother used to drink. A lot," she continues.

"What are you talking about Lauren?"

I look back at the son of a bitch, Clay.

"What the hell is she talking about?" I snatch the tape off of his mouth and he gasps for air.

"Talk and talk fast," I growl at him, the gun still at his face.

"She didn't used to drink. Before you were born, your mom was a CNA. She got a job through the welfare programs at this big hospital in the city. She was the happiest I had ever seen her. Our family was actually doing okay . . ."

"You're on a time clock," I say impatiently.

"A—after a few months there she started having a lot of extra money. She started having these fancy clothes and jewelry. I'm not the smartest man in the world, but I knew that wasn't coming out of her check. I knew something was going on, but I never said anything. She was happy, we were happy. Then she got pregnant. She lost her job, but she kept saying everything was going to be okay. That we would be taken care of. After you were born, whatever she was waiting on never came through. She got real depressed, started drinking a whole lot, she was only sober half the time,"

"You're lying," I growl at him, releasing the safety on the gun

"Listen to him, Cal!" Lauren screams at me, and *poor* Clayton starts to cry.

"Do you want to know how we adopted you?" William shouts.

"We had wanted a baby for so long. Everyone knew it, even my estranged stepfather! Dexter Crestfield Sr. brought you to our door. He told us that you were his illegitimate son whose mother killed herself."

"You're lying!" I shout.

"I'm not. Call Gwen. She'll confirm it," he says, ushering out his phone. I look over at Lauren.

"That's why Collin asked for a third of his company. He remembers what you don't. He knows you're Dexter's son," Lauren pleads.

No. No, fuck, no!

"Okay, let's say you're right. I'm Dexter Crestfield's fucking son. This asshole found out she was sleeping with him, and he shot her for it," I yell at them.

"No. That's not what happened," Clayton says, crying like a little girl.

"No, Cal," Lauren pleads. Think. Please try to think. I feel dizzy, my thoughts crash together, and my vision blurs.

Instantly, I'm back at the house, this time she's alive. She's drunk. My mom . . . I'm on the floor watching television. She's yelling at someone on the phone.

'You lied to me. You ruined my life. You promised you'd take care of us. I see your little ugly fucking kid whenever they show you on the news. How could you not love ours . . . you don't love him, if you did you'd get me out of this hell hole . . . I don't give a shit about a trust fund for him. We have to live now. I won't keep living like this!

I rub my temples. I feel my heart pounding.

She's drinking more and more. Soon she goes in her room. Me and two other kids are in front of the TV. I get up and open the door to her room. She's sitting on the bed bawling.

I ask her what's wrong.

"Nothing. I have a toy, you want to play with it?" she asks me. Her voice is so sweet and nice. It hardly ever is. I nod my head, and she goes in a drawer and pulls out a gun. She kneels down on the floor in front of me. It's heavy, but she helps me hold it.

"We're going to play a game. When I count to three, you're going to pull this, okay," she says showing me the trigger. She then aims it at her chest.

"One, two . . ."

I drop the gun out of my hand.

"I killed her? I killed my mom," my chest feels tight. I can't breathe.

"Babe, it's okay," Lauren says, running over to me and hugging me. I cry so hard I'm shaking.

"It's okay, babe. You were only a baby," Lauren says rocking me like I'm a baby now. I killed my mother. I almost killed an innocent man because I was wrong. I killed her. I'm a murderer.

"I found you, in the bedroom. She called me right before it happened and told me everything. How she had an affair with Dexter Crestfield, that he promised to marry her and take care of her the rest of her life, but he didn't, and that you were his son. She said she couldn't live in squalor anymore. That you and your brothers and sisters were better off with her dead. I tried to get home as fast as I could. When I did, it was too late. I figured out what had happened," Clayton's voice explains but it doesn't matter.

Everything I believed. Everything I held on to was a lie . . .

Except her. She's my truth.

chris

I T SUCKS WHEN you have to be filled in on things that happen in your own life. When the transition finished, Lauren and Dr. Lyce filled everything in for me. It turns out I'm actually a Crestfield. It still makes me cringe to think about it.

My birth mother was so sick, she used me to kill herself. Clayton, her husband, eventually told them she grew up Catholic and believed if she killed herself she'd go to hell. I wonder how much better off she thought she'd be having her five-year-old do it for her. He also told us Isabella left a note with Dexter Sr.'s information on it the day she killed herself. Clayton called Dexter Sr. and told him what had happened. Dexter Sr. came and had everything, right down to the last detail, swept under the rug. Clayton says he told him family had always been important to him, and he had to know his son was taken care of. Can you believe that? Dexter also gave him a pretty nice chunk of change for him to disappear with my half brothers and sisters. Dexter had to keep everything quiet since at the time he was married, and the pre-nup would be void if infidelity could be proved.

It made perfect sense for him to give me to the Scotts since my mom couldn't have children. She couldn't care less what led to the mysterious circumstances of Dexter bringing a child to their door. My dad wanted to make her happy, and Dexter purchased the land that they lived on, which they wouldn't have been able to pay off for years.

Collin, the other guy inside my head, it turns out had been popping up on occasions long before he made his presence known to Lauren. He was the one who told the Crestfields about Cal and how he needed their help when Cal surfaced and took over. The Scotts thought all along it was Cal who reached out to them, and really it was Collin who took over after Cal's break and started talking to Helen in these sessions.

We've been in therapy the past few weeks. After everything happened with Cal trying to kill Clayton Rice, I guess he needed a break because I woke up and Lauren explained everything that had happened. To think how many lies were hidden from both of us, and the fact that I have another alter that not even my parents or Helen knew about is mind-boggling. Therapy has been going okay. I still feel numb a lot, like a part of me is missing. Lauren is great. She is there each step of the way. My mom has been staying with us the past two weeks. I've even talked to my dad one or two times. I'll have to slowly try to build that relationship back, if it can even be rebuilt. Helen's recommended that I try to avoid anything that brings on stress or anxiety, to try not to think about it until our sessions.

I've started to have more memories of Lauren and me when Cal was in control. They're not as frequent as they were, but they've been coming back slowly but surely. Lauren comes to these sessions sometimes, but Helen asked that today it just be me.

"Okay, Christopher, before we begin I want to show you something," Helen says, turning on the big television in her office.

"Are we watching another testimonial?" I ask her, trying to sound more interested than I am. At first it was interesting watching videos of other people with DID share what their experience has been like. The hardest part was listening to how their family members cope with it. Seeing the sacrifices everyone has to make makes me feel guilty.

"Not today," she says, and I look up and see myself on the screen.

"So, we on?" The moment I hear the voice I know it's not me. It's him. He lets out a deep sigh and sort of leans over his knees.

"It's me. The guy you think made your life a living hell, right?" he laughs. "Well if you think that, you're fucking delusional—without me, Caylen and Lauren wouldn't be in your life. You'd probably be married to that stuck-up bitch, Jenna."

"Cal, come on, you said you'd be nice," I hear Helen's voice in the background. He rolls his eyes and huffs.

"Okay, let me get straight to the point. I want to do right by Lauren. I left her once because I thought I was doing the right thing. I wanted her to have someone better than me," he says solemnly.

"Well not better, because let's be honest it doesn't get any better than this, but more responsible, reliable who didn't have the shitload of baggage we do," he shrugs. "I never wanted Lauren to know you. It always seemed like everything in life came so easy for you. I thought you'd be easier for her to love than me," he continues. It's one thing for you to hear a recording of yourself and not recognize your voice or remember saying the words, but to see it, to watch it yourself, it hits you that it is real.

"Since I met her . . . before I officially met her, I've been trying to fix things for her. Make things right, give her everything she deserves," he sighs. "She doesn't deserve us fighting against each other. Telling her to pick and choose all the time. Confusing the hell out of Caylen when she gets older," he shrugs. "You are the responsible one. The selfless one. You could be a good dad. But God, sometimes you're a fucking pussy, man," he says with a groan.

He's such an asshole.

"I mean you are, and I can't leave my girls with someone who acts like a pussy."

"I want to give her something she always wanted. I sure as hell can't do it by myself. But maybe both of us together, we can give her the prince charming she deserves," he says. "Helen and I have been talking, and I'm starting to think maybe this integration thing won't suck ass completely. So what do you say, Chris? You in, or you going to pussy out?" he asks cockily.

I don't care what he says. I'm not a pussy.

lauren
six months later

A NEW START.

That's what he asked for. I told him no, because I don't think we need one. Our history wasn't the best, but it's made us who we are. Each and every bumpy step of the way has made us who we are today.

When he got on one knee and asked me to marry him again—that I agreed to.

We thought there was no better way to start, than renewing our vows on a beautiful July day on my Aunt Raven's property. I glance over and smile at Aidan and Hillary who, as it turns out, had been secretly dating since they met at the disaster of a dinner party at the Scotts. Raven sits proudly next to the man she's been seeing, they may be walking down this same aisle next. Angela is next to her, one hand intertwined with Stephen's, the other wrapped around Caylen. It turns out that I was never his perfect girl, but Angela seems to be. I look back at Mr. Scott who did the honor of walking me down the aisle.

It's funny how time and life-changing events can heal wounds. Well, some of them. He and Mrs. Scott are separated. They are working on their friendship even though Gwen plans on proceeding with the divorce. Mr. Scott is hoping she changes her mind. I tried to get Lisa to come to the wedding, but she respectfully declined. My husband still hasn't forgiven her, so it's probably for the best, even though he has warmed up quite a lot to Willa, who is our flower girl.

"Christopher Calvin Scott do you take this woman to be your law-fully wedded bride to have and to hold as long as you both shall live?"

"I do," he says. Holding my hand, he gives me a wink that still sets butterflies off in my stomach. He asks me the same thing, and I nod enthusiastically with a smile as wide as a Cheshire cat.

"Yes," I say simply.

"LAUREN WILL YOU do me the honor of having this dance?" Dexter asks, extending his hand out to me.

"Of course, Mr. Crestfield," I say with a laugh. The band is playing a slow but upbeat song as we make our way onto the dance floor between my groom and Raven, and Mr. Scott and Helen dancing.

"You know when Cal first told me about you, I was worried about him."

"I was harmless. You should have been worried about me," I retort playfully.

"You're the best thing that ever happened to him," he says, sincerely.

"Thank you, Dexter. That means a lot coming from you. Thank you for everything, as well," I tell him. Then I notice my hubby has gotten up on stage with his guitar. Everyone around us stops dancing and looks at the stage.

"I'd like to dedicate this song, to my beautiful, amazing, smart, and extremely sexy wife. Who for some reason, agreed to get on this roller coaster with me again. This is for you, babe," he says looking me in the eye and beginning to play the song we first danced to all those nights ago in his apartment. You always hear the phrase 'fall in love all over again' Before I met him I didn't think it was possible, but I've fallen in love with him three times. Once when he called himself Cal, again when he called himself Chris, and right now as he plays his heart out for me in front of everyone, keeping eye contact the entire time. When he's done, everyone applauds and catcalls. I start to make my way to the stage when

Hillary grabs me and leans over in my ear.

"I know I've asked you this a thousand times, but come on, you've got to tell me, which one is he? He's got to be Cal, right? But you said Chris knew how to play the guitar, Cal didn't?" she asks, and for the thousandth time I roll my eyes at her playfully.

"I told you he's both," I wink at her. Once I reach the stage, he holds a hand out for me and pulls me up on stage with him.

"I love you, Mrs. Scott," he grins at me.

"I love you more, Mr. Scott," I tell him, before he pulls me into his arms. I kiss him with all that's in me, and he does the same. Some days I see more of Chris, others he's more Cal-like. Sometimes I even see bits of Collin, strangely. Really, I've learned they're all just titles to different facets of his personality, categories of his moods.

We dance right there on stage, surrounded by our family and friends. As we sway to the music, I feel that familiar trace on my back. I glance up at him, and he winks at me, and I wink back. I love this man every day, every part of him, and I will for the rest of my life. My beautifully broken Prince Charming, and I wouldn't want him any other way.

The end . . .

author's note

Hey there! You reading this!

Thank you for sticking with me through the twists and turns, tears and laughs of the Scotts. These characters have been with me for almost ten years in the making. They sat stagnant for almost four years, and Lauren haunted me every so often to give her a happy ending after I wrote the first draft of *If I Break* back in 2004. These characters have literally changed my life.

You all have changed my life. To think that I have had my dreams come true, telling stories for a living. I cannot say how grateful I am to you all, and I thank God each and every day for sending you all my way.

I hope you enjoyed Cal/Chris and Lauren's story. I wanted to end their journey the right way. I hope it met your expectations.

Lisa and Gwen's story 'What Happens After' releases November 30th on all platforms.

I hope you stick with me for all the other stories that play in my head. I do have one favor for you. If you enjoyed the book, please take time to leave a review on whatever site you purchased on and/or Goodreads and don't forget to tell a friend about the series. Remember that the first book is free. I appreciate anyone who takes the time to do so. If you'd like to reach me, I check my Facebook everyday so feel free to connect with me there facebook.com/portiamoorebooks. Or email me at portiacmoore@gmail.com . Though this is a work of fiction DID (Dissociative Identity Disorder) is a very real disorder that affects thousands of people. If you'd like to learn more about it, see my webpage. Until the next one.

God bless!

Portia xoxo.

about the author

I'M OBSESSED WITH blowing kisses. I guess that makes me a romantic. I love books and cute boys and reading about cute boys in books. I'm infatuated with the glamour girls of the past: Audrey, Dorthy, Marilyn, Elizabeth.

I'm a self confessed girly girl, book nerd, food enthusiast, and comic book fan. Odd combination huh, you have no idea . . .

Like Portia Moore on Facebook
www.facebook.com/portiamoorebooks

Follow on IG
www.instagram.com/portiamoorewrites

or visit
www.portiamoore.com

books by

portia moore

For a sneak peek into my most recent novel What Happens After continue reading.

WHAT HAPPENS AFTER

prologue

HOW CAN YOU love someone when you know they will never truly love you back because they can't ever love you back? Your brain should stop you from loving them. There should be a defense mechanism embedded deep within you to stop your soul from allowing you to give your heart to someone who doesn't deserve it, who doesn't even want it, someone who *couldn't* have it even if they did want it.

Unfortunately, there's no fail-safe for love, no brake to stop you from throwing your life—and the lives of those around you—completely out of balance. There are no warning lights or flashing danger signs. There's nothing to stop the planted seeds from growing and taking root. And once they grow, there's nothing you can do about it. Your desire to water those wretched seeds only increases. Once you realize those seeds weren't supposed to grow, it's already too late. At seventeen, you haven't got a clue . . .

chapter one

gwen

HE LIED TO me. What's worse than him lying to me as my husband and the father of my child, my so-called soul mate, is that he lied to me as my friend. Our history, our bond, our love, didn't stop my best friend from lying to me all these years. He kept secrets from me, and it hurts. It hurts so badly—the half-truths, the deception, the words I never ever thought I'd use . . . it all hurts.

I never thought that anything associated with love could be so painful, but love betrayed definitely is. This unfathomable heartache snuffs out all of my urges toward forgiveness because now I know the truth. At least what I *imagine* the truth to be—those images run continuously through my mind.

The love that once was so sure has been replaced by anguish . A pain that erases the joy and closeness we shared, pushing it further and further away, like a mirage—unreal. Our history seems more like an illusion. Only vague images of our love and life together remain, but those spectral images are tainted.

While my own memories are like a half-forgotten dream, those moments I *imagine* are all too vivid. Everywhere I look, I see betrayal, and I can't get his duplicitousness out of my head. My faith has been shaken to the core. Those thoughts become an unbearable weight, a sickening fog that suffocates me, a stench so bad it chokes all the beauty and joy out of life. All that remains is blinding rage, anger, bitterness, and hatred. These thoughts turn my consciousness into an abyss that I can't escape. I secretly pray for the moment I'll feel nothing because anything is better than this.

Adultery.

Affair.

Betrayal.

Words I try to escape from as the hours tick by. It feels like time has slowed down, but in reality it is moving so fast it sneaks up on me—like a thief in the night. I look in the mirror at the fine lines that have formed around my mouth and eyes, things I overlooked before but are like flashing lights now. I wonder when this happened. When was my youth stolen? Did it happen when Christopher turned ten, or did it happen when I first saw my grandchild? Is today just the first day I noticed them? This morning when I looked in the mirror, I didn't see them, but they were there. Right? I just never noticed until now. I wasn't even alarmed by the increasing number of grey hairs I've accumulated over the years. Why should I worry over trivial things like that anyway when there's so much more to regret?

I always knew life was precious. You realize it when you find out you'll never be able to produce it. When you find out that you're unable to do the one thing you believe you were put on the planet to do—our God-given right as a woman to bear children. I have come to appreciate that fertility is a gift, not a right, even though I'm slightly resentful. The realization of just how precious the gift of life is became even more evident once I heard the words, "You have stage-three breast cancer." Aging, living is a blessing, not something to worry about. When I was able to say, "I beat cancer," I quit worrying about the small things. If I could survive cancer, I could survive anything. To wake up in the morning and take a breath became so much more of a welcome event than one would ever think.

So it isn't a wonder why today, of all days, I notice the things I didn't use to care about but *today* mean everything.

I wish I were just being dramatic, but without hesitation, I can say being alive doesn't seem as important as it once was. These badges of maturity feel less like an honor and more like a punishment, a cruel inside joke I'm not in on.

What else could I think of it as?

My husband, my dear husband, the man I love more than anything in the entire world, has always made me feel beautiful. When I said wrinkles, he said laugh lines, and not only that, he said they made me more beautiful than the day he first met me. I believed him.

I believed him because he's my best friend, my confidant, my own personal superhero . . . or at least he was yesterday. Today, he's my personally-crafted villain. One who knows my weaknesses and knows me better than anyone else in the world. I've shared my deepest secrets with him. He's been my glue when my world was on the cusp of falling apart several times over—at least I thought he was. Maybe he wasn't, or maybe he was for a while, or maybe it was all a façade.

Maybe I was just a fool. I must have been a fool, an arrogant one. Because until today, I never understood why the women I grew up with felt self-conscious about their appearances as each birthday passed. Because I knew it all, I had it all figured out—they'd married the wrong man. I thought that if you married your soul's true mate, a life partner, they should appreciate who *you* are *now*, who you've grown to become. My husband, my best friend, told me that, and like a fool in love, I never once questioned it—until today.

Because today is the day I found out that my husband—my best friend, the man I turned my world upside down for, whom I gave my youth to, my best days, my joy, my entire self—has not only been screwing my son's best friend but also has a child with her. Before today, I considered her—the twenty-seven-year-old without a single laugh line who grew up before my very eyes—like a daughter. But now I know her as my husband's *lover.*

So today, I look in this mirror and see every single thing that makes me different from the girl he fell in love with *and* the girl he betrayed me with. Today, I question all the times I stood in front of this mirror, pulling myself together to greet each day with a smile while I fought the flesh-eating monster living inside me, to make life easier for him. Today it all seems pointless, worthless! If I'd just given in when death came for me, I wouldn't be experiencing the pain I'm in now, a fate that seems worse than death. I hate thinking like this! I hate these thoughts, but they're honest and feel more real than anything else today. Truer than love, more honest than forgiveness, and more authentic than the last twenty-five years of what I thought was an unbreakable marriage.

I want to cry and vomit at the same time. Maybe I could just crawl into myself as if I didn't exist. Here I stand, forty-nine years old, a woman and mother who beat the odds of advanced cancer. Yesterday morning, I felt invincible. Now I feel as fragile as a seventeen-year-old whose heart has been broken, crushed, demolished.

A grown woman decimated and paralyzed.

It's hard to remember how to move. Not so much in the literal sense, even though my limbs feel heavy, but how do I get out of this space I'm in? How do I escape from what feels like a prison? My husband has cheated, broken my trust, and produced a child with my *son's* best friend.

When I think about Christopher, all of this feels so much worse. He had to be the one to tell me. The words that came from his mouth crashed all around me. They were the worst words I've ever heard, words so jarring, so life-altering, so unbelievable my psyche couldn't comprehend them. My soul sang out to God, *Please, please let what he just said, what was just released into the universe, be a mistake.* Somewhere in my mind, I believed it could be changed, that there was an error that could be easily fixed. That it could be taken back. But it couldn't. It couldn't ever be taken back.

I'd give anything just to have found out first so my son wouldn't have had the burden of delivering the message from hell. To say things that had to have been almost harder for him to say than for me to hear . . . my baby . . . their baby. My son has a sister, a half-sister.

My husband has a child, a biological one. One I could never give him, no matter how much I wanted to, but she could. A twenty-seven-year-old who can barely remember where her keys are was able to give my husband a child.

"Mom?" Christopher's voice comes from the other side of the bathroom door, where I've been for I don't know how long. A half hour, or has it been two hours? "Mom, can I come in?"

His voice is low and laced with sorrow, like when he was a little boy who'd done something bad and was coming to tell on himself.

I try to muster up sound from my dry, constricted throat. "Umm, one minute, honey."

I move quickly and turn on the sink to splash water on my face. I try but fail miserably to mask my pain, the dull, throbbing ache coursing through me that has my breath tightened and my head heavy. I attempt to break out of the catatonic state I've been trapped in and conjure up any amount of strength to hold myself up, to keep my emotions from pouring out of me. My son . . . my son needs to see that I'm not a complete blubbering mess even if I have to fake it. I take one more breath before opening the door.

I open it and look at the man I've raised since he was five years old. He used to be so small. Now he's a foot taller than me, broad-shouldered, and can appear intimidating but wouldn't hurt a fly. When I look into his eyes, I never know who I'll see: the mild-mannered gentleman with a heart of gold or the person who's built a wall around himself to protect himself from being hurt. I should've taken notes on how to build that wall.

His big green eyes find mine. They shift from my face to his feet several times before I force myself to give him a smile and hug him the way I did when he was a little boy.

"I'm so sorry, Mom." His voice quivers.

I rub his back and open my mouth to tell him everything will be okay, that this all will work out, but I can't bring myself to do it. I can't lie to him, because I know how it feels to be lied to, betrayed, and treated like a child who can't handle life's realities.

"I shouldn't have told you like that. I-I—"

His voice gives in, and I pray for him to have the strength he needs—that he doesn't fall apart. He has his own daughter he has to be strong for now. My and his father's problems should be just that—ours. But I know life doesn't work like that; love doesn't allow you to just shift burdens that you want to help carry.

"You have nothing to be sorry about," I say, commanding my voice to steady.

"How could they do that to you, to us? How could he do that, Mom?"

I can see his distress as I continue to rub his back, hoping to calm him down. "I don't know."

I've been trying to figure out how he could lie and betray me and his son, how he could do so without guilt, how he could continue to live as if nothing had changed, and I can't come up with anything. Christopher lets me go and turns his back toward me, grabbing a towel and wiping his face. I walk past him out of the bathroom and sit on the settee in my bedroom.

"Is your dad still out there?" I ask quietly, gesturing to my bedroom door where his father has been camped out.

"Yeah, he fell asleep." He's cross, his jaw tight and his hands clenched into fists.

As angry as I am with William, I loathe what I've just seen, the look of hatred and bitterness that flashed across his son's face at the mention of him.

"You should come back to Chicago with me and Lauren. You can't stay here with him."

My thoughts haven't even gone beyond what I heard tonight, but he's right. I can't stay in this house with him. I don't know if I can stay in this house at all, where they . . . where he and Lisa . . .

"This is my fault. If I wasn't friends with her . . ." he mutters.

I gently grip his chin and make him look at me. "This is *not* your fault. You had nothing to do with this." My voice is stern, but he shakes his head. I see his anger intensify.

"That's the thing. He didn't think about me. He didn't think about you! I can't forgive him for this. There's no way we can get past this."

I put my face in my hands and try to think of life without William. A day without William. To think that the William I believed in is no more. He's a lie, a distant memory. No longer my protector, my confidant, my best friend. I squeeze my eyes shut and rub my temples. How do we get past this? How do I save my family when the damage is beyond repair? I fought cancer with all I had to save my family. I knew the family would crumble without me. At the time, William and Chris had been at odds because of Cal, and without me as their buffer and mediator, I knew they'd be lost. Now at least Chris has his own family, a beautiful little girl and a wife who loves him the way I loved William.

Loved William?

I wish after all of this I could truly use past tense with confidence. At least whatever happens, Christopher will be fine. He has to be.

"Do you want to leave in the morning?"

His question interrupts my thoughts.

"I just want to sleep right now, I think. We'll figure everything out tomorrow," I tell him, squeezing his hands.

He looks at me with worry and concern, and a moment later, his face is hard and his expression has gone cold. "Do you want me to make him leave?"

His voice is low and bitter, which makes my stomach drop. I can't take more fighting, more confrontation, confusion, and anger. Is this all that's left of my family? No. It can't be. I want to fix it, but how do I fix it when I'm broken? How do you fix yourself *after* you break?

chapter two

I T'S SEVEN IN the morning. I've been sitting in the chair by my window since five. I've been dressed and ready to go since before then, but I can't seem to bring myself to walk out the door. I watched the sun rise, leaving the darkness of the previous night behind, and living on a farm, early mornings are normal. If only I had a miracle to do the same with my life. I dread the idea of leaving my room. I haven't seen William working outside, so there's a good chance he's still outside my door—camped out, wanting to talk, wanting to apologize, wanting to explain. There's no way to explain sleeping with your son's best friend.

There's no explanation that can make this better, nowhere to move forward. I barely know any details about the how or when. Then again, anything that increases my knowledge isn't going to help either; it's only going to hurt. I can't take any more hurt than I already have.

I still have a son and a family. A family that needs me, that I can't run away from. My faith teaches forgiveness, but how can I forgive this? How can I forgive *him* and mean it? How can I forgive him for having a child outside of our marriage? How can I forgive betrayal, lies, and secrets? I should have had Chris ask him to leave last night. How can I face him without wanting to rip off his head or bursting into tears?

I open the door and sigh with relief when I see that William isn't sitting next to it. I'm relieved, but I also feel disgusted with myself because I'm disappointed by his absence. I haven't felt this conflicted since I was a teenager. I close the bedroom door and cautiously make my way down the stairs to the kitchen. I usually cook breakfast every morning no matter what. This is the first time I haven't since I was sick. No, that's not right. There was also that time when Chris went missing and I left Lisa to wait on him while Will and I went looking for him, and . . . I feel sick.

I try to push her name out of my mind because whenever I think of it, I feel rage boil up from the pit of my stomach. I'm angry at her, at him, at myself. How could I not see it? How could I not have a clue that something was going on between them? How could I not notice my husband was having an affair right under my nose? I have to be the biggest idiot on the planet. Before I step over the kitchen threshold, the smell hits me. As I step in, I see a plate already fixed with waffles, grits, fresh fruit, and sausage.

"Good morning."

I look up and see Will step into the kitchen from the pantry. He looks a mess. He looks how I feel. I try to speak, but no words come out of my mouth.

"I-I made breakfast. I tried to make it healthy. You've been talking a lot about that lately, and I've listened," he says, his blue eyes encapsulated by puffy eyelids. His hair is completely disheveled, as if he's run his hands through it a thousand times. His five o'clock shadow is pronounced and his dimples absent because his lips are pressed so firmly together.

This is the first time I've looked at him since I found out. The first time I've ever looked at the man I married and felt anything but love, hope, and strength. It's funny how a few hours have changed everything for us.

Seeing him makes my emotions crash against each other. Each second I stand here, I become more enraged. How could he do something so stupid, so selfish, and so . . . unforgivable? And he stands here like nothing has happened, as if we're going to eat breakfast together and everything will be okay?! Nothing will be okay. I realize this as I stand in my kitchen in front of him, the same place he and his whore ate with me and sat with our family.

"I can't believe you did this to us." The words are automatic, as if triggered by his presence. They hurt to speak but hurt even more to hold in.

"Gwen."

His voice breaks as he tries to approach me, but I step back and push my arms out to let him know to stay back.

"Please, just let me explain," he begs. His voice sounds pained, and my heart aches for him—for me

"I can't. I can't. I don't want to hear it, and there's nothing that you can explain. Anything you say will only make things worse!" I'm frantic. It's a lie; I want to know everything, but I don't think I can survive hearing it.

"Gwen, you're my best friend," he says with tears in his eyes.

I have to turn away. I grab a chair to keep my balance. To see him like this hurts, but I can't hurt for him. He didn't hurt for me. I don't even know if he hurts for me now. I'm sure he hurts for himself.

"I never meant to hurt you. I know how that sounds, but if I could take it back—"

"You did hurt me! Worse than anything I've ever experienced, and you cannot take it back." My voice is loud and unrecognizable.

His gaze isn't on me but set on the floor instead.

"In our home, William. How could you? With Lisa of all people!" I'm close to screaming at the top of my lungs.

"There's no excuse for what I did," he whispers.

His words make me want to throw something. To see him broken . . . I haven't seen him like this since I was sick. A chill shoots down my spine.

"Were you seeing her when I was sick?" I ask cautiously. I don't know if I can take hearing the answer. His eyes widen, and he approaches me; I retreat again.

"No. I stopped before I found out you lost our child," he promises.

The pain of that memory shoots through me. I know he thinks what he said should give me some consolation, but it doesn't. It tears open a wound I've tried to forget, a wound that has become purulent. "You stopped out of pity. You stopped out of a sense of duty, guilt, and a mournful promise but not out of love. Do you love her?"

He shakes his head. "It's always been you, Gwen—"

My eyes narrow on his. "Except when you were screwing her."

He looks defeated, as though he's given up and realized there's absolutely nothing he can say to fix this. I feel as though my soul is beginning to crumble. I can't talk to him about this. I can't think about this.

"I need you to leave."

"Gwen, please. I'll give you time. I owe you that, but we can get past this." His voice deepens with each word to the more familiar, authoritative tone I'm used to from him instead of the sad, broken one.

"How dare you!" I scream. "You have a daughter, William! A daughter! How can we get past that? Tell me?!"

He covers his face. "I didn't know." He attempts to touch me again, and I swat him away.

"You didn't know? You think that makes it better?" My whole body shakes as I shed angry tears.

Tears are falling down his face now too. He gets on his knees and grabs my waist. "What can I do? Tell me—what can I do? I'll do anything. Please!"

I try to get out of his grasp, but he holds me tighter.

"We can get through this. I promise you we can," he cries against my stomach.

I realize getting him to let me go will be futile unless I hit him on the head with one of the table utensils, so I gently grasp his face and make him look up at me. "*We* don't have to do anything, and *you* don't get to decide that. *You* decided to ruin us—everything we had, our family, our history, *you* decided that. *I* get to decide whether I can even consider the possibility of looking at you without seeing you as the person who hurt me more than anyone in my entire life.

"You have no idea how this feels, how badly I hurt. You can't, because if you got it, if you understood, you would leave me alone. You'd know how much it hurts me to see you, to hear your voice as I look around our home and think about how you desecrated and disrespected the place where we built our family. And the very worst part of it all is that I was completely oblivious. I thought we were fine, that we were okay. I've been happy!"

"I've been happy too! I haven't been involved with Lisa in years!" he shouts, and hearing him say her name makes my stomach churn.

I cover my face, trying to catch my breath.

"Is everything okay?" my son's wife, Lauren, says from behind me. "William was just leaving."

His face falls, his expression crushed. "We have to talk about this."

"I need you to go now! Right now, William." My screeching makes even me flinch.

He glances behind me at Lauren, then he nods. "If that's what you want."

He wipes the tears from his face. I've only seen William cry once in his life besides today, and that was when his mother passed away. Now I have to squelch the instinct to go to him and hug him and tell him everything will be okay. A task made easier as my urge to lash out at him consumes me.

"I'm just going to get a few things, and I'll go. If that's what you want," he says quietly, his eyes on mine.

After taking a deep breath, I say, "There isn't any other choice."

His eyes fall to the floor, and he walks past me. As I hear him leave the room, I feel my spirit shatter. The wail I release is embarrassing. I cover my face with my palms, immediately soaking them with tears. I feel two arms wrap around me.

"Is there anything I can do?" Lauren asks.

I can't speak because I can't stop crying.

～

"HERE YOU GO," Lauren hands me a cup of chamomile tea. She cautiously sits across the table from me.

In the short time we've known each other, we've grown close. She has my granddaughter, so that automatically puts her near the top of the list of my favorite people, and she makes my son happy, happier than I've seen in such a long time. Things had been going so well until yesterday. When everything came to a head—no, that explanation is too mild. When the volcano erupted and destroyed everything near it.

"Thank you," I say, breaking myself from my thoughts. I can't imagine how awkward it is for her to be here right now. I know that she and Lisa had grown to like one another. Now to be in the middle of all of this . . ."I'm sorry you're here for all of this. We're usually quite the normal family."

My pathetic attempt at levity falls flat. Her eyes widen, and she shakes her head.

"No need for apologies. I-I can't imagine what it's like to be in your shoes right now," she says earnestly.

"It's not the greatest place to be right now," I say, successfully coming off a little lighter.

She nods again and lets out a deep breath. "Chris and I talked, and we would love to have you come back to Chicago with us if that's something you would like." She sounds hopeful.

"Thank you for the invitation. As much as I'd love to have more time with my Caylen, I just don't think it's the right time," I say before taking a sip of tea.

She nods understandingly.

"I hate to run from my own home, you know?" I swallow as hard as I can to keep my voice from breaking. "But how can I stay here? Everywhere I look . . ." I lift my hands off the table in disgust. "I don't know where they . . ." I'm too exhausted to complete my thought.

"Maybe it wasn't as bad as you think," Lauren says lightly, and her face scrunches up immediately. "That was a stupid thing to say. I just think sometimes our imagination, the unknown, is so much worse than what actually happened." She gives a small shrug.

"It's almost funny. Yesterday we sat here and ate breakfast, and everything was fine. All was well. Now today—" I stop as my voice breaks. I hate who I've become, a sobbing pitiful mess. I push the tea away as I rest my head in my hands on the table. "I shouldn't have told William to leave. I can't stay in this house."

"Where are you going to go?" she asks.

That's the question. I don't want to intrude on my son and his family just as they're settling into their life together. I surely don't want to be around my granddaughter in the state I'm in now—hating her grandfather. She's only one, but I'm sure she'll still pick up my feelings rather than my words. I don't want to be the cloud over them. They've had enough gloom to last a lifetime.

"I have a sister. I can stay there until I get my bearings," I murmur. "Gia's great. She'll be able to put up with my moping."

Lauren stands and walks over to me. "I think you're allowed to sulk." She gives me a warm smile and a big hug. I can tell her smile is an attempt to cover her worry. "And it's great that you have someone who can be there for you. I always wished I had a sister or brother."

"It's funny, I always wanted Chris to have a sibling. Now he does," I say, unable to mask my bitterness.

"Do you want me to help you pack or drive you to your sister's?"

"No. The drive will clear my head. I know I look like a mess, but I'm fine. I've been through worse." Before I leave the kitchen, my feet stop, unable to move, and I feel embarrassed about what I'm about to ask. "Lauren, did you—was there anything you noticed between them since you've been here?" I feel more pathetic than ever.

Lauren walks closer to me and looks me directly in the eye. "No, not once."

I laugh at myself. She isn't his wife. Whether she noticed anything or not isn't important. I was the fool. I was blind, and what bothers me the most is the little voice in my head that tells me I had this coming . . .

◌◟◟◞

lisa

LOVE IS LIKE a parasite rooting within you. It affects every part of you that matters, tainting it. A virus that spreads so quickly that by the time you realize you've caught it, there's no stopping it from gaining ground. It's a drug that changes how you feel, how much you eat, what you hear, and the decisions you make. A good day on love is better than any high imaginable; a bad day on love immobilizes you. Love unrequited is even worse than love unspoken. Love—something that you've tried to forget about, a door that had been shut though not locked. Yesterday I blew that door wide open, and every foul thing it hid became visible for all to see.

It's my worst nightmare. My deepest, darkest secret revealed. My worst fear confirmed. I had to tell the one person who has been one of the only real friends I've ever had. A person who never judged me, who loved me like a sister, and I told him something that would destroy him. That did destroy him. I thought that since telling him was the right thing, it would at least make me feel better, my conscience satisfied for the first time in years. But it didn't.

It didn't make him feel better, and with the way he looked at me, I know he'll never ever forgive me. Time won't heal the hatred he had in his eyes. The thing I feel worst about is the small glimpse of disappointment he showed before pure malice consumed him. That hurt more than anything, the thought that all the things everyone has said about me and my family—the rumors, everything he refused to believe about me—were true. I didn't live up to his expectations. Turns out I'm nothing but a whore's daughter who grew up to be just like her mother. I'm worse actually because to my knowledge, my mom never slept with her best friend's married father. She never did something so careless to someone she called a friend.

When you're young, you don't think; you just feel. You crave, you want, and you take. I wish I could just blame that on my age, on being a stupid hormonal teenager, but I can't. Because I'm still like that. As much as I don't want to, I think of myself first, and as much as I wish I could convince myself that I told Chris the truth because it was the noble, right thing to do, I didn't tell him because of that. I told him because it was eating away at me. The secret, knowing what I caused to happen, and I was afraid—afraid of being responsible for raising a little girl alone and even more afraid that she'll turn out like me.

That scares me more than anything as I look at her sleeping. The same long blond hair as mine, the blood running through her veins that was passed down from my mother and her mother. I want her to stay peaceful, sweet, and innocent. I want her to hold on to the lie that she isn't a Garrett. I wish more than anything that the lie she knows were real, that her real mother was a sweetheart, that her real mother was selfless and would do anything in the world to make her happy. I wish more than anything to trade places with the woman who deserves to be her mom. I don't even want to call myself her mother. I don't deserve that title.

I gave my daughter away before she was even born. I abandoned her before she was even thought of. I wish more than anything I could trade places with the woman who deserves to be her mom so that she could raise her to be the woman she's capable of, but I can't. She's stuck with me, and my punishment is telling her that the world she knew was a dream, a lie. My daughter's reality is that she has a mother with no clue how to be responsible for anyone besides herself and a father who didn't even know she existed.

I fight back tears because I know out of everyone involved in this, I deserve tears the least. I never meant to hurt anyone, but I guess that's what every fucked-up person says after they hurt so many people. You don't mean it though. In that moment, you don't think about someone else's hurt—you think about pleasure, your own pleasure. Something that feels so good can't be that bad, right? That's what you tell yourself at least, and when you're young, you believe it.

"Hey." My friend, or anti-friend, Aidan stands in the doorway. His expression's unreadable, and I'm grateful for that. "I've got to head out."

He looks tired. I'm sure he didn't get much sleep last night with all my crying and him coddling me. Aidan isn't a coddler. He's the friend you call when you want someone's ass kicked. He's the doer, not the one who stops and thinks. Aidan is anything but the person you call to sulk with.

"Are you going to be okay?" he asks, looking at me, but his eyes don't reach mine.

I can't blame him for being unable to look me in the eye. Chris is his real best friend, not the anti-friend he and I are. Enemies who have been friends with the same person for so long we had no choice but to become friends in the most unfriendly way possible. We argue, we tease, but the reason we even tolerate the other is Chris—was Chris. Now that Chris wants nothing to do with me, I wonder how much longer Aidan will be around.

"I'll be fine. I have to be, right?" I ask with a fake laugh.

He frowns at me. "I'll come back and check on you after I get some sleep. Your couch has fucked up my back. I need to sleep in my own bed." He massages his shoulder.

"Thank you for everything, A," I say, getting off the bed and walking over to him.

A small smile creeps across his face, showing two dimples. His blue eyes are soft and comforting, unlike the wide grin he usually flashes me after an insult. "You're good. Well, *you're* not good, but no thanks necessary." He nudges me playfully in the shoulder.

It's comforting, our banter. Our petty arguments are the only things I'll have to remind me of my best friend.

"C-can you let me know how he is once you talk to him?" I say, sounding desperate even to myself.

"I-I don't know," he says hesitantly.

"Please, Aidan. I just want to know he's okay."

His eyes fall from my face to the floor, then he puts his hands on my shoulders. "He'll survive this." He gives me a reassuring squeeze, and I nod. He opens the door to leave, sweeping his hand over the blond hair that's grown out from the buzz cut he had during the tour he just finished. "I don't know a lot of people who can forgive what you did, but if there's anyone who can, it's Chris."

I nod.

"I'll see you later, okay?" he says before heading down the stairs of my porch.

I shut the door and rest on it once it's closed. I take a deep breath and wish for my head to stop pounding and for the thousand-pound weight on my chest to give me just a little bit of a break. I sink into my couch and pull a pillow onto my lap. My thoughts are going in slow motion. Everything that happened yesterday consumes me. My mind tries to drift to before yesterday, to a time I've done my best to block out.

I'm thankful when my doorbell rings. Aidan must have left something. I push myself off the couch, open the door, and my heart clenches when I see him standing on my porch. His usually bright blue eyes are dim and squinted at me. His golden brown hair, which is so much longer than the days I used to run my hands through it, looks as if he hasn't touched it all day. His facial hair has grown since I saw him a couple of days ago, a far cry from the five o'clock shadow covering his rigid face. His presence is overwhelming. Anger and sadness radiate off him, his emotions so strong that if they were a physical being, I'd be knocked down. It's been so long since we were this close, since we were alone. I don't know why I haven't prepared myself for this moment, but I'm completely vulnerable.

"I thought you understood, Lisa," he says, his voice not matching his heated gaze. His voice is quiet, somber, and broken.

"I don't know what to say to you, Will," I force the words from my throat.

He pushes the door open and stalks past me to the center of the living room. I shut the door and cross my arms.

"I didn't have a choice," I say, cautiously approaching him.

"We all have a choice!" he roars.

I don't say anything. I know that he's not done, and I don't want his yelling to wake up Willa. With how he is now, they'd have an awful first meeting.

"You could have talked to me first. Given me some type of warning. I was blindsided! Chris will never forgive me for this!" he says frantically, walking closer to me so we're only inches apart.

"We haven't talked in a very long time. You wanted it that way, remember?" I say harshly.

His eyes widen. "So this is your way of getting back at me? Years later and at the worst possible time?"

"This isn't about getting back at you. How could you think that? This is about doing the right thing. I thought that it would help Chris!" I yell back.

"Help him? You think destroying his family is the way to help him?" He laughs condescendingly.

"I thought that—I just thought that maybe if he knew the truth, about us and what he saw before he started to act differently, that it would help his treatment." Tears start to fall from my eyes. Not for William, not for me, but for Chris.

"Him not remembering what happened between us was the best thing that ever happened. Not just for you and me but for him! You broke him. That was something that never had to be brought up. He was doing fine. You saw it!" His tone is desperate and I don't know if he's trying to convince me or himself.

We are both guilty. We relished in the secret that was gratefully forgotten. It was almost like a do-over with Chris. When I came back home after college and realized that not only had he forgiven me but, it was like it had never happened, it was a gift. Or so I thought then. I let out a deep breath.

"Chris hasn't been fine since he saw us that night. He's been seeing a therapist on and off for years. Him not remembering seeing us together wasn't a blessing, it's *his* curse, a repressed memory that has been tearing him apart. We always knew it. No one just simply forgets seeing his father fucking his best friend!" I yell back at him. He lowers his head and shakes it.

"I thought that maybe he had really forgiven us. That he chose to not ever bring it up because he didn't want to hurt his mom. I didn't literally think that he repressed seeing us together," I say pleadingly. He looks up at me with a scowl.

"Well, let me just say, Dr. Lisa, that he is still not fine. None of us are after your confession," he says with a forced laugh, and tears slip from his eyes. He wipes them away quickly.

"Is he okay?" I ask desperately.

"What do you think?" he asks.

"Lisa, I can't sleep with all the yelling," Willa says quietly, standing in the doorway.

"I'm sorry, honey. My friend is just upset. Go back to bed and watch some cartoons, okay?" I say before ushering her back to the bedroom.

When I return to the living room, Will's face is expressionless. His wide blue eyes glisten. "Is that her?"

I feel butterflies in my stomach. I've imagined this moment so many times, but it was never like this. In my imagination, the daydreams of a nineteen-year-old girl, I would call him right before I went into labor. He would rush to my side and tell me everything would be okay, and I would have my family. Then it didn't matter if I had to share him with the other one. When you're young, you don't see life for what it is. You disregard its harsh realities. You think if you just wish hard enough and say your wishes aloud, believe in them long enough, you can give them life and they can be granted. Life doesn't necessarily turn out like that.

"Yes," I say quietly.

He nods, makes his way slowly to the couch, and sits. I look at the man I had my first crush on, whom I gave myself to, whom I wanted to not just love me but be in love with me more than anything. After he ended us, he ended me for a while. I was heartbroken, I was lovesick, and I went into mourning.

"Why didn't you tell me?" he says, his eyes finding mine.

For the first time in years, I'm drawn in once more. I remember everything between us, everything I've pretended for eight years never happened, and I close my eyes to break the spell. "I thought I was doing the right thing."

I sit next to him, keeping the requisite inches between us. He puts his head in his hands and lets out a deep sigh.

"For who?" he mutters.

"For all of you. For Chris, for Gwen," I say, feeling guilty even saying her name. As much as I grew to love Will, my love didn't stop the guilt growing inside me, knowing what I was doing to her. A woman who had only shown me kindness. She never looked at me as anything other than Chris's friend. She didn't judge me based on who my mother was or what she did, and knowing that I was what everyone said I would be hurt more than anything.

"Does she know that I'm her—her father?"

I sigh. "She doesn't even know that I'm her mother." I chuckle sadly.

He looks at me questioningly. "How is that possible?"

I roll my eyes. It's funny that he thinks I could balance a life as a preschool teacher and bartender and secretly be a mom. "She hasn't been with me, Will."

"Where has she been?" he asks, his eyes zeroed in on his hands.

"With Aunt Dani. I went to live with her after I found out I was pregnant. I knew she'd make a better mother than me," I say honestly.

His head snaps up. I now have his full attention.

"And what about her father?" he asks angrily.

"What father? The father who was married and had a family? The father she'd have been a bastard to?" I say, tears falling from my eyes.

"That's not fair. If anyone knew how much a child would mean to me, it would've been you," he says.

I ignore the stab of guilt. "Tell me, if I had come to you and told you that I was pregnant—or better yet, after she was born—what would you have done? Would you have accepted her with open arms, or would she have been a secret love child? Is that what you would have wanted for our daughter?"

"And now? Now what life do you want for her?" he asks, his eyes boring into mine.

I look away as memories of touches trying to fight their way to the forefront of my consciousness, feelings that I've fought to keep down for so long. "I want her to have a better life than I did," is all I can say.

"Gwen kicked me out of the house. Chris is furious with me. I don't know how he's going to handle all of this." His deep sigh contains palpable anguish as he runs his hand through his hair. "I've got to figure out a way to fix this. I can't lose my family."

I feel anger rising in me. This man whom I loved and gave my youth to, whose child I brought into the world, is talking about how he has to save his family as if the little girl in the next room isn't his family. I try to calm my anger—I'm being selfish and unreasonable. I have to stop myself from lashing out at him.

"I'd like to meet her when I'm not like this," he says, standing from the sofa. I immediately stand as well.

"Where are you going?" I ask him as I follow him toward the door.

"Right now, I don't think I'd be a good father to anyone. I need to—I just need a little time. I'll be back. I promise."

When he leaves, I do something I haven't done in years. I cry over him and hope this isn't the beginning of a trend.

What Happens After is Available Now